Praise for A Very Importa

A curiously magical thriller with
sparkle.

Helen Lederer, author of *Losing it*, comedian and founder of
the *Comedy Women in Print Prize*

This is a thriller, a chase, a buddy story, a mystery (certainly
for Dawson, who starts out off the back foot but manages to
survive several rugged encounters), all smoothly told with
hugely engaging characters, and rips along at a hectic pace. If
you like some smiles, even chuckles, with your reading, this is
great fun but doesn't dissolve into slapstick.

Adrian Magson, author of *Hostile State*

My goodness! What a hilarious, energetic and entertaining
roller-coaster of a read this is. The pace never lets up. Dawson
(for he is our hapless hero – and never was a man more lacking
in hap) starts off in the UK, hops over to Australia and there is
chased by a colourful collection of Germans and Russians, Brits
and Aussies. Some are goodies, some baddies, and some lurk in
the grey area in between. All are intent on solving the mystery
of the eponymous teapot, or preventing others from doing so.
It's as clever and witty as its title. I certainly enjoyed the ride!

Sue Clark, author of *Note to Boy*

A very entertaining read that kept me guessing all the way
through. I needed to have my wits about me as there is a large
cast of characters and the chapters switch rapidly back and
forth between them, but this only added to the book's fast
pace. Steve's skilful storytelling and sense of fun made this a
rollicking good read.

Imogen Matthews, award-winning author of *The Hidden
Village* and *Hidden in the Shadows*

Bored to Death in the Baltics

Owen

Thanks. I hope
you enjoy it. (Read
this one second).

Steve Sheppard

STEVE
SHEPPARD

CLARET PRESS

ISBN paperback: 978-1-910461-31-0
ISBN ebook: 978-1-910461-32-7

A CIP catalogue record for this book is available from the British Library.

This paperback can be ordered from all bookstores as well as from Amazon, and the ebook is available on online platforms such as Amazon and iBooks.

Cover and Interior Design by Petya Tsankova

www.claretpress.com

Acknowledgements

Once again, I find myself indebted to a number of people for helping me get this second book out into the world. Primarily, the purchasers and readers of *A Very Important Teapot*, especially those who kindly took the time and trouble to leave largely complimentary reviews. Without them there would have seemed little point in trying to write a sequel. Secondly, my deepest thanks to thank Anna Pitt, Imogen Matthews and Rob Sheppard, who willingly and smilingly ploughed through the extensive first draft of *Bored to Death* (or whatever it was called then) and who each somehow contrived to come up with completely different observations, queries and positive suggestions. Many of which I heeded. Obviously, without the unwavering support of Katie Isbester and her small but diligent cohorts at Claret Press, especially Madi Simcock-Brown, you would not be reading either this paragraph or the book itself. And without the design expertise of Petya Tsankova, many of you would have passed *Bored to Death* by on the bookshelf, either physical or digital.

Thank you all.

I also feel I should acknowledge the part played by Covid-19, which managed to hold itself off just long enough for me to visit Estonia in March 2020. It was a close-run thing as they closed the border pretty much as my plane hit the tarmac again at Gatwick.

__ In which a tree sheds some
leaves, and Dawson walks
into a shop

Dawson had the tree to thank, so he did.

'Thanks, tree,' he said.

He would have liked to be more specific but he wasn't an expert on trees, so didn't know what variety it was. He couldn't therefore say, 'Thanks, oak.' It wasn't an oak, anyway, he knew that at least. So, type, genus, classification: all unknown. Size, however, was another matter. It was a substantial tree, substantial enough to have shielded Dawson almost entirely from the blast.

The tree was one of many planted on both sides of South Street in Stallford. They were an attractive sight, although also the subject of a good number of regular diatribes to the letters page of the *Stallford Sentinel*, complaining about roots pushing through the pavement, making pedestrian travel hazardous at night, or for the blind at any time.

It was a sunny morning in early June and, until the explosion, all was well in Dawson's world. Mostly well, anyway. His girlfriend, Lucy, was away in Dorset visiting some old school friends and staying in her parents' stately pile. That being so, Dawson had spent rather longer than usual the previous evening in The Cricketers, and was under par this morning, sunshine or not. However, the mild hangover was not preventing him strolling down South Street to his local paper shop to swap his usual Saturday badinage with Zaheer, the proprietor. Also, he was working – after a fashion.

He wasn't expecting the explosion. Why would he be? Why would anyone? Stallford was sleepy at the best of times, and at 9.30 on this particular morning, with the pavement already heating up under his sandalled feet and a clear blue sky heralding a glorious day to come, it was positively soporific.

Dawson picked himself up and dusted down what few clothes he was wearing. He appeared quite miraculously to be unhurt but as the smoke cleared, he began to realise that the elderly gentleman who'd been a short distance ahead of him had been less fortunate. Looking around, he spotted a brown homburg hat perched daintily atop the adjacent war memorial. He'd noticed the homburg sitting on its owner's head when he'd left his flat a few minutes earlier and remarked to himself that the wearer seemed a tad overdressed for the climatic conditions, with a padded jacket below the homburg and a pair of brown tweed trousers beneath that. Of the jacket and trousers, Dawson could see nothing and the wearer of all this clobber was, distressingly, also invisible.

He leaned against the tree which had protected him. 'Bugger,' he said.

Dawson was pretty sure no one else had been within fifty metres at the time of the explosion but, predictably, the area was becoming considerably more populated as people emerged from neighbouring buildings. One of them approached Dawson, a woman, middle-aged, blonde hair with dark roots, one blouse button too many undone, a worried look on her face.

'Are you all right?' she asked.

'Yes, thanks, I think so,' replied Dawson. 'I believe I may have this tree to thank.' He peered around it and saw that the bark had been stripped off completely on the side that had faced the blast. There was a pile of leaves on the ground and not many on the tree itself.

'It's just that you're bleeding,' continued the woman. 'From your head.' She pointed to Dawson's head in case he'd forgotten where it was. Dawson put his hand up and felt a spot above his left ear, pushing an unruly mop of mouse-brown hair out of the way. He looked at his fingers. There was a small amount of blood on them. It didn't seem too serious and there was no pain.

'Come into the shop and I'll clean you up,' said the woman, pointing again, this time across the road. She obviously enjoyed pointing and Dawson felt it impolite not to look. The shop was called Mr Bojangles and didn't appear to be the sort of place he would ever willingly enter. For one thing it was painted purple and yellow. Dawson would rather have backtracked up South Street to The Cricketers but the pub would be shut so probably wasn't a viable option. He also felt, from a professional standpoint, that he ought to hang around at the scene of the explosion. After all, he was an employee of MI6, albeit in an indeterminate capacity, and it seemed possible that the police might want his help, if only as a witness. And in any case, there was somebody at MI6 he needed to report to. Nonetheless, he found himself being dragged quite urgently across the street.

Before he could force himself to refuse the woman's kindly, if over-insistent assistance, he was inside Mr Bojangles. It was quite dark in the shop, and his eyes seemed to be taking an age to adjust. He was surrounded by displays of largely unidentifiable trinkets and jewellery and he became dimly conscious of a rather sickly, sweet smell pervading everything. He looked around for the woman. He failed to spot her immediately but finally noticed her standing towards the rear of the shop. He couldn't be absolutely certain, his brain didn't seem to be functioning properly, but she seemed to be holding something up to her face. He started to call out but stopped as he observed the floor of the shop, which was covered with some sort of swirly-purple-patterned material, rushing towards him.

'That's odd,' he murmured indistinctly to nobody in particular. He didn't feel the floor make contact with his face.

A bomb had exploded in Stallford. That much was clear as soon as I switched on the television news. There was no mention of any casualties, but the secret service part of me immediately thought "targeted" and then moved on to "Saul", so I reached for my phone. I was a little surprised to find my hands shaking. Saul didn't answer and eventually his voicemail kicked in. That was a worry. He never knowingly refused my calls, so the alarm bells were jangling full pelt by now.

I had to get to Stallford, and quickly, but it was a two-and-a-half-hour journey back to Surrey from my parent's place in west Dorset. It would be lunchtime before I got there.

—

The four months since Australia had been disappointing, at least as far as I was concerned. Back in February, our boss, Jason Underwood, had been full of praise and promises following the successful recovery of the Nazi diamonds, but suddenly he was gone, promoted to bigger and better things. His replacement was a woman named Elspeth Arundell, and we were rebranded as G22, ostensibly to do with search and recovery, but in fact more about search-and report-back-to-someone-else-for-filing-and-forgetting.

It all seemed rather unfair. In just a few months, we had located two or three items of possible usefulness and, on one memorable occasion, one person of more than possible usefulness, an Estonian scientist by the name of Viktor Nurmsalu, in possession of important knowledge, *the nature of which I had not been made privy to. His discovery had been a personal triumph for Saul, whose determination and legwork had uncovered him hiding in Snowdonia. That alone should have been enough to get at least a round at the pub. But apparently not as far as Elspeth Arundell was concerned, who made it clear that she was keen to eradicate even the tiny amount G22 was costing from the service's budget.*

If so, there was of course an alternative, albeit one without any guaranteed income, and that was to leave MI6 and open a private intelligence agency. I believed we could make that work, what with my resourcefulness and Saul's enthusiasm, but the start-up capital was somewhat lacking. There seemed to be only one thing for it – a visit to Bank of Mum and Dad, embarrassing at my age, but worth a try.

Which was why I was now inconveniently in Dorset instead of with Saul.

__ In which Dawson remembers he
hates ships, and chats to a
young woman

When Dawson woke up, he was on a ship yawing in a heavy
sea. Was yawing a word? He was sure he'd heard it before in
some sort of maritime context. Whatever the ship was doing, it
was making him feel sick. Dawson hated ships, had done since
one dreadful cross-channel ferry trip when he was twelve. As
he remembered it, he nearly hadn't made it to thirteen.

There was also a considerable amount of heavy engineering
work going on inside his head. He looked at his watch which
told him it was approaching half past six. But did that mean
half past six in the morning or half past six in the evening?
And on what day?

He was still wearing shorts and sandals but someone
had thoughtfully slipped a thick, rough-wool sweater over his
upper body so he wasn't especially cold. The room, cabin he
supposed, was cool and dim, but not completely dark. He forced
his aching head to look upwards and immediately found the
light source, a small, square porthole high up in one corner.

He discovered he wasn't restrained in any way, no
handcuffs, ropes or heavy weights to help when throwing
captives overboard. Even so, he felt too unwell to move and
decided not to try, figuring that even if the cabin door proved
to be unlocked, he was on a ship in the middle of a violent sea,
so escape was unlikely. He guessed something was bound to
happen sooner or later, so he shut his eyes and tried to think.

There had been the explosion in Stallford. Wait a minute.
There was also a woman, wasn't there?

And suddenly there *was* a woman, standing in front of
him. He hadn't heard her come in. Probably, he'd drifted off.
He couldn't make her out clearly in the half-light, but she
seemed quite young. The woman in Mr Whatsits hadn't been

young, he recalled that now, so he was pretty sure this wasn't the same person. She was keeping her distance as though she thought he might be dangerous, and had placed a tray on the floor with a plate of food and a plastic beaker on it. Noticing Dawson was awake, she said, 'Stay where you are. I have gun,' and she waved a small automatic up and down a couple of times to prove her point. Even without the appearance of the gun, Dawson wasn't planning on going anywhere.

But he did have some questions. Articulating them, though, was an issue. His throat didn't seem to work, and he was immediately caught up in a paroxysm of coughing.

'Do not try to talk,' said the woman or, possibly, girl. She was still only dimly visible but she sounded no more than nineteen or twenty. 'Drink,' she continued. 'Here. Water. Drink.' She pointed with the gun towards the beaker. Dawson shuffled forwards until it was within reach and took a large mouthful. That was a mistake. The coughing started again. It took a few more measured sips spread over a minute or so before he was able to bring it under control. The woman was still standing and watching him when he was finally able to speak.

'Where am I?' he asked. It wasn't very original but seemed to get to the nub of the matter.

'You are on ship,' she replied.

I walked into that one, Dawson thought. 'You sound foreign,' he said. 'Who are you?'

'No, it is you who is foreign. I am Latvian and this is Latvian ship.'

Dawson was beginning to cheer up despite the banging in his head. His visitor appeared willing to talk and didn't seem particularly villainous, gun or not. And as far as he knew, Latvia was not a country that Britain had troubled diplomatic relations with.

'What day is it?' he asked.

'Is Saturday evening. Eat.' She pointed with the gun to the plate of food, some sort of pale meat, chicken possibly, and some even paler boiled potatoes.

So, the same day then. Eight or nine hours in which he had been rendered unconscious – and now he remembered the odd smell in Mr Oojamaflip's shop – and transported from Stallford to this ship.

'Are we on our way to Latvia?'

'Yes, Russia.' The reply was rather confusing but Dawson reflected that Russia did seem a whole lot more likely than Latvia in the circumstances. Worrying, but more likely.

'Why?'

'Perhaps you important.' She looked Dawson up and down with an expression that suggested that she may have been speaking sarcastically. 'I go now,' and she started to back towards the door. 'Eat. You will feel better. I will bring breakfast tomorrow. Oh, and there is bucket there, for your you-knows.' She waved her gun again towards another corner.

Dawson decided he probably needed a friend and ally, and this girl seemed to be his best bet. Also, as he hadn't actually met anyone else yet, she was currently his only bet.

'Wait a second,' he called, forcing a smile. 'What's your name?'

'I cannot tell you.'

'Why not? Don't you know it?'

'You funny.' But she didn't crack a smile. She stood with her back to the door, the gun hanging loosely by her side. 'I am Sofija. My father is captain of ship. Why do Russians want you?'

'I can't imagine,' he replied. But he could. He knew that the Russian SVR held him and Lucy Smith responsible for the capture of their agent, Valentin Prokofiev, in Australia. Prokofiev himself might well be holding a personal grudge against Dawson for shooting him. It had probably hurt quite a lot. They clearly couldn't forgive and forget, and the prisoner exchange of Prokofiev in April with a member of the London Philharmonic Orchestra who had hidden a rocket launcher in his trombone whilst performing before President Putin in Moscow had presumably moved Dawson's capture up the agenda. He only hoped that Lucy was safe, but he could do nothing about that and she was more than capable of looking after herself. For now, his own plight was his main consideration.

'Why are you doing this?' he asked.

'Money.' She shrugged. 'My father has little. You cannot make money with small cargo ship like this, sailing around North Sea and Baltic. He has no choice. You are passenger, cargo, he not know you so why should he care? And Russians pay large amount. We go to Riga anyway. Is not far out of way.'

'And what if I said they will kill me when they get me to Russia?'

'You do something very bad if that is true.'

'You speak excellent English.'

Sofija laughed. 'Of course. All Latvians speak English. Nobody speak Latvian. English is language of business. What little business is left anyway.'

'If things are so bad, why can't your father sell the ship and try something else?'

'What else? He know nothing else. And ship not ours. Is leased. We would get nothing.'

'The Russians must have paid your father quite a lot to make it worth his while.'

'Will keep us going for two, maybe three months. Anything can happen in three months.' She paused. 'I am sorry. My father is sorry. He not want to do this, you understand. He hate Russians.'

'Thanks, Sofija. It must be hard for you both. And thanks for the food too.' He picked up the plate and a fork. Sofija nodded and left. Friendly or not, she did not forget to lock the door behind her. It involved a lot of creaks and clunks.

Still, thought Dawson as he chewed on the chicken, she would be back in the morning, and he could work on a plan overnight.

The first person I saw was Mabel Scutt. Having parked next to Saul's Golf, I would have been hard pushed to avoid Mabel, who had ears like antennae and a nosiness to match. She oversaw the six flats in Church House with a rod of some material considerably stronger than iron.

'Hello, Mabel,' I said, trying to be calm and friendly even though my insides were churning like a one-woman cheese production line. I'd made it up from Dorset in a world record two hours and was frantic with worry, so being calm and friendly wasn't easy.

She stared back at me with gimlet eyes. Mabel didn't like me. Back in the day, she'd managed to persuade Saul to let her have a spare key to his flat so that she could "keep an eye on things". I soon put a stop to that, although not before she had caught us one Sunday afternoon, if not exactly in flagrante delicto, then approaching the point of no return, let's say. She had been completely unfazed by the discovery. As an active member of the nation's security services, I shouldn't have been as fazed as I was. Unfortunately when I'm fazed I tend to hit out. Not physically, you understand ("Naked Girl Assaults Pensioner" headlines would not have gone down too well back at MI6), but verbally. Quite a lot of verbally. Saul had hidden under the bedclothes.

So, all in all, I wasn't happy to see Mabel and she wasn't happy to see me.

'You have parked in my parking space, Miss Smith,' she said through thin lips, failing to acknowledge my smiling-through-gritted teeth greeting. 'Again.' I should point out here that Mabel does not actually own a car.

'Sorry,' I lied. I could sense my smile turning slightly

sinister under the strain but managed to keep moderately civil. 'It's an emergency. Have you seen Dawson?'

'Perhaps you should try his flat.'

'Yes, of course.' It did seem the obvious thing to do. I brushed past her and took the front steps two at a time. 'Saul?' I called as I opened the door. And then, 'Are you here?' It wasn't a large flat and frankly, if he hadn't answered my first call, which he would have known was important by my use of his hated first name, he wasn't going to answer my second one.

Mabel had followed me slowly up the stairs. 'Oh, he's not here,' she said.

I spun round. 'What the f...!' I yelled. 'You said he was.'

'No, young lady, you misheard.' Only the fact that I tend not to hit old ladies stopped me hitting this one. 'I doubt if you know,' Mabel continued, 'but there was an explosion in the town earlier today.' Of course I knew. Why in the name of all things demonic did she think I was so frantic? 'Someone may have detonated a bomb.'

'Yes, I heard,' I managed to get out through even more gritted teeth. I wouldn't have any teeth left to grit at this rate.

'There may have been a fatality.'

That information, from everything I had heard on the radio on the way up, was not yet in the public domain, but it wouldn't surprise me to learn that Mabel had a hotline to the Chief Constable. She knew what I was thinking, of course, but made me ask anyway.

'Dawson? Please Mabel.' I vowed I'd make her pay for that please if I lived to be as old as her, which was admittedly unlikely in my line of work.

'Mr Dawson left to buy his newspaper shortly before the bomb exploded.' She paused, as if for dramatic effect. 'The explosion was by the war memorial. The newsagent *is further along South Street. I usually go to WHSmith's myself.' I could have done without the geography lesson and her diary notices, neither of which had the slightest relevance. Especially with my stomach threatening to fall on the ground.*

'I had also decided to go for my usual Saturday morning stroll around the town. I was some way behind him, and luckily the explosion left me unaffected.' Luckily? 'However, when I got closer, I saw Mr Dawson entering Mr Bojangles.' At last, some good news. How much time had she wasted keeping me waiting for that, the witch?

'Mr Bojangles?' I was already ushering Mabel out of Saul's flat as I spoke. 'I know it.' I set off down the road at a run.

'You're welcome,' came a thin, satisfied voice from behind me.

__ In which Dawson discusses
   portholes, and finds out
   what heads are

Four nights had passed, four nights during which Dawson had managed to sleep a little, despite the yawing and the fact that Sofija and her father had apparently decided that a thin, smelly mattress, clearly fished up from the seafloor, would suffice as a bed.

He had not seen Sofija since that first evening. Or rather, he had not seen most of her. There was a slot in the door with a hinged flap and she had merely banged on the door and passed him the food tray wordlessly through the slot and stomped away. Probably she was under instructions from her father not to get too friendly with the prisoner.

But this morning, Wednesday it must be, there she was, standing in front of him when he awoke. How did she do that? It was as though she could materialise at will. Locking the door behind her that first evening had been a particularly noisy undertaking but the unlocking process had not been loud enough to rouse him.

'Are you awake?' asked Sofija, somewhat pointlessly as she was watching him haul himself to his feet. The ship appeared to be stationary, and a bright sunlight was streaming in through the square porthole high up to his right, if portholes could actually be square and this wasn't just a plain old window. He wondered inconsequentially what porthole was in Latvian. '*Iluminators*,' said Sofija.

'What?'

'*Iluminators*. Porthole. You ask what is porthole in Latvian. *Iluminators*.'

'Did I say that out loud?' Perhaps he wasn't as rested as he'd thought.

'No, I am mind reader.' And she laughed.

Dawson studied her, now that the light was good enough to do so. She was older than she had sounded on Saturday evening, early twenties maybe, quite short, sturdily built with cropped, untidy dark-blonde hair. Strong-looking. He supposed that hauling around the sub-Arctic on an undermanned tramp ship could build muscle in a girl. She had a round, naturally smiley face, with cheeks reddened by wind and rain. There was no sign of the gun.

'Where's your gun?' asked Dawson.

'Why? Do you want to overpower me and have wicked way?' She sounded as if she wouldn't be too disappointed if he did. It wasn't quite the response he was expecting, especially as he hadn't washed for four days and he was certainly not the first, nor possibly even the fifteenth person to wear the woollen sweater since its last visit to a washing machine.

'Who's driving the ship?' he asked.

'No one. We are stopped.'

'What about the crew?'

'You look at her.'

'You? You're the whole crew? On a ship this size?'

'How you know what size it is?' A fair question.

'How big is it?'

'Not big. Small cargoes. Of course, we like more crew, but we cannot afford them.'

'May I have my belongings?' Dawson's phone and the small amount of cash he'd had on him had been taken away. He knew this because he'd felt in all his pockets. There were only two. 'And a wash and some clean clothes, perhaps?'

'Clothes, yes, I will get you fleece and trousers. The sweater you wear is very smelly.' She made it sound his fault. 'We have clean ones. Also shoes. What are these things on your feet?'

'Sandals.'

'I not know this word "sandals". Where is rest of them?'

'That's all there is, sorry.' Why was he apologising?

'They stupid shoes for ship.' Dawson was going to explain

that, had he known he was to be kidnapped and transported across the North Sea on an old cargo ship, he'd have been sure to pull on some Wellington boots when he got up on Saturday, but Sofija carried on talking. 'Come and I will show you heads.'

'Heads of what? Who are they? You just said it was only you and your father on board.'

'Heads are toilets. You not know this? Have you not been on ship before?'

'They're not called heads on cross-channel ferries. Still, thanks. Is there hot water in these heads?'

'Soap also, yes. You smell too. Not just sweater. You must wash. Do not try to attack me or you will regret it.' She allowed Dawson to lead her out of the door into a dank, echoing corridor.

'Don't worry. I'm not going to attack you. I'm not sure that diving overboard into the middle of the North Sea is my best plan of action at the moment.'

'Not North Sea, Baltic, in fact Gulf of Riga. Anyway, you would not dive overboard. I would hit you and stop you.' Dawson suspected that she probably would hit him and quite hard too. She certainly didn't look undernourished.

They arrived at a door indistinguishable from half a dozen others they'd passed, except this one had a small pile of clothes and a pair of stiff, heavy boots sitting outside it.

'Heads,' said Sofija. 'You go in and wash. Here are clothes. Old but clean. I will lock door.'

'So, you don't trust me.'

'Of course not. You are English. I have heard all about the mad dogs and the Englishmen. And I will not be here to hit you. If you jump into sea, you will die of cold, and we not want you dying before we give you to Russians. If they want to kill you, they will be unhappy if you are dead before they get here.'

___ In which Elaine Bates watches
television, and decides she
doesn't like paperwork

Elaine Bates was bored and fed up. New Scotland Yard was all endless corridors and harassed men and women in uniform, together with self-important ones in plain clothes. She looked down at her own jeans and fleece hoping she didn't look self-important herself. Before arriving, she'd been assured that the Met was a vibrant force where everyone had each other's backs, where the social life was inclusive and where anyone – even a young, relatively inexperienced female copper from the hickier parts of Hicksville, Australia – could make a real difference. The only difference she'd been able to make so far was to obtain the key to the store cupboard so that the ladies' toilet wasn't perpetually out of loo paper.

She stared out of the window into the bright sunlight reflecting off the steelwork of the London Eye across the river and shivered involuntarily. Transferring to England in the spring had seemed like a great piece of timing but as far as she was concerned, sun or no sun, spring had failed to spring and although it was June, summer had yet to summer. Not that she was an expert on British seasons – where she came from, there was simply one that lasted all year round and which could most accurately be described as hotanddusty.

It had appeared to be a great opportunity when the call had come from the Police Commissioner's office in Melbourne two months ago. A prisoner swap had been arranged between the United Kingdom and Russia and as one of the prisoners, Valentin Prokofiev, was currently languishing in a secure facility in Melbourne, he would need to be transported back to England to allow the swap to take place.

'Constable Bates,' the Commissioner had said foisting an unwanted cup of weak tea upon her. 'I have two pieces of good news for you. First, in view of your meritorious conduct in helping Agents Dawson and Smith in February, you're promoted to Acting Sergeant.' Only Acting? Still it was better than nothing. 'Second, I want you to escort Valentin Prokofiev to London, where he will be taken off your hands by some Pommy bastards from MI6 for onward transportation. The English love to transport people.'

'Why me, sir?' she'd asked. 'And do you mean just me?' It was a reasonable question. Prokofiev was a dangerous hitman, and the wound he'd received when Dawson had shot him two months earlier was probably healed by now. So, dangerous and fully fit.

'Well, not just you, no, but now that you're a sergeant,' – sort of – 'you'll be in charge. I'm sending a couple of burly types with you, don't worry. And as for why, apart from the fact you'll be able to talk over old times with Prokofiev, you've put in for a transfer to the UK police so this is an opportunity for you not to have to pay your own fare.'

True. Foreseeing a long and tedious career patrolling the highways and byways of Victoria, Elaine had indeed applied for a transfer, although more in hope than expectation.

And the journey had gone smoothly in a dull sort of way. Prokofiev had been tight-lipped and brooding, and Elaine's two male police companions had a conversational spectrum that started at Aussie Rules football and finished at Rugby League.

She looked at her watch. Her break was over. She smoothed herself down, attached a professional smile to her small, sharp face, brushed her hands through her short, brown hair and set off for the operations room to see what further unimportant work her inspector had lined up for the morning.

The place was an unexpected hive of activity. Puzzled, Elaine looked up at the line of tv screens on the wall. It looked like there had been some kind of terrorist event in her absence. A bomb had exploded in a small town thirty kilometres south of London with one apparent fatality.

'Who got killed?' she asked the officer next to her.

'Don't know,' he replied. 'Powers that be are still working on who and why. Religious extremists, probably. Or a Russian hit, maybe, like Salisbury.' He shrugged.

'But Salisbury wasn't a bomb.'

'No, but the Novichok thing wasn't exactly the brightest assassination the Russians have ever attempted, so maybe they thought blowing up the victim would stand a better chance of success. Who knows?'

Elaine was still looking at the live feed on the screen when suddenly a face she knew appeared, an attractive face beneath blonde hair tied back in a familiar ponytail. It was Lucy. Elaine hadn't seen her or Dawson since Australia. A surge of joy went through her. She'd like to see Lucy again. And Dawson. But especially Lucy. Right, she thought, it made sense for Lucy to be there. She was, after all, an MI6 agent, and if the Russians *were* involved in this incident, then she was probably there on official business. Lucy was talking to a police officer who was presumably trying to prevent her crossing the police tape strung across the road to keep out members of the public. Elaine couldn't imagine anything as trivial as a tape, or for that matter a policeman, being enough to stop the Lucy she remembered. Elaine slightly high-fived herself as the blonde girl ducked under the tape and marched up to a knot of other people including the giant figure of a chief inspector.

Elaine sought out her own inspector. 'Excuse me, sir,' she said. 'Is this a security matter now?'

'What? No, not yet. Surrey Police are officially in charge still. That may all change though when we know what the hell's going on.'

'So why are MI6 involved?'

'What do you mean?'

'I've just seen someone who I know to be Secret Service on the television.'

They glanced up at the screen but Lucy had disappeared. 'Are you sure? You're probably mistaken. Anyway, never mind, I need you to go up to the third floor and find PC Johnson. He's snowed under with paperwork. He could do with some help.' He turned away, discussion over.

'Of course, sir,' said Elaine, and left the ops room. However, when she reached the stairs, she turned down instead of up and soon found herself outside on the Embankment in the sunshine. She lifted her chin to the sun, letting the rays beat on her face.

'That's more like it. Stallford, here I come.' And she strode off in the direction of Waterloo Station. She may have been slow to catch up with Lucy Smith, but now seemed as good a time as any. She hadn't flown 19,000 kilometres just to help PC Johnson with his paperwork.

There was a police Do Not Cross tape strung across South Street just before the war memorial. I paused as I passed The Cricketers fifty metres before the tape and ducked into the pub, as Saul might well have taken refuge there. But why would he not have phoned me if he was sitting inside nursing a pint? The place was less full than usual. I imagined most of its Saturday lunchtime regulars were chewing the fat by the Do Not Cross tape. Anyway, it was immediately clear that the place was Dawsonless, so I carried on down the road and pushed through the throng of people busying themselves inventing a wide selection of unlikely conspiracy theories.

Police tapes, I was pretty sure, didn't apply to MI6 agents, so I started to shimmy under it. A large hand rested on my shoulder. As far as I'm concerned, that's sexual assault so I turned swiftly, prepared to shove the heel of my own hand forcefully up my assailant's nose. Luckily, I managed to abort at the last second and not damage the young copper whose hand it was. Maybe I should calm down a little.

I smiled at the copper, those gritted teeth coming into play again. I find a winning smile usually works with men, whether or not they're wearing police uniform, and this time was no exception.

'Sorry miss,' he said, beaming at me in a most unprofessional manner. 'I'm really sorry, but you have to stay this side of the tape.'

'I don't think so,' I replied, fishing my MI6 ID out of a pocket and flashing it at him.

He looked startled, although I'm not sure why. He

surely didn't think secret agents were all James Bond lookalikes.

Giving the young copper no time to think of an excuse to keep me out, I ducked under the tape and walked up to the most senior policeman I could see. I wasn't 100% clear on police rank insignia but he looked at least superintendent level if the gold on his cap was anything to go by. He was massive, tall and broad with a chest you could have packed all your worldly goods in.

'Excuse me,' I said. The possible superintendent turned and glared down at me. A senior-looking fireman with a tired face also turned but with a more non-committal expression.

'Yes?' said the giant.

He sounded belligerent. I supposed that was understandable given that a bomb had gone off on his patch, and on a Saturday too, so it had probably put paid to a relaxing round of golf. Still, it wasn't my fault and I could be as belligerent as the best of them given that my boyfriend was missing and his proximity to the explosion was unlikely to have been a coincidence. I waved my ID as close to his face as I could reach and dived straight in. 'What can you tell me about the victim of the explosion...' I looked at the name badge pinned to his portmanteau chest, '...Chief Inspector?'

Chief inspector? Is that all he was? Surely I outranked a chief inspector?

He stared at my ID. I must say he seemed less than impressed by what he was reading. That was strange: I was impressed every time I looked at it. A year ago, I'd been dealing with insurance claims from pensioners with flooded bungalows, so being a spy seemed an unlikely hike up the job ladder.

'MI6?' he said. 'You're kidding me.' Again! I ask you.

What is it about being small, blonde and female that makes working for the secret service seem so unlikely? 'Who sent you? This is a police matter. If we need any help from you or any of your spooky mates, we'll let you know.' He turned away, muttering over his shoulder, 'Don't hold your breath.'

I took a chance. I needed information and I wasn't going to get it from this plod by coming over all damsel in distress. 'Clearly you're not in the loop, Inspector...' I glanced at his chest again, which was an easy thing to do as it was at my eye level and currently about six inches from my face. '...Downton. Perhaps I'd better speak to your superior officer.'

The fire brigade bloke had a broad grin on his face by now. He was obviously enjoying the exchange hugely. Perhaps he too had been the victim of Chief Inspector Downton's man-management skills. A couple of paramedics and a youngish guy in medical greens were also taking a keen interest.

'Go away, young lady, or I'll have you arrested for obstructing the police,' said Downton, trying to sound important. 'I'm in charge here.'

'Oh, I think Chief Superintendent Gulliver's still around somewhere,' chipped in the fireman ingenuously. 'Yes, there he is,' and he pointed towards the war memorial to a nondescript man of indeterminate age in clothes so plain they could have been bought from a pikestaff catalogue. He was talking to a woman in the white papery outerwear of a forensics officer. The fireman called across. 'Superintendent! There's someone here wants to speak to you.'

The Chief Superintendent glanced over. Given his name was Gulliver, he was a surprisingly short man, positively Lilliputian in fact, even shorter than me and

I'm not exactly a giraffe. I knew there was no longer a minimum height requirement for policemen but this was taking things to ridiculously low levels. Possibly he had been sitting down during the job interview. Like the fireman, he also appeared very tired but unlike Chief Inspector Downton, he'd obviously read and memorised the Manners Maketh Man booklet.

'Yes, young lady, what I can do for you?' said Gulliver. Once again, I brandished the MI6 ID and, unlike everyone else, he didn't flinch or look me up and down disbelievingly. 'OK, Miss Smith, I'm not surprised to see you, if I'm honest, although I wasn't told you were coming. You'll be wanting to know if the victim was anyone you'd be interested in, I take it. Come over here.' He turned towards the chief inspector. 'Okay, Abbey, I'll take it from here.' Abbey? No, I must have misheard.

Gulliver steered me away from the less-than-warm environs surrounding the simmering Downton and across to the war memorial. I glanced across at my friendly fireman, who grinned back. I resisted the urge to smirk at the chief inspector. As a senior member of MI6, it would have been unbefitting.

_ In which Sofija and her father
exchange insults, and Dawson
gets in a boat

'Come with me,' said Sofija, when Dawson re-emerged, refreshed, re-clothed, re-booted and at least moderately re-energised from the heads, which had contained a shower capable of intermittent spurts of warm, brackish water. 'You have been long time. I think you try to escape through porthole.'

Dawson hadn't thought about trying to open the porthole. He wasn't a bad swimmer, so perhaps he could have risked trying to make it to the sliver of grey land he had seen in the distance. It was June, so surely the water wouldn't have been cold enough to kill him.

'Yes, you would last not more than thirty minutes and not reach land for two hours. Is further than it look,' said Sofija, who had apparently read his thoughts for a second time.

'I decided to have a shower. You didn't tell me there was a shower.'

'I not your mother. Follow me. My father want to talk with you.' Sofija led Dawson to some steep steps and trotted up them two at a time, despite her shortish legs and the near vertical nature of the climb. Dawson followed more carefully. When she reached the top, she stopped and looked at him with a quizzical expression on her open, ruddy face. 'You not very fit, Mr Dawson. How you think you swim ashore? Come. There is not much time,' and she took him by the arm as he finally reached the top of the steps and hurried him to what he could see was the bridge. At least Dawson knew what a bridge was.

A stocky, grey-haired man with about a week's growth of beard and wearing a stiff-looking sweater that could have been the twin of the one that Dawson had recently worn, was standing with his back to the spray-soaked front windscreen of the bridge.

'This is my father,' said Sofija. As she had already indicated they were the only three people on board, Dawson thought the introduction unnecessary, but he walked towards the man and held his hand out. The gesture was not reciprocated.

'You, Misteer Dawsing,' said Sofija's father in a virtually incomprehensible growl. 'You be pick up half one hours.' He consulted his watch. '*Jā*, half one hours,' he repeated.

When Sofija had said that all Latvians spoke English, she obviously wasn't including her father. Nevertheless, the gist of what he was saying was clear. Clear but discouraging. The Russians would be rendezvousing with the ship in thirty minutes.

'The Russians don't like me,' said Dawson. 'They're not inviting me for a holiday. You'll have my death on your conscience. Can you live with that? Whatever they are paying you, the British government will double.' He suspected that the British government would fall down in a collective heap, laughing uproariously at the prospect of paying anything at all to keep him alive, but it was worth a try. The captain shrugged, turned to Sofija and started yelling in what was presumably Latvian. Judging by the spittle flying from his mouth, Latvian may not be the language of business but seemed to be pretty effective for cursing.

Sofija spittle-shouted back in the same language. Dawson wondered why he'd bothered to shower. He hoped the argument wouldn't go on for too long; he had only about twenty-five minutes to think of a way of avoiding an uncertain future in Russia. Actually, not uncertain. Certain. Certain death.

Finally, the two ran out of insults and Sofija grabbed Dawson muscularly by the arm and hauled him off the bridge to a cabin a few doors down the corridor. She pushed him inside and followed, pulling the door shut behind her. Her already reddish face had gone a few shades more crimson and she was breathing deeply, her not inconsiderable chest heaving.

'My father is idiot,' she said. 'He could avoid Russians if he want. They not pay him yet.'

'You said they had.'

'Yes, I think this, but now he say no, they bring money in boat when they take you. I think they lie. Russians!' She spat on the floor. Dawson was moderately impressed by the volume of liquid in her mouth. 'We must escape. We have little time.'

'We?' said Dawson. 'It's me they want, not you. Is there a lifeboat or something I can take?'

'Yes, this good idea, we take lifeboat. But you cannot do it alone. And you say British will pay me to save you from Russians.'

Dawson felt that it was not the right time to comment on this.

Sofija opened the door a crack and peered up and down the corridor. 'Ssh,' she said. The door to the bridge was open but there was no sign of her father. Sofija gestured to Dawson to keep quiet and then edged out into the passage, away from the bridge and back down the steep steps they had climbed earlier. From there, the two of them made their way onto the lower deck, on the side furthest from land, and Sofija started to fiddle with the fixings of a smallish open lifeboat. 'Get in,' she whispered.

'What about you? I thought you said you were coming.'

'I must launch lifeboat. This old ship. I cannot do it from inside boat.'

Dawson clambered into the lifeboat, wondering about the quality of an escape system that left one person on board a sinking ship. With a sudden whoosh, the lifeboat plummeted downwards and hit the water with a huge splash. A second later, Dawson heard the smaller splash of Sofija, who had jumped into the sea next to the boat. He reached out and grabbed her arm.

'Let go,' she hissed. She slithered over the side like a dumpy mermaid and immediately set to work on the outboard motor attached to the stern. Before she could start it up, Dawson heard the sound of a powerful engine, partly muffled by the bulk of the ship but getting steadily and rapidly nearer.

'Russians are here,' she said, and amazingly she was grinning. She pulled the cord of the outboard, which spluttered into life, then produced a vicious looking knife from nowhere and hacked through the two ropes still connecting the boat to the cargo ship. Immediately, she was back at the stern, gunning the outboard into action, and the lifeboat started to pull away from the ship. It didn't possess the acceleration of a Formula 1 car, nevertheless, the gap between the two vessels widened quickly. Sofija was careful to keep the ship between them and the approaching speedboat. The vessel's name, *Astrid*, came into view as they drew clear. She saw Dawson looking at the name. 'My mother,' she said, with a note of sadness. 'She die when I was child.'

The roar of the unseen speedboat suddenly ceased.

'They will soon find out we escape. I know where we must go but will be hard to outrun them. We pray.' Then she laughed. Dawson couldn't see anything especially funny about their situation, but he looked at Sofija's red, wet, grinning face and laughed too.

Unfortunately, Chief Superintendent Gulliver hadn't been particularly helpful. Despite his outward friendliness, he obviously couldn't understand what I was doing there, and he was hindered by the fact that he didn't really know very much and wouldn't until forensics had been able to identify the little that remained of the person who had been exploded.

However, he did say that a local woman had suggested that the victim might be an elderly gentleman with a possibly Eastern European accent who had recently moved into a top-floor apartment in a nearby block of flats. I immediately put the sixes and sevens I was currently at together and came up with thirteen.

'Would the local woman be a Ms Mabel Scutt, by any chance?' The unguarded look of respect Gulliver gave me was a giveaway. MI6: we know everything.

I asked Gulliver if he would tell me when the victim had been identified, but he clammed up at that point. 'Perhaps I could call one of your senior colleagues tomorrow,' he suggested and, on a whim, I gave him the name of Jason Underwood, even though I had little clear idea what Underwood's current remit might be. I sure as hell wasn't going to get Elspeth Arundell involved though.

For a bomb that had completely obliterated an entire human being apart from his hat, which had been found on top of the war memorial, very little structural damage had been done, even the memorial itself surviving intact. A lime tree had completely lost its leaves and much of its bark, and two parked cars had their windows shattered, but that seemed to be about it.

There weren't any obvious hiding places for a bomb.

No bins for example. And no smoking remains of vehicles. Nothing in which to secrete an explosive device. That suggested that the bomb may have been strapped to the victim himself rather than hidden somewhere. I put this to Gulliver but he was non-committal. Why would the victim have chosen to blow himself up? Suicide bombers usually have mass casualties on their mind but from all accounts there had been few other people around.

Except Saul, of course, but it did look like he'd probably survived. There was certainly no evidence, no traces of anything Dawsony lying around, that would suggest otherwise. Anyway, I wasn't going to get much more out of the Chief Superintendent, so I thanked him and walked across the road to Mr Bojangles.

A bell over the door jangled in an old-fashioned and coincidental way as I entered. The shop was dark and musty and smelt of joss sticks. It was a smell I hadn't experienced since university and it brought back unpleasant memories of drunken evenings and bad hangovers.

'Hello!' I shouted. 'Anyone here?'

'Can I help you?' The quiet voice came from behind me and made me jump, which in turn made me annoyed. Well, more annoyed. I was annoyed already and taking my annoyance out on Inspector Abbey Downton hadn't quite assuaged it, so I was ripe for another victim.

I turned sharply and came breast to almost-exposed breast with a middle-aged bottle blonde standing well inside my no-fly zone. For someone who looked likely to move with the silence of a herd of wildebeest, she had arrived behind me surprisingly noiselessly.

I fished out the picture of Saul's lovably ordinary face that I kept in a less-than-security-conscious sort of way in my wallet.

'Have you seen this man at all today, madam?' I asked in my most official-sounding voice, which was remarkably similar to my most annoyed-sounding voice.

'No, I'm afraid not.' Even in the dim interior of the shop, I could see that she hadn't so much as glanced at the photo.

'Perhaps it would help your memory if you actually looked.' I thrust the picture closer to her chubby, over-powdered face.

'Who wants to know?' It was a reasonable sort of question but I wasn't feeling reasonable. I thought rapidly.

'Police,' I said.

'I've already spoken to the police. I'm not repeating myself to a flibbertigibbet like you.' Oh dear, wrong answer. I'd long since left my flibbertigibbeting days behind.

I pinned her by the throat up against a purple-painted pillar. The hours of combat training with Bulldog and his cronies down in the MI6 dojo were at last proving useful, although the woman actually looked as if she would come second in a fight with a particularly flimsy paper bag.

I relaxed my grip slightly. The powder wasn't completely hiding the fact that she had turned slightly green. I didn't want to strangle her, not until I'd got some information out of her anyway.

'How' – pant – 'dare' – pant – 'you!' she panted.

'This man,' I thrust my face to within a few inches of hers, 'was seen entering this shop shortly after the bomb went off this morning. Why? And where did he go afterwards?'

The woman at last looked at the photo of Dawson I was holding up with the hand not currently round her throat. 'Oh, yes,' she said. 'I remember now. He did come in earlier. He bought a dreamcatcher and left again. Now, let me go or I'll scream.'

I tightened my grip again to stop her doing that. I didn't want to fall out with Chief Superintendent Gulliver this early in proceedings and, friendly or not, he probably wouldn't take kindly to me attacking a local shopkeeper.

I suddenly realised that the woman's gaze had shifted to a point over my left shoulder, but no one had come in through the door to the street, that was certain. The bojangling of the bell would have been a dead giveaway. However, as I started to turn my head, something very hard and very painful struck me over my right temple.

Bloody amateur, I thought in self-disgust as I blacked out.

___ In which Dawson has only a foggy
    idea of events, and he and Sofija
    drink beer

'Do you still have your gun?' asked Dawson.

'No. I have this knife. I good with knife,' and Sofija tossed the nasty-looking weapon nonchalantly into the air and caught it again by the handle, whilst still looking at Dawson. It was extremely impressive, especially in the unstable lifeboat, but Dawson still felt a gun would be more use. Or two guns. A hand-held rocket launcher had its attractions too. 'Gun would not work after I jump in water,' Sofija continued. Dawson wasn't sure that was true but he *was* sure that leaving it behind gave their pursuers an extra weapon, not that they were likely to be short of firepower.

He heard the sound of the speedboat's engine starting up behind them. It hadn't taken the Russians long to discover that their bird had flown. The noise was curiously muffled, however, and looking back towards the *Astrid*, he realised that the ship had disappeared. A bank of fog was rolling across the sea towards them. This could surely only be good news.

'Look, fog!' he shouted to Sofija, who was sitting in the stern, one hand holding tightly to the juddering arm of the rudder. The lifeboat was bouncing around and making only slow headway. 'They won't find us in that.'

'I think they have ears on side of heads. They will hear us.'

'But their engine is much louder than ours. It'll drown us out.'

'Please not to use word drown. And yes, louder, but different. They will hear us. We have maybe ten minutes before they catch us.' The bank of fog had now reached the lifeboat and all at once, Sofija's face was not much more than a blur.

'Turn the engine off. They won't find us if they can't hear us.'

'I know what I do, Mr Dawson. You trust me, please. We nearly there.'

'Nearly where?'

'You should always look forwards, not backwards. You cannot change what is behind you.' So Sofija was a bloody philosopher now, was she? Philosopher or not, she was right. He turned his head to face the front. All he could see was fog and spray but no, wait a minute, there was something else, a darker smudge in the greyness. And suddenly they weren't chugging along on the sea but scraping the bottom and lurching to a halt. They had hit land. Whilst Dawson was still taking this in, Sofija was out of the lifeboat, hauling him bodily out after her. Then she gave the boat a mighty shove back off the shelving beach on which they had arrived, turned it to face the open sea again and stood back as, with engine still running, it lolloped slowly off back into the fog and disappeared.

'Good,' she said. 'Come.'

'What is this place?'

'Island. I know place to hide.'

'What island?'

'Does it matter? You have particular island in Baltic you prefer?'

Dawson had to admit that his preferences in this respect were quite limited, so he shrugged and followed the solid but fog-shrouded figure of Sofija up the beach and into a line of windswept trees at the top. She was making a good pace up a steady incline and he struggled to keep up. He didn't want to risk losing her in the fog and getting lost. Abruptly, she stopped and he nearly cannoned into her. He suspected he would have come off worse in the collision.

'Stop,' she whispered, overlooking the fact they already had.

'Why are we whispering?' he whispered back.

'Sound. It travel in fog. Russians not far away, listen.' It was true. Dawson realised the sound of the speedboat's engine had altered and was just a gentle puttering in the middle distance behind them. Perhaps the island was not as well hidden as Sofija had hoped.

'Follow me. Be careful,' said the girl, and Dawson suddenly realised they were standing on the edge of a cliff. Another good reason not to have cannoned into her, he reflected. He peered over the edge and saw waves crashing on to the rocks about ten metres below. The drop didn't seem to concern Sofija, however, who slithered over the edge with the agility of a compact mountain goat. Dawson didn't much like the idea of following her and falling to a soggy death, but the alternatives seemed even less promising. So he shut his eyes, took a deep breath and, trying not to look down, slipped clumsily over the precipice.

Immediately his feet landed on solid ground.

He risked a glance down. He was standing on a ledge. A very narrow ledge, admittedly, no more than forty centimetres wide, but enough to allow him to take a second breath. He looked around. The fog seemed thinner on this side of what must be, he realised, an extremely small island, but thinner or not, he could see no sign of Sofija. She had completely disappeared. He dared a look to the rocks below but she didn't seem to be there and, tough as she was, she would have been likely to yell out had she fallen.

'Sofija,' he called, remembering despite everything to keep his voice down. 'Where are you?'

'Sssh,' he heard in reply. That seemed a bit unfair. He'd thought he was ssshing. 'In here, quick,' and suddenly there was her round, ruddy head poking out of what at first glance appeared to be solid cliff-face. He shuffled along the ledge and saw she had crawled into a crack in the rock that seemed hardly wide enough to have allowed her admittance. She wasn't exactly skinny. Not only was the crack completely indiscernible from above, it could hardly be seen from just a few feet along the ledge. Dawson hoped that it was equally invisible from the sea should the Russian speedboat venture round to this side of the island.

He squeezed through the crack and found himself in a dim but dry space a few metres square, with a low ceiling that wouldn't even allow Sofija to stand upright, let alone the taller Dawson. Sofija was squatting at the back of the cave, and he hoped she was simply avoiding banging her head and not engaged in a more basic function.

'Beer?' she said, holding up a can. Dawson realised he was very thirsty. Hungry too. He had not received the usual slot-delivered breakfast that morning and it was well over twelve hours since he had last eaten.

'Thanks,' he said. 'You don't have any food hidden away in here too, do you? You never brought me my breakfast.'

'Breakfast less important if you dead.' This seemed a logical argument. 'I have food here. Tins only.'

'What have you got?'

'Beans and fruit. Prunes. Not much. We can have a little.'

'Beans then.' Dawson felt that eating prunes might result in an undesirable outcome, given the lack of toilet facilities. It seemed an odd foodstuff to choose. She was busy opening two tins with the words *Ceptas Pupiņas* written on them. Not Heinz then, he thought.

'What is this place? Why have you got this stuff hidden away?'

'I find it, I not remember exactly, six, seven years ago. As girl, I like to explore. My mother was dead and my father, he always busy. So.' She shrugged. 'Is my secret place. Russians not find us here.'

Dawson had a lot of questions to put to this sparky, capable but also strangely vulnerable Latvian girl. He wasn't sure what to ask first so tossed a mental coin.

'What is this island called?'

She shrugged again. 'I do not know. Perhaps it has no

name. Big island out there,' and she pointed out through the cave entrance, 'is Saaremaa.'

Dawson hadn't noticed a big island; he'd been too busy trying not to fall off this small one. 'Saaremaa,' he repeated. 'Is that part of Latvia?'

'Estonia. Next country over. This island too, probably.'

'Don't you know?'

'I not care. There is no customs.' She laughed again. Dawson wondered what manner of disaster would cause her to lose her good humour.

'Why are you helping me?'

'Bored. I want adventure. This is adventure, no?' Dawson thought that adventure might be too optimistic a word for whatever this was. 'Also, I like you. You very nice. You not deserve to be killed by Russians.' He was grateful for her help but found himself hoping that she didn't like him *too* much. He had a Lucy waiting for him back home and knowing Lucy, doing a hell of a lot more than just waiting.

'So do you think the Russians will give up?'

'Maybe. Or maybe they think we go to Saaremaa.'

'And then what?'

'Perhaps we do go there. Is double-bluff, yes?' And again she laughed. Dawson smiled back at her, though it was a little strained. If this was her idea of fun, he'd opt for boredom.

___ In which Elaine watches some cows
   sunbathing, and PC Sam Bunter is
   flustered

During the few weeks she had been in England, Elaine Bates had experienced nothing of the daily traumas suffered by railway travellers in and around London. She was surprised and irritated therefore to discover how long it took her to get from Waterloo to Stallford. She counted fifteen official station stops, where the train hung around, motionless, for endless minutes as if hoping that a throng of latecomers would miraculously appear out of thin air. For reasons of his own, the driver also made three more, random stops, which at least gave Elaine the opportunity to watch herds of cattle basking in the afternoon sunshine.

Eventually, a full two hours after Elaine had stormed out of New Scotland Yard, she alighted at Stallford Station and turned her thoughts towards making contact with Lucy, although it occurred to her that Lucy could be back in London by now.

At the far end of the High Street, a police tape was stretched across the road and a harassed, untidy-looking young police constable in a high-vis jacket was diverting the traffic down a side road that seemed too narrow for the task. Elaine marched up to the tape and flashed her Met badge at the young copper.

'Gosh,' he said. This wasn't a figure of speech known to Elaine. She doubted if it was a word that had ever passed an Australian's lips. 'First it's MI6, now the Met are here. Popular, aren't we?'

The mention of MI6 grabbed Elaine's attention. 'MI6? Blonde woman, my sort of age, annoyingly attractive?'

'That's her,' said the copper, smiling a big, white-toothed smile. He looked happy to be taking a break from redirecting angry car drivers. 'Attractive yes, gorgeous in fact. Not that you're not, of course,' he added hurriedly, his face reddening.

'Yeah, mate, you can cut the bullshit.' Elaine knew that her pointed little face and sharp, dark eyes were not the stuff of male fantasies, and she had long since learned to live with that. 'When did you see her?'

'Couple of hours back, I suppose.' He glanced up the street, where there was still some forensic activity going on under a tent that had been erected by the war memorial. A few other police officers were standing around looking bored. 'Your friend, er...'

'Lucy Smith,' said Elaine helpfully. 'And no, I'm not giving you her phone number.'

'Oh, er, no, I mean, that's not...' He took a deep breath and composed himself. 'Miss Smith was talking to the Super and then she went into that shop up there on the right.' He pointed to Mr Bojangles.

'Keeping an eye on her, were you?' said Elaine, glad that he had. She smiled at his embarrassment. 'Don't worry, I would too.' That turned up his embarrassment levels several notches. 'And did your eye-keeping extend to noticing where she went when she came out?'

'She didn't come out.'

'What? And this was two hours ago?' He nodded. 'How can you be sure of that? You've been directing this traffic, haven't you?'

'Trust me, sarge, if she'd come out of that shop, I'd have noticed.' Elaine didn't doubt it for a second.

'Didn't you think that odd?'

'Course. As soon as I'm done here, I'm going to look for her.'

'For professional reasons of course.'

'Yes. What do you take me for?'

'A bloke. I'm going to look now. Care to come with me? What's your name, by the way?'

'Sam Bunter, sarge. And yes, I'm with you. Hang on a mo.' He gave a whistle and waved at one of the coppers by the memorial, who wandered across. 'Joey, mate, can you take over here? I've got to go with this Met sergeant.'

Joey nodded. 'Sure thing. No probs.'

'I'm Elaine, by the way,' said Elaine as she and Sam walked up the road. 'Sorry if I come across a bit abrupt. I can be like that sometimes, especially where friends are involved.'

'So this Lucy's a friend of yours, is she?'

'Yeah, although I haven't seen her for a while. Oh, and er, better get this out there straightaway – I'm afraid she's taken.'

'I'd be amazed if she weren't.' PC Sam grinned a big-toothed grin. 'Don't worry, it was only lust at first sight. Happens all the time.'

Not where I'm concerned, thought Elaine ruefully, reflecting that more than a year had passed since her last serious relationship, if a three-night vacation to Uluru and a couple of trips to the Village Cinema in Shepparton could be called a serious relationship.

Arriving at Mr Bojangles, Elaine tried the door, but it was locked. 'That's unusual, isn't it?' She looked at the two shops either side, both of which were open despite the shortage of customers due to the road closure.

'Yes,' said Sam, 'but maybe business is a bit slow, what with the bomb and all. Come on, let's try next door.'

The next-door shop was a small newsagent. A dark-skinned man of about seventy with twinkly eyes and pure white hair hurried out of a back room to greet them.

'Good afternoon, officer,' he said to Sam. 'Are you here to tell me that the road is reopening? I have lost so much in takings, so much. It is a terrible day.'

Elaine wasn't sure if the terrible day referred to the death of a man in a bomb explosion or the dent in his daily takings but decided not to rush to judgement. 'Can I have your name sir?' she asked.

'My name is Zaheer Abbas and, yes, officer, before you are asking, this is my shop and has been for nearly thirty years.

I have very many loyal, regular customers who do not wish to be going to Mr Smith's or Mr Waitrose's shops, where the service is not, you understand, as personal as...'

'Thank you, sir,' interrupted Elaine. It had been a simple opening question, not a request for his full life story. 'Next door, Mr Bojangles. It's shut. Do you know why?'

'Ah, yes, Mrs Marjorie, she is often shut. Saturday afternoons, always by this time. Very little business. I ask her once, do you make a profit? I could not be seeing how she can, not here in Stallford. Her shop should be at the seaside, I am saying. She was very rude, said it was none of my business, but I was only making conversation. Not very nice lady, not nice at all, very vulgar.'

Zaheer Abbas did not appear to possess a stop button but Elaine was impatient to get on. 'A young lady entered Mr Bojangles around lunchtime and hasn't been seen since. You didn't happen to notice her, did you?'

'Yes, indeed, very pretty lady, yellow hair, not like you.' Elaine presumed Abbas was referring purely to the difference in hair colour, not to any variance in prettiness. He didn't seem the type of man who would go around wilfully insulting female police officers. It was hard though to see how Lucy could be a successful secret agent when she stood out like the least sore thumb in the world to every Tom, Sam, Dick and Zaheer who clapped eyes on her. Abbas hadn't finished though. 'The lady, she left by the back door, long time ago. One o'clock maybe, just after, something like that.'

'What?' Elaine and Sam spoke together, but once again, Abbas hadn't finished.

'She was not well, I could see this, they were having to carry her to the van.'

Elaine and Sam looked at each other.

'What van?' said Elaine.

'Did you recognise the men who were carrying her?' chipped in Sam simultaneously.

Zaheer Abbas looked from one to the other, unsure who to answer. He finally plumped for Elaine who was half the size of her male companion but rather scarier. 'Mr Bojangles' van,' he said. 'Purple with yellow writing, very garish indeed, very vulgar, like Mrs Marjorie, a small Ford maybe, I do not know about vans.'

'And did you report this?' asked Elaine.

'No, of course not,' said Abbas. 'Why would I be doing that? The lady was being carried by a policeman. Very big policeman. Mrs Marjorie, she was helping.'

__ In which Sofija lies on top of
    Dawson, and Dawson pees over
    a cliff

Several hours had gone by in companionable silence. At some point the speedboat had passed in front of their hiding place and Sofija had put her finger to her lips as if she thought Dawson might cry out. Now though, the only sound was the muted crashing of the waves on the rocks below. Daylight was still streaming through the crack and it seemed somehow brighter than earlier. Probably that meant that the fog had lifted.

'How long are we staying here?' he asked the girl lying on her back next to him. Judging by the slight wheezing noises she was making, she had somehow managed to fall asleep in the cramped, uncomfortable cave. There was no answer, so he prodded her lightly with his foot and without warning she sprung up and on top of him and had her hand on his throat before he even realised what was happening.

'What the...' he gasped.

Sofija's face was only an inch or two from his own and there was a coldness in her eyes he had not seen before. She seemed to be staring straight through him. Her neck muscles were tensed like steel hawsers. Gradually, she relaxed. 'I am sorry,' she said, easing her grip. 'I was asleep.'

It didn't seem much of an excuse to Dawson. He'd woken several people up over the years and hardly any of them had felt the urge to strangle him. Sofija's expression returned to its more usual smiliness.

'Do you normally attack people for waking you up?'

She gave this more thought than strictly necessary. 'Not often.'

'Would you mind getting off me?' She was heavier than she looked. Probably all the hidden muscle.

'I do not know,' she replied. 'You very comfortable. I would sleep better on top of you than on ground.' She laughed, but rolled off him anyway and lay, breathing heavily, next to him.

'I was wondering how long we should give it before we make tracks.' A thought occurred to him. 'Do you have a phone on you? My phone perhaps. You forgot to give me my things back.'

'No, no phone. Same reason as no gun. Baltic Sea not good for phones.' It seemed more plausible than the gun story and he certainly hadn't seen any sign of a phone but he nevertheless had the feeling she was lying. 'We stay until it get darker. Not yet.'

Dawson looked at her. There was something about her that didn't add up but he couldn't work out what. 'Do you think they've given up?' he asked.

'Russians? Maybe. Maybe not.'

'I could do with relieving myself.'

'What of?' Sofija sounded puzzled. It was obviously not an expression she knew.

'I need a pee,' Dawson tried.

'No peas,' said the girl. 'Just beans. And not many. We must save these. There are lots of prunes though,' she added brightly.

'Piss,' said Dawson. 'Toilet, lavatory, khazi. And I'll need it a lot more if we start on the prunes.'

'Why you not say about piss?' She shuffled agilely to the cave entrance on hands and knees and peered out. 'Yes, is safe, be quick.'

Dawson found, on trying to move, that a few hours of inactivity had stiffened several muscles, including a few he hadn't previously known he possessed, so his progress across the cave was considerably less agile than Sofija's. He edged out of the entrance and found a bright sun burning low down to his left out of a cloudless sky. Seabirds wheeled and skittered overhead. It was a surprisingly warm evening. He had always supposed the Baltic would be permanently chilly at best, even in midsummer. There were no boats in sight but what was presumably the island of Saaremaa filled the horizon ahead of him. How could he not have noticed it earlier? It only seemed to be a mile or two away, almost within touching distance. He could even see traffic moving along a coast road. He peed over the edge of the cliff and edged back into the cave.

'If that's Saaremaa,' he said, 'then it looks like we could probably come up with a way of getting across. See if your bluff idea works.'

'Is further than it look. You cannot swim across, even in daylight. Very bad currents. But, yes, you are right, is only place we can go. We must wait until night. Three more hours. In June in Baltic, night is very short.'

'How do you propose we get there?'

'Propose? I not think we know each other long enough.'

'What?' He turned and saw she was grinning at him again.

'Is joke,' she said, 'but ask me again when I save you from Russians. I might say yes. You are thin and, what is word? floppy, but I can make man of you.' Yet again she laughed.

Dawson hoped that floppy was not the word. He was quite proud that no one had ever mentioned any inherent floppiness to him before, especially Lucy, but he shrugged it off. He wasn't sure if this short, stocky, smiley Latvian girl genuinely was talking about marriage or whether she was, as she suggested, joking. Either way, he didn't feel that this was the best time to tell her about Lucy. Not while his safety was so completely in her hands.

'You said that swimming is out of the question and I certainly wouldn't want to try it in the dark. And as you decided that the lifeboat was superfluous, how are we going to get to Saaremaa?'

'Super...? I not know this word.'

'Not needed. You pushed it back out to sea. You remember?'

'Yes, if Russians spot boat, they know we here. Do you not understand this?'

'Yes, of course, I'm not stupid.'

'If you say so. Not that boat. We use raft.'

Dawson had never built a raft and wasn't sure how they would go about it without tools. An axe for example. Or a saw. Hammer and nails. Something that might help to turn a tree into a raft capable of holding two people on an open sea with bad currents without capsizing. It sounded like a difficult and time-consuming task at best, and night would fall in three hours. 'OK,' he said. 'We'd better get started.'

'No, we wait until dark. Did you not hear?'

'We can't build a raft in the dark. And what do we build it with anyway?'

Sofija put her hand to her mouth in mock horror. 'Oh, no, I not think of that. Lucky that I already have raft. It is hidden. Down there,' and she pointed over the cliff edge.

This made no sense. Why had Sofija not mentioned the raft before and why would she have one hidden on the island anyway? According to her, she hadn't been here for years, and would always have come in a boat in any case. And what state would the raft be in, after lying concealed for goodness knows how long close to, or even submerged in, saltwater?

Contradictory wasn't the half of it. Dawson was beginning to convince himself that Sofija and the truth enjoyed a very tenuous relationship.

_ In which Sam looks in some
   recycle bins, and Elaine
   spots a manhole cover

The empty car park at the rear of both Mr Bojangles and Zaheer Abbas's shop was hardly big enough to be described as such, especially as it also had to make room for two large recycling bins.

'What happens if they both want to get their cars in here at once?' Sam wondered. Outside the back door of the newsagents, chained to a drainpipe, was an old sit-up-and-beg bike, complete with handlebar basket. It looked like the sort of contraption that Abbas would ride.

'I think that may be Abbas's car,' said Elaine.

'Yes indeed, Miss Police Lady,' said Abbas, who had joined them uninvited. 'I do not like cars. Mrs Abbas used to drive but she is no longer with us, *Allahu Akbar.*'

'I'm sorry to hear that, sir,' said Sam politely. 'Did she die recently?'

'Oh, no, officer,' said Abbas, shaking his head vigorously. 'She is not dead. She ran away with her driving instructor. It was extremely fortuitous, indeed it was.'

Elaine decided to take charge of the situation. 'If we need any further assistance, we'll ask,' she said to Abbas.

Meanwhile, Sam had crossed to the nearest recycling bin and peered inside. He repeated the exercise with the second bin. 'She's not going to be in there, is she?' Elaine snapped. 'He's a pretty reliable witness so we can assume Lucy's been driven off in the purple van. We need to get a search going for it. I guess that's not something you can authorise and for all I know, I've been suspended by now, so we'll need to find your boss and let him know what's going on.'

'I wasn't looking for Miss Smith. I just wondered, being secret service and all that, whether she might have managed to dump a clue of some sort in a bin as she was being taken out.'

'And did she?'

'Doesn't look like it. Both bins are empty. It was bin day yesterday.'

'How the fuck is she going to dump a clue in a bin while she's unconscious? And what sort of clue? A map she's miraculously drawn while out cold pointing to a place she doesn't know?' She took a deep breath. 'I'm sorry, Sam, but we're wasting time. Who's your chief?'

'That's sort of the point, really. It's Chief Inspector Downton and he's, well, a big man. A very big man.' And in case he had not made himself entirely clear, he added, 'A very big policeman.'

'What? Are you suggesting your inspector could be the copper who put Lucy in the van?'

'It's possible. He's an absolute bastard, 'scuse my French, and actually I haven't seen him all afternoon.'

'While I'm not sure that a high level of bastardness would necessarily make a copper bent, it's certainly worth pursuing. So, if Inspector Downton is in it up to his neck, who else do you report to?'

'Well, there's a Chief Super across from Guildford in charge. I saw him over by the memorial not long since, although...'

But Elaine was already striding back into the shop, manoeuvring Zaheer Abbas carefully but firmly out of her path. 'He's our boy then,' she said over her shoulder. 'Let's go talk to him.'

Sam trailed after her. 'I can't just go up to Chief Superintendent Gulliver and tell him all this, there are proper channels.'

'That's his name is it? Gulliver? Well if you can't, I will,' said Elaine. Jesus, she thought, proper channels. Bloody tight-arsed poms. 'Don't be such a drongo,' she added, forcibly.

'Drongo? Are you calling me a dog?'

'No, you drongo, that's a dingo.'

Exiting the shop, they saw that South Street had finally been reopened to traffic, but there was a small group of officials still hovering near the memorial, looking as though they were about to make tracks. Apart from a denuded tree, there was little to suggest that a bomb had gone off only a few hours earlier.

Elaine pointed to a small man who wouldn't have stood out in a crowd of one. 'Gulliver, I presume.' Sam reluctantly nodded. But twenty feet short of the small group of Gulliver, a senior fire officer and a middle-aged woman in plain clothes with a police holdall slung over her shoulder, Elaine stopped suddenly. 'That's odd,' she said, looking at her feet.

'What's odd about your feet?' asked Sam, joining her.

'Not my feet, you dipstick. This manhole cover. Look at it.' She bent and stared more closely, her dark eyes narrowed against the afternoon sun. Sam looked too but wasn't sure what he was supposed to be looking at. It was a manhole cover. The road and pavement were full of them.

'What have you found, young lady?' came a voice. Chief Superintendent Gulliver, who didn't miss much, was certainly not going to miss a woman accompanied by a uniformed constable squatting down in a crime scene peering at the ground.

Elaine looked up. 'This manhole cover's new,' she said.

Sam still didn't understand what she was on about but Gulliver did. He bent down. Being so small, he didn't have to bend very far to get a good view. 'And you are?' he asked.

'DS Bates, Met Police, sir. You see what I mean?'

'I do, sergeant. How come there's a completely unmarked, shiny new manhole cover right where there's just been a bomb go off?' They glanced around at the surrounding blackened and scarred pavement. Gulliver, who didn't miss much, was annoyed that he had missed that. 'Now why didn't any of us spot that? Good work. And now we've got that off our chests,' he added, straightening, 'what exactly are you doing here?'

He recalled asking a similar question of another young lady a few hours earlier. It seemed any number of young ladies wanted a piece of this particular action.

Elaine decided that it was probably not the time to explain that she was supposed to be back in New Scotland Yard holding PC Johnson's hand while he wrestled with the filing, so skipped that bit and jumped to something more relevant. 'My friend was here, and she appears to have been sloshed over the head and kidnapped by one of your officers. We need to get a spot out for the van she was driven away in.'

This wasn't exactly what Gulliver had expected to hear, but he wasn't a man who wasted time. 'Who is your friend and why do you think she's been kidnapped?'

Elaine, with her traffic cop background, was used to explaining things pithily, and took no time to go through what they knew and what they guessed. Gulliver listened without taking offence at the pithiness. He looked less than impressed at the mention of Chief Inspector Downton but perked up when Elaine mentioned Lucy.

'So, let's get this clear, it's the MI6 woman who you say has been abducted by my chief inspector.' Elaine nodded. 'That's a very serious accusation to make of a police officer, especially as you didn't actually see the kidnapping take place.' No shit, thought Elaine. 'Anybody can buy a fake police uniform and they come in all sizes.' Nevertheless, he turned to the forensics woman. 'When did we last see Inspector Downton, Anne? Not for a while, I'm thinking.' She shook her head, which was confusing as she was presumably agreeing with him.

Gulliver pulled his phone out of a pocket, stabbed at a button and spoke quickly into it. 'Gulliver here. Get a search started for a small purple van with the name Mr Bojangles in yellow on the side. VRM unknown but there can't be many vehicles of that description. A Ford of some kind possibly. Yes, that's right, Bojangles, as in the song. Before your time maybe. Do it now, please. Also, can you put Chief Inspector Downton on the line?' There was a pause. 'Has he been there at all this afternoon?' Another pause. 'Give me his number, please. Thank you.' He rung off and punched a number quickly into his phone. It was clear to all four people watching that no one was answering. Eventually the voicemail kicked in. 'Abbey? Call me back as soon as you get this.' He hung up and looked around the small group. 'I need you to do your stuff with this manhole cover, please, Anne. Can you get your guys back again sharpish? This cover, the old cover if we can find it or what's left of it and the drain itself. Don't stop until you find something. I'll be at the station. Sergeant Bates, come with me. Constable, you can go back to your friend in the paper shop and check if he's got any CCTV out the back.'

'We didn't see any, sir.'

'Were you looking?' Both Sam and Elaine had to admit that they had not been looking. 'So, go and ask, will you?' Gulliver paused and looked up at Elaine and quite a bit further up at Sam. 'However, good work, both of you. Sergeant, we'll see if we can't square this with your bosses at the Met. What you did seems entirely reasonable to me.' He tried to force a smile but, remembering that he quite probably had a crooked inspector on his payroll who might turn out to be a terrorist, he couldn't quite manage it.

I was woken up by another thump on the head, this one caused by my diving headfirst onto the filthy floor of a small van that, judging by the bucketing, jolting and sliding going on, was not currently travelling along a road. It felt as though it was careering out of control down a steep embankment. I tried to find something to cling on to, but I was probably at 75% functionality at best, so wasn't especially successful. Just as I saw something that I could grab, it slid away from me, or me from it, one of the two. The result of all this banging about was a couple more bruises, this time on my left elbow and right buttock.

Eventually, after what seemed like half an hour of this barrelling progress, but which was probably less than half a minute, the ground levelled out and the van stopped. There were no windows, but an air vent in the roof cast just enough light for me to make out that there was nothing in the back of the van apart from me and a metal bench running along one side, on which I had presumably been lying before being hurled to the floor.

I heard a door open and someone got out of the van. Then there was a clang and a creak. Gate, I thought. By now I was getting up towards 90% of full fitness, even allowing for the bruises and the headache. I'm a lot tougher and more resilient than I used to be.

Bulldog, he of the MI6 dojo, had repeatedly and forcefully informed me that pain only exists if you allow it to. He had introduced quite a lot of pain into our sessions to emphasise the point. 'Convert the pain into anger,' he'd said, and after the fifteenth bit of pain he'd inflicted on me, I'd managed to convert it into so much anger that Bulldog himself had failed to turn up to our afternoon appointment, which had been taken from quite a distance away by his number two, Snape. The next day, Bulldog had reappeared, trying to disguise a limp, but he at least had the decency to buy me a drink that evening. 'I thought you said not to show pain,' I'd remarked, wittily. I hadn't been sure whether I was expected to apologise, so didn't. Snape told me later that had been worth another five points on my scorecard, leaving me, extraordinarily to my mind, as their best ever female pupil, and the best of any gender for four years. I hadn't told Saul that of course. 'How d'you get on?' he'd asked. 'I passed,' I'd said. 'It was fine, you'll be fine.' His own stint in the dojo had been delayed by Elspeth Arundell, another reason to suppose she was looking to get rid of him. Saul, of course, had not pushed the matter. 'It doesn't need both of us to be all butch,' he'd said when I'd offered to chase it up. I'd made him regret that butch, although not in a butchy way.

The van moved off again, slowly and not for very long. We stopped for a second time and the engine was switched off. I could hear voices. I couldn't make out what they were saying, but there were two of them and I thought I recognised them both, one for sure. It was a female voice, whiny, sounding tense. Definitely the woman from Mr Bojangles. I was itching to get my hand at her throat again and, as they hadn't bothered to restrain me in any way, I couldn't see any reason why that happy eventuality should not come to pass. Assuming someone opened the rear door of the van and let me out. It suddenly occurred to me that permanent incarceration might actually be their plan. Or perhaps they'd just set fire to the van in what, judging by the recent barrelling down the embankment, was probably quite an out of the way spot. 'Snap out of it, woman,' I said out loud. I needed to get a grip.

When had I heard the other voice? Today, I decided, definitely today. Male, gruff, touch of arrogance perhaps. Oh, wait a minute. No. Surely not. Chief Inspector Abbey Downton? I listened again but could only hear low muttering now. Let's think. Downton was a copper, a senior copper and he must be genuine because Superintendent Gulliver and everyone else around him had accepted him as one. Bona fide coppers, however, don't go around biffing people over the noggin for no reason. True, I was holding Mrs Bojangles by the throat at the time, but a polite verbal remonstration from a policeman would have made me stop. Probably. And even if he had decided that he liked me so little after our discussion in South Street that hitting me would give him some sort of satisfaction, a true bastion of the law was unlikely to have bundled me into a van and taken off to wherever we were now.

I no longer had anything in my pockets, no phone, no ID, nothing, but I was still wearing a watch which had survived the buffeting rather more successfully than I had. I had to hold my wrist close to the air vent in the roof to see the time but was astonished to note that it was only two o'clock. It was less than an hour since I'd entered the shop. My head must be tougher than I'd thought. We couldn't be more than about twenty miles from Stallford. It was something, but it didn't help much.

My thoughts were interrupted by the sound of both front doors opening and then, suddenly, a third voice, getting closer. Now that my captors were out in the open, I could hear them much more clearly.

'Marjorie, stay by the van.' That was Downton. Definitely.

'What the fuck you doin' 'ere?' This was the third voice. Whoever he was, I could see I'd have to have a word with him about his grammar.

'Change of plan. Some bimbo claims to be secret service, got too close, so we've had to bring her along.'

'You're still in fuckin' uniform. Anyone see you?'

'Not doing anything I shouldn't. Don't worry. Nobody'll miss me. We'll get her in the house and you can take care of her. Marj and I'll get back to Stallford. She can drop me on the edge of town. No one'll know I've gone. Gulliver doesn't want me around anyway.'

'Why not? 'E don't suspect nuffink, does 'e?'

At this point, I heard a key being inserted in the lock on the rear doors, so I nimbly sprang back on to the bench and feigned unconsciousness, watching through hooded eyes. If I was going to have to fight my way to freedom, I'd rather not be doing it from a confined space. Better to be taken somewhere with a possible escape route.

It was just as well I'd made that decision, as the first thing I saw when the doors opened was a gun. A big gun. It looked like the sort of shotgun that could be used to down several elephants, and it was pointing straight at me.

It was hard to describe the man who was doing the pointing. Well, I say man, but he was more a walking tattoo. It was genuinely quite difficult to spot the human under all the ink. He was shortish, squattish, completely bald (you can't easily tattoo skin covered in hair) and sported a brow as low as a limbo bar. He was also, as far as I could see, the possessor of no more than half a dozen rotting teeth, scattered randomly around his mouth, and that was six more teeth than discernible nails on the end of the ugly fingers pointing the shotgun at me.

Chief Inspector Abbey Downton was standing a few paces behind him, still wearing full uniform and with a look on his monolithic face that was hard to determine, especially with my eyes half shut.

'Oi, you, bitch, shift yer arse and get out 'ere.' That was the mobile tattoo parlour. I felt it politic to open my eyes fully at that point. I groaned theatrically and clasped my hands to my head. I don't know how convincing a performance it was, but Inkman didn't seem to see anything amiss with it and Downton wasn't actually taking much interest in proceedings. I didn't know whether he'd had anyone killed before, but he'd told Inkman to take care of me and he hadn't been asking him to run me a hot bath and make me a cup of cocoa. I knew who he was, so if he wanted to go on pretending to be an upright enforcer of the law, he obviously couldn't afford to have me stick my hand up and suggest criminal or terrorist tendencies. It might come down to my word against his and I was confident that my word would triumph, especially if Marj Bojangles proved as easy to break as she looked.

I'm making this sound as though I was full of bravado here, but in truth I was terrified. Nothing in Australia, and nothing since, not my time with Bulldog and Snape, not even my interviews with Elspeth Arundell, had prepared me for a showdown with the ugliest man in the world holding a cannon-sized shotgun with orders to "take care" of me.

_ In which a van disappears, and
Elaine and Gulliver start down
a slippery slope

Back at Stallford Police Station, Gulliver phoned Elaine's inspector at New Scotland Yard to explain her disappearance from her important work assisting PC Johnson to file traffic reports. It was a wasted call, the inspector not having noticed her absence. 'Yes, sir, keep her by all means,' he said. 'As long as you like.'

'You don't seem to have made too positive an impression,' remarked Gulliver, hanging up.

'Bit of racism, I reckon, sir.'

'Accusing a senior officer of racism half an hour after you've accused another one of terrorism is unlikely to make you many friends.'

'If it's true, it might.'

'Probably not even then. You'd better hang around here for a while.'

There was a knock on the door and a young constable entered. 'The purple van was spotted at Leatherhead, sir,' he said without preamble. Elaine thought that the atmosphere was a whole lot more relaxed here than up at the Yard. 'But it disappeared somewhere around junction 9 of the M25.'

'What do you mean, disappeared?'

'Well, sir, the cameras picked up the van heading on to the motorway, going west, but it doesn't seem to have reached the next camera.'

'And how far's that?'

'Less than a mile, sir.' Elaine tried to translate that into normal worldspeak. Bloody miles. It was about time the Brits caught up with the rest of the planet. It was like speaking in tongues.

'And you're saying, if I'm not mistaken, that that's before the next exit,' Gulliver said.

'Right, sir.'

'OK, sergeant,' Gulliver said to Elaine. 'Let's go look for this van. You and me'll see if we can't find ourselves an MI6 agent. And if Chief Inspector Downton's with her, you'll still probably have a job.' He turned to the constable. 'Point any backup in our direction when they get here, would you?'

'Hang on, sir.' Elaine had been staring intently out of the window as the unremarkable grey Mondeo, unremarkable that is apart from the blue flashing lights in the front grille and rear window, edged slowly up the hard shoulder of the M25. Gulliver braked sharply.

'What is it?'

'Back up a bit, sir.' He did so and Elaine got out. 'Gap in the barrier.' Gulliver checked to see he wasn't going to be wiped out by a passing lorry and followed her. She was already peering closely at the ground between the gap in the safety barrier, a gap that should not have been there. 'A vehicle's been through here, sir. Today, I reckon. Look, the grass has been flattened. It's only just starting to rise again.'

Gulliver looked but saw nothing apart from long grass dotted with dandelion and cow parsley. If there was a flattening of the grass, he couldn't spot it. 'OK, I'll take your word for it. Traffic policing Down Under involves a lot of tracking through the bush, I presume.'

Elaine ignored the comment and moved slowly forwards, still looking down. After ten metres there was a small rise in the ground. The small rise was immediately followed by a long drop, not steep but a steady if undulating downward gradient through a large meadow full of wildflowers and with a small brook at the bottom. Clearly visible, heading down the grassy slope, were some tyre tracks. There appeared to have been quite a lot of skidding, if their zigzag route was anything to go by. 'I think we may have struck gold, sir. What now?'

'Now we slide down the meadow, I should think. You OK with that?' He glanced at her feet but needn't have worried. Elaine was wearing a pair of sturdy trainers. She rarely wore anything else now that her uniform days were, at least for the time being, behind her. The only things sturdier than her trainers were Gulliver's own shoes, which might have been purchased from a shop called "All-Weather Footwear for the Discerning Policeman."

Elaine was definitely up for sliding down the slope and as quickly as possible, aware that Lucy had been missing for several hours. 'Of course, sir. What about the car, though?'

'It's fine; it's locked. If some idiot chooses to drive into it on the hard shoulder, that's their lookout. Also, it'll tell our backup where we are when they finally get here. Come on, let's go.'

___ In which Dawson is sick on
a beach, and Sofija mentions
an abnormal snowman

At first glance, the raft that Sofija had retrieved from the bottom of a shallow pool amongst the rocks resembled nothing remotely raftlike. The only thing that gave Dawson any confidence in its buoyancy was that it was made of wood, but he suspected that a few years' submergence was likely to have had an adverse effect on its floatability.

'It doesn't look very seaworthy.' As he was about to entrust his life to the raft, he felt he had a right to venture an honest opinion about whether it was up to the task.

'Will be fine,' said Sofija. 'Help me carry it to sea.' Dawson thought she could probably manage that on her own but maybe she didn't want him to feel inferior. As far as he was concerned, that ship had long since sailed, even if the raft might not be about to follow suit.

'A torch would be useful,' he said, when they reached a small beach and were staring out into what was by now near blackness. The island of Saaremaa was presumably still in front of them but there was no sign of it.

'Torch can be seen from many miles away. You do not think before you speak. How you know Russians gone? They may be hiding, waiting for us. Is what I would do. Dark is good.'

'And what happens if we miss Saaremaa? What's the next land after that?'

'Zviedrija.'

'Which is where exactly?'

'Sweden.'

Dawson thought Sweden sounded a much more friendly destination than Saaremaa. There was a British Embassy in Sweden. 'Why don't we try and get there?' he asked.

'You not make sense. First, you say raft not get to Saaremaa, and then you say go to Sweden. Saaremaa we can reach. How far you think Sweden is?' Dawson didn't know but realised she was making a valid point. 'Anyway, is hard to miss Saaremaa, even in dark. Is big island. You have seen this.'

Three hours later, after the most frightening journey Dawson had ever undertaken, they were lying on their backs on a narrow strip of shingle with the early dawn lightening the eastern sky. The raft was consigned to the same waves from which they had lately hauled themselves. First the lifeboat, now the raft, thought Dawson; Sofija clearly didn't believe in hanging onto things. Bits had fallen off the raft at regular intervals during their journey, bits that had included Dawson, twice. The first time, Sofija had reached out with a powerful hand and grabbed him by the unmentionables. Whilst he had admired both her quick thinking and the tenacity of her grip, he had had to inform her, once he'd stopped screaming from the pain, that he was actually a decent swimmer. He hadn't been completely certain whether the part of him she had grabbed had been deliberate or happenstance. She claimed the latter, without going so far as to apologise but, judging by her behaviour towards him earlier, she may just have been sizing him up.

The second time he'd fallen off, he could see surf breaking ahead, so he'd pushed off entirely and half swum, half waded ashore, leaving Sofija and the raft to make their own way.

He rolled over and retched a stream of seawater into the shingle. Suddenly there was Sofija, standing over him, dripping water, tugging at the back of his collar. She had a thing about necks, Dawson concluded.

'We must move. Day is nearly here. Russians may be keeping watch.' She pulled harder and, despite his best efforts at resistance, Dawson found himself being dragged to his knees.

'I get it,' he said irritably. 'Look, we need to find somewhere a bit warmer. We'll catch pneumonia if we don't.' He inched himself slowly to his feet and looked around. There was a keen wind coming off the sea. In the half light, he could see a rough slope of sandy grass with tufts of unidentifiable vegetation stretching up towards a low stone wall about fifty metres away. He guessed there might be a road the other side of the wall but it was far too early for any traffic. He started up the incline, not bothering to look back to see if the girl was following. Reaching the wall, he eased himself over it and sat down.

'East is to the right,' he said, but then he noticed that Sofija was only now heading up the slope towards him. As she arrived, he pointed towards the sun peeping over the horizon. 'Estonia is east of Latvia, if I've got my geography right, and west is, as you pointed out, the way to Sweden, which is a long way away with a lot of sea in between. So I suggest we head as near east as we can.'

He hoisted himself to his feet and looked at the girl. His main target was to locate some source of officialdom, a police station possibly, which could contact the British Consulate. And he didn't really care if Sofija came with him. In fact, if she did, there was a good chance she'd contradict the story he planned to give the authorities. Not so much a story as the absolute truth, and as he had more than a strong suspicion that Sofija wasn't what she was claiming to be, she might put a gigantic wrench in the works should any local police question her separately.

'OK, but we must be careful. Will be busy soon.'

'Busy's good. We could use a lift. We might be miles from any sort of town.'

'You forget Russians.'

'Yes, these Russians you say are after us. I've only got your word for that, haven't I?'

Sofija marched up to him, with a glare that would have turned a sphinx to sand. Dawson ignored it, although he was glad she had her hands down by her sides.

'Who you think is chasing us? Abnormal snowman?'

Despite himself, Dawson laughed. 'I think you mean abominable.'

'Abom... You invent this word. Shut up. If Russians not after us, then who? You tell me.'

'That's the point. I don't know. You say it's the Russians, you say the Russians paid, or didn't pay, or were going to pay your dad to bring me here, but it all seems a bit unlikely, doesn't it? If they want me dead, they aren't without resources closer to home. They could have had me killed anywhere. Bit of Novichok and Bob's your uncle.' Then he realised, they had tried. With a bomb. This might be their Plan B.

Sofija stood watching him, the ferocious glare replaced with a more open, questioning expression, with her arms crossed in front of her chest. She spoke. 'You know I am right, yes? You have, how is it? worked it out, yes? With your Uncle Bob, maybe.'

Dawson still wasn't sure though. If the SVR had tried and failed to blow him up in Stallford and had then gone to all the trouble of hiring Sofija's father to transport him to the Gulf of Riga, a journey taking four days, just so they could bump him off there, it still didn't explain why Sofija had decided to go rogue. What did she expect to get out of it? However, it seemed on reflection, and with her blue eyes boring into his with that same questioning look on her open face – a face so open it was hard to believe it capable of duplicitousness – that the Russians probably were behind all this. They would still be after him. And therefore Sofija as well. Being an English gentleman, in a common or garden sort of way, it was surely Dawson's responsibility to ensure that his young female companion, tough as she was, came to no harm.

'Right,' he said decisively. 'This is what's going to happen. I'm going to take my chances and try and make my way to civilisation, to the nearest police station or equivalent. I won't accept any lifts and if I hear a car coming, I'll simply scoot off into the woods until it's gone. I don't imagine it'll be like Piccadilly Circus.'

Sofija started to say, 'Pick a what...?' but Dawson hadn't finished.

'As for you, thanks, really, you've been amazing, but the next town is where we part company. You need to make your way back, apologise to your dad, and forget all about me and this little adventure you've led me on. Not adventure, no, escape. This escape.' He hadn't looked at her while he was speaking, but now he did. The questioning look she'd worn a minute earlier had gone again and the glare was back. She advanced two steps until she was breast to stomach with him.

'Have you finish now? I thought you were idiot, nice idiot but idiot. Then I think, no, maybe not. Not idiot. Now?' She spat at his feet. 'Idiot again. Still idiot. You need me. You think Russians will not be watching police or paying police even? I can get you to your so-called civilisation and find you honest officials to hand yourself in. And anyway, how I get back to my father, who probably killed anyway if you remember? I have no boat.' She looked at Dawson accusingly as if the lack of a boat was entirely down to him. It certainly sounded more important than the possible death of her father. 'I not swim back to Riga.' Dawson wouldn't have put it past her but nodded. 'I come with you to Kuressaare, capital of island. Is less than ten kilometres from here.'

'I thought you said you'd never been on Saaremaa.' She ignored him.

'There is no British Consul, but I know person who can help. Not police. And, no, it was you said I had not been here. I never say that.' Dawson tried to think back. There had certainly been an implication that she had never been to the island before but maybe nothing more than that. But she had definitely never suggested that she knew a "person who can help". Although, come to think of it, why else would she head for Saaremaa in the first place?

'OK then, you win,' he started to say, when the noise of an engine being heavily gunned broke the early morning silence. It was coming from the east, from the direction of Kuressaare, and it was coming fast. He grabbed Sofija by the arm and pulled her across the road and into some bushes on the other side. Peering out through the leaves, they saw an elderly, long-wheelbase Land Rover Defender roar towards them around a bend fifty metres up the road. Then, for no obvious reason, it stopped with a screech of brakes and two men got out. The driver was a solid man dressed in black, probably in his twenties, with a shaved head and wide Slavic features, and holding an automatic pistol. The man who emerged more slowly from the passenger side was in his late thirties, of medium build, wearing a pale grey suit and open-necked white shirt. His fair hair was cropped short and his pale blue eyes possessed a piecing stare that looked capable of seeing through walls, let alone a bush or two.

Dawson drew a deep but silent breath. Valentin Prokofiev had arrived.

I'd now been called a flibbertigibbet, a bimbo and a bitch within the space of about an hour, which wasn't the sort of thing any self-respecting woman should have to put up with, especially not a self-respecting woman who was also a fully paid-up member of Her Majesty's Secret Service, albeit a member not yet in possession of a licence to kill. I'd asked about that. They'd laughed. Actually laughed. When they'd stopped laughing, they reminded me that after two weeks in the company of Bulldog and Snape I shouldn't need a gun. And anyway, people toting guns were statistically far more likely to be shot by other people toting guns than those who were unarmed.

They'd had a point. If I'd had a weapon in my hand when the rear doors opened, the hideous tattooed troll would have splattered me all over the wall of the van with his giant shotgun. It would probably have taken a while to clean me up. So, I decided to calm down and use my brains. I knew I had some of those, my First in Modern Languages from Cambridge told me as much, and I couldn't believe that I didn't possess considerably more brain power than old Inkman. Mind you, Bulldog had also warned me not to rely on first impressions. Anyway, I decided that retribution for the Flibbertigibbet (Marj), Bimbo (Downton Abbey ha-bloody-ha) and Bitch (the aforesaid nameless monster in front of me) would have to wait.

So I got out of the van, hands in clear sight. I glanced across at the giant who, assuming I stayed alive long enough to tell the tale, would soon be not so much inspector as inspected by various gentlemen incarcerated at Her Majesty's pleasure, who would probably quite enjoy having a bent copper in their midst. Downton didn't return my glance. Instead, with his eyes staring at a spot several feet over my head – not difficult, admittedly, as his eye level was considerably higher than my head – he strode back to the passenger side of the van, yelling 'Marj!' as he did so. She scurried to the driver's side of the van and got in beside Downton. The van began to move but, by that time, Inkman had ushered me to the wooden door of the badly maintained, red-brick bungalow in front of us. When I say ushered, that's a polite way of saying that he prodded me there with persistent over-heavy use of the gun barrel into the small of my back.

I could both hear and smell his heavy breathing behind me. I'm not as good with interpreting breathing patterns as I am with a handful of foreign languages but something about what I was hearing suggested to me that he perhaps wasn't as confident as he had previously seemed. It was understandable. He was, after all, alone in a secluded spot with a highly trained secret agent and, if the cinema has taught us anything, it is that British spies always come out on top in run-ins with the bad guys. I was hoping that his wariness would not result in the shotgun being emptied into my back before we made it inside. I also hoped that he wouldn't want the neighbours, if there were any, to hear the gun as it cut my promising life short.

'Open it, cow!' he rasped from close to my ear. Cow now, was it? The evidence was mounting. No jury would convict me of anything other than a mercy killing.

I turned the handle and pushed open the door, prompted by another firm prod from the shotgun. The bruises were multiplying. Entering, I found myself in a dim corridor leading to a closed door at the far end. There were further doors, one on each side. The decoration was more shabby than chic and the smell was hideous, as if all hell's washing and food compost had been left untended for twenty years. My immediate impression was that once Inkman had "taken care" of me, my mortal remains would be added to what must surely be a pile of other cadavers which, if the stink was anything to go by, had been there for a considerable time.

'Straight ahead, through the door.' It seemed he'd run out of rude names to call me.

I reached the door at the far end of the corridor and put my hand on the knob. 'It's locked,' I lied, and half-turned my head to see that my unexpectedly sudden stop had caused my repugnant custodian to come a little closer than he ought to have done.

'No, it's fuckin'...' he managed to get out, accurately it must be said, before I dropped abruptly to the floor, swivelled and punched him hard in what for politeness' sake I could call his midriff, at the same time swinging a leg hard towards the back of his left knee. I was actually quite surprised by how effective this manoeuvre turned out to be. Kudos to Bulldog. I must have scored a bullseye on his paraphernalia, judging by the noise he made, somewhere between a bellow and a shriek, the upper registers of which could have been a rallying call for the entire local canine population. He let go of the shotgun and had already started to clamp his hands to the affected region when my leg connected with the rear of his knee and he toppled sideways. The shotgun, however, beat him to the floor. It landed butt first and the impact set it off. I hadn't foreseen this happening because time to plan my little stratagem had been rather tight, and if Inkman had known what was going to occur, he would probably have tried much harder to keep hold of the gun, the pain from his balls notwithstanding. Because what was going to occur, what actually did occur, was that as he fell, his face came hard up against the business end of the shotgun just as it went off.

The result wasn't pretty. I mean, he hadn't been pretty to start with, but even his heavily inked, sparsely toothed face was more attractive than a bloody pulp, which was what was left after the gunshot. I was lying, completely unharmed, with my back resting up against the door and my erstwhile attacker was stretched across my feet next to his still-smoking gun. I didn't know for sure if he was dead but I sure as hell wasn't going to take his pulse. I'd need to wash my hands afterwards and I didn't know where the bathroom was.

I was just congratulating myself on not throwing up, when there was a crunch of gravel from beyond the still half-open front door and a shadow appeared. A very large shadow. Downton stepped into the corridor, stooping slightly to avoid banging his head on the lintel. Ye gods, he was big. And ye gods, why the fuck hadn't he and Marj driven away like they were supposed to?

'Thank goodness you've arrived, officer!' I cried. 'There's been a terrible accident.' If I'd thought my attempt at humour would make him pause, I was wrong. He walked slowly towards me and the mortal remains of Inkman, and glanced dispassionately down at his ex-colleague, careful to keep any blood off his shiny police boots. He kept his pistol pointed at me.

'Tricksy little slut aren't you?' he growled.

So I was a slut too, was I? It would have been cleverer if any of the insults had a grain of originality in them. 'You really should stop calling me names, Abigail,' I said.

'You've seen what happens when you do,' and I nodded towards the body.

He leaned towards me and I was briefly aware of the butt of his gun heading rapidly towards my head. Fuck, I thought as I started to turn away. Not again.

___ In which Elspeth Arundell
   discusses geology, and Dawson
   starts to feel useful

Dawson had spent some of the interminable hours locked in the bowels of the *Astrid* reflecting back to a cold, wet Monday in mid-May. He had been alone in G22's small, down-at-heel office in Bulstrode Street, trying to figure out how he could usefully fill the day while Lucy was on her self-defence course at Vauxhall Cross. She called it self-defence anyway, but Dawson suspected there was more than a little attacking involved too.

'Don't worry,' she'd said. 'I've left you lots to do and when I come back, I'll be fully prepared to watch your back when I send you into dangerous situations ahead of me. We generals always take the rear.'

'I thought that was back in the First World War.'

'I don't recall Eisenhower storming the beaches himself on D-day either and I doubt things have changed much. You can't have important people like me getting mown down first.' And she'd kissed him, laughed and left, dressed to kill in what she considered appropriate training clothing. There was quite a lot of Lycra involved and, as far as Dawson was concerned, it just made her look sexier than ever.

In the office, he'd discovered that Lucy may have left him "lots to do" but she had forgotten to send it to him, and it was all on her computer, which was locked. He didn't know the password, which he thought showed a disturbing lack of trust. The Secret Intelligence Service was insistent that passwords must not be shared, presumably considering secrecy to be intrinsic to their title.

Dawson had tried several passwords without success and was about to give up and walk around the corner to the Golden Eagle when there was a voice from behind him. 'Try "I love

Dawson"," said Elspeth Arundell, witheringly. The suggestion worked. Dawson found himself blushing. His own password was still "Letmein123". Perhaps he should change it.

'Coffee, Miss Arundell?' he asked.

'Ms,' she replied. 'And no.' Dawson couldn't ever remember hearing her say thank you. Or please for that matter. She didn't seem inclined to sit down so Dawson stood up. It seemed the polite thing to do even if the politeness was not reciprocated.

'What do you know about karst?' she said.

'Cast?' said Dawson, doubtfully. 'Cast what? Fishing? Of thousands?'

'Neither, nor cast about wildly in a facetious manner, which is what you are doing.'

'I often do that when I'm nervous,' agreed Dawson.

'Why are you nervous?'

'Because I imagine you're about to sack me. And, even if you aren't, you make people nervous. You just do.'

'That's not a particularly nervous thing for a nervous man to say.' She looked at him levelly for a few seconds then sat down anyway. Dawson followed suit. It all felt a bit like musical chairs without the music.

'Should Lucy – Miss Smith – be here to hear you sack me?'

'No, and I'm not sacking you. If Miss Smith were present, I would not be. This is not for her ears. I am aware that she is at HQ for a few days learning how to beat people up. A rather outdated skill, frankly. This is a dump, isn't it?' she added, changing the subject. Dawson could only agree. The two tiny, adjoined offices and cramped kitchen really were a dump, a far cry from Vauxhall Cross. 'I'll start again. Can we take it that I am not trying to get rid of you?'

'I'm not sure. In your shoes, I probably would be.'

'You don't have a very high opinion of yourself, do you?'

'It's positively stratospheric compared to a few months ago.'

'And so it should be. You handled yourself very well in

Australia in extremely difficult circumstances.' Was that a compliment? Dawson wished he was recording the conversation. 'Without you, there would still be an unidentified Russian assassin at large.'

'He still is at large. He's gone back to Russia, hasn't he? Anyway, it wasn't just me.'

'Yes, Prokofiev is still at large but we now know who he is. And yes, other people helped. But it was mainly you.' Dawson wondered if he could surreptitiously fish out his phone and press the record button. 'Anyway, we were talking about Karst. K A R S T, not C A S T. Karst landscapes and karst aquifers to be more specific. I do not wish to give you a detailed geology lesson but karst landscapes are composed of a variety of soluble rocks – gypsum, limestone, dolomite, quartzite and so forth – and, because they produce a rapid flow of water through karst aquifers, are potentially a huge source of green energy. However, they also present a number of challenges, not the least of which is that they are underground. Thus far, the costs involved have been hugely prohibitive when it comes to any sort of wide-scale commercial production of electricity.'

'Right. Great. Go green go.'

'Before I proceed any further, how are you at keeping secrets?'

'I don't know. It doesn't sound as if this karst stuff is particularly secret, so I guess you're coming to something else. And I have signed the Official Secrets Act.'

'This is more secret than that. You must, for example, not share what I am about to disclose with Miss Smith.'

'She's my girlfriend. And my boss.'

'And she may or may not remain your girlfriend. Affairs of the heart come and go. But she will not be your boss for long.'

'Is she the one being sacked?'

'No one is being sacked, but I have other plans for her. It will be up to her if she chooses to share those plans with you. You, however, will not share this with her.'

'Or?'

'Or, Wormwood Scrubs is not a particularly comfortable home address.'

'Point taken.'

'Good. Now, I have to tell you about a gentleman presently going by the name of Victor Naismith. And that is a name that you will never, ever allow to pass your lips.'

'Who's Victor Naismith?' said Dawson, allowing the name to pass his lips.

'Nobody in any real sense.' Dawson decided that Arundell would have made a lousy teacher. Obtaining information from her was like squeezing a brick out of a soap dispenser. 'Naismith is really a gentleman by the name of Kaspar Nurmsalu, an Estonian national. Another name you must never ever say aloud.'

'Is Kaspar Nurmsalu important?'

'No, but his brother, Viktor, is.'

Dawson realised that whatever this was about, it sounded increasingly as though Elspeth Arundell might be giving him a job to do, which in turn might delay his inevitable sacking. 'Why's Viktor important?'

'You do not need to know that.' Of course not. 'However, whilst Viktor does not concern you, I am reluctantly prepared to tell you that he is a scientist holding information which the government is extremely keen to acquire. You will not ask me what that information is. We need to make Viktor Nurmsalu invisible and to help us achieve that, his brother Kaspar has kindly agreed to take his place temporarily.'

'What's in it for Kaspar?'

'An astute question. Briefly, money. Kaspar has not made such a success of his life as his brother and could do with a fresh start, shall we say. We will enable him to do that.'

'If Viktor needs to be made invisible, then you clearly believe he is at some risk. So the risk is being passed to Kaspar. Is he aware of that?'

'Kaspar will be paid a great deal of money. He is not asking any questions.' That was a no then.

'What do you want me to do?'

'It is not a request, Mr Dawson. You will "find" Kaspar Nurmsalu and deliver him to a safe house.'

'Where will I find him?'

'North Wales. Snowdonia.'

Dawson smiled. He was at last beginning to feel quite useful. Arundell didn't return the smile. 'Soon after delivering Kaspar Nurmsalu to the safe house, you will transport the new Mr Naismith to Stallford.'

'Stallford? That's where I live.'

'Of course it's where you live.' She really was unnecessarily snappy. 'We need you to keep an eye on him until things sort themselves out. And it will be considerably easier for you to do that if he is close at hand. Very close at hand, in fact. There is an empty flat above yours, I believe.' It was true, there was. The young couple living there had moved out very suddenly a week before.

'So, Viktor Nurmsalu or rather Kaspar, known as Naismith is going to be placed in that flat? Mabel Scutt's not going to be too happy.'

___ In which Elaine and Gulliver
    smell something disgusting,
    and walk down some stairs

'So, what is this place?' said Elaine.

'Old farm cottage maybe. I imagine the M25 did away with the farm, and this dump and the field we slid down is all that's left.'

'Dump is right.' She surveyed the bungalow, scrubby red-brick walls with severely degraded pointing struggling to hold the bricks together. Broken windows with near-rotten frames from which the paint had long since lost contact. Moss covering most of the roof and a gap where a chimney stack had once stood. Weeds growing steadily and unrestrained up the walls, obscuring the lower halves of the windows. The whole place didn't scream neglect so much as post-apocalypse. It wasn't a great advert for Leatherhead, truth be told.

Gulliver and Elaine followed the poorly laid concrete drive that led down the side of the bungalow. It continued past the building, through a small copse and on towards a road that they could hear more than see a couple of hundred metres away. Elaine was puzzled. 'So why did they go to all the trouble of driving the van off the motorway and down the field when they could just have used this drive?'

'They were trying to hide,' said Gulliver. 'Remember, they disappeared between the motorway cameras. They didn't want anyone to spot them turning off the road at the front. Which means there must be something here.'

'Maybe it's just a cut through, sir. Maybe the bungalow means nothing.'

'Could be. Best if we find out for sure though. We've still got the search for the purple van ongoing and perhaps our backup will arrive to help.'

'Odd property this. Front door at the back and no door at the front.'

'If there's only one door, that's the one we'll use.'

Elaine tried the door. The knob turned easily.

'Me first, I think,' said Gulliver. 'You're a guest in our country. I don't smell a trap but, if it is, it would be discourteous in the extreme for me to let you go first.' He moved in front of her and pushed open the door. There was no welcoming gunfire, just a disgustingly putrid assault on their nasal passages.

'Jesus, that's ripe,' said Elaine, as they both took an involuntary step backwards.

'I've smelt worse,' grunted Gulliver. 'Come on. Breath through your mouth.'

Throwing the door wide open to allow light into the passage that stretched out in front of them, they entered cautiously. They were immediately aware that the epicentre of the odour lay at the far end of the passage, where a swarm of flies was engaged in an enthusiastic investigation of something on the floor. They edged forward. On the tattered remains of what had once been wall-to-wall carpeting was a large pool of congealed blood containing bits of something Elaine didn't much like the look of. Gulliver bent down and examined it more closely.

'Not very nice, is it?' he said.

'What is it?' asked Elaine although she suspected she knew the answer.

'Slivers of bone and bits of flesh, I'd say. Judging by that thing there which looks like it might once have been part of an eye, someone's had their face shot off.'

Elaine gagged and was quite proud of herself that she managed to stop before it became more than just a gag. 'God, sir, you don't think that's...'

'Lucy? Don't know. We'll get forensics down but we need to carry on looking first. Whoever this was, people with their faces shot off don't get up and walk away.' He glanced up at

Elaine, whose own face was preternaturally pale. 'Are you all right, sergeant?'

Elaine nodded, stepped past the superintendent and opened a door in front of them. She found herself in what had once been a kitchen, but if the estate agents' blurb had said "needs some modernisation", it would have been subject to scrutiny by Trading Standards. The filthy window to her right, partly obscured by undergrowth, let very little light into the room, but she saw a further door in the far corner and walked over to it. She didn't have to try the handle to see that this door wasn't going to open easily. The padlock was a dead giveaway.

Gulliver joined her and then started sifting through drawers in the kitchen units. He soon found what he was looking for, a hefty screwdriver. 'That doesn't look like the most secure padlock I've ever seen,' he said. 'This should do the trick.' He inserted the screwdriver into the padlock and gave it a sharp twist. The lock snapped open. Elaine pulled on the door and revealed a flight of stone steps leading down into the darkness. She slipped out her phone, switched on the torch and edged down the steps. There were thirty-nine of them, which didn't sound very original, and at the bottom she came across another door.

'I reckon this hasn't been here long, sir,' she said. 'Looks new to me.'

'Who installs a new door in an old wreck of a house?'

The light from the phone torch revealed a lock and handle. Elaine pulled on the handle. Nothing. 'Don't think your screwdriver's going to be much use here, sir.' She kicked the door in frustration, perhaps understandably given the likelihood of there being a dead Lucy the other side of it.

At that moment, Gulliver's phone started buzzing in his pocket. He plucked it out. 'Reasonable signal,' he said, sounding surprised. 'That's a selling point, could add a few hundred quid to the value of this place.'

'Making it worth a few hundred quid,' muttered Elaine.

'Gulliver here,' he said into the phone. He listened briefly and spoke again. 'Get a fix on this phone and haul yourselves here sharpish. We need cutting equipment for a solid wooden door. Not a battering ram, no, there's no room to get a run-up.' He paused and glanced at Elaine before continuing. 'And you'd better bring an ambulance with you as well.'

He put the phone back in his pocket and they stood there irresolutely for a few seconds in the enveloping silence.

And then they heard a noise, muffled, hardly audible at all, but a noise nonetheless. It sounded like a very high-pitched scream and it was coming from the other side of the door.

___ In which Sofija turns into
    somebody else, and Dawson
    climbs into a box

'We meet again, Mr Dawson,' said Valentin Prokofiev, sounding just like the villain in a spy novel. The Russian assassin was looking straight at him as if he could see clear through the thick undergrowth. Perhaps he could. Dawson could certainly see Prokofiev through a gap in the foliage, so it was reasonable to suppose Prokofiev had spotted at least a small part of him. Or Sofija of course, who, although shorter, was rather more substantial. How the Russian knew where they were hidden and had managed to draw up at exactly the right spot, Dawson had no clue.

He turned to Sofija and was astonished to see her begin to stand up, another broad grin infusing her broad face. He grabbed her sleeve to try to pull her back down but the only effect was that he found himself being dragged involuntarily to his feet as well. He let go of her arm and fell back.

'Hello, Valentin, my darling,' said Sofija.

Darling? So she hadn't been after Dawson's body after all. He couldn't decide if he was relieved about that or whether there wasn't just a trace of jealousy surfacing. However, that wasn't his primary concern. By now, Sofija was at her full, less than considerable, height and pushing through the bushes into the road.

'Move to one side, Galina,' said Prokofiev. 'Alexei would not want to shoot you by mistake.' Alexei grunted as if to suggest he didn't care one way or the other.

The girl took three adroit steps to her left, well out of the likely route of any bullet travelling in Dawson's direction. Dawson decided there didn't seem much point continuing to crouch so he stood up slowly. He'd seen lots of films and knew that the courteous thing to do in these circumstances was raise both hands over his head, so that's what he did.

Despite adopting this position of surrender, he could see little reason why Prokofiev should not have him shot anyway. Mind you, the Russian had taken an awful lot of time and trouble if all he wanted to do was kill him. He was certainly stringing things out. Why, though? Dawson hadn't exactly been bombarded with top secret information since he'd joined MI6, so would be less than useful as a mole, if that was the correct term.

However, Alexei didn't pull the trigger and Prokofiev himself appeared to be unarmed. Still keeping his hands airborne, Dawson turned to the girl who had been calling herself Sofija. In the five months since he had been thrust inadvertently into the murky world of espionage, Dawson had encountered several people who seemed to think it was a little dull to be the bearer of a single name. His girlfriend, for example, wasn't really Lucy Smith. Dawson smiled at her. 'Well done,' he said. 'You had me fooled. You should be on the stage.' The grin had disappeared from her face and her eyes were restless. 'Galina, is it? So, what are you? Latvian? Estonian? Or Russian, I'm guessing.'

Sofija-Galina shrugged and moved towards the Land Rover, but she stopped short at a command in Russian from Prokofiev. '*Podozhdite!*' he said. 'You will drive, Galina Dimitrovna. Mr Dawson and I will be in the back.'

'Galina Dimitrovna now, is it?' said Dawson. 'No wonder you're confused.'

'Patronymic,' she said. 'You still idiot. And I not confused.' She hoisted herself into the driver's seat and Dawson, with Alexei's pistol a persuasive influence, got in behind her, followed by Prokofiev. Alexei sat beside Sofija-Galina, swivelling in his seat to keep his pistol trained on Dawson, who was experiencing *déjà vu* all over again. This was the third time this year he had been forced to ride in the back seat of a car against his will, and the second occasion he had had a gun pointing at him to encourage his obedience. The lack of originality was disturbing.

'Going to a lot of trouble, aren't you? Why don't you just get Alexei here to pop me one in the shoulder and call it quits? I only shot you because you were about to kill a policeman I was quite fond of. It was nothing personal, so no hard feelings, eh?'

'Shut up, Mr Dawson,' said Prokofiev quietly. 'I have not brought you here to kill you now. You will be coming on a small journey with me. Later, who knows? You are merely a pawn.'

Sofija-Galina turned the Land Rover expertly in the narrow lane and sped back eastwards. Dawson could see her eyes in the rear-view mirror. She seemed to be looking at him more often than was strictly safe bearing in mind they were driving down a narrow country road at over 70 kph. He thought there was a troubled expression behind her eyes, and even with all her previous contradictions, this new development didn't feel right, somehow. There was something else too. If Prokofiev and Alexei had been on Saaremaa all along, how could it also have been them in the speedboat? And if it wasn't them, then who was it? In any case, why would Galina, or Sofija, have gone through all the palaver of helping him to escape, hiding in the cave on the small island and then risking both their lives on the decrepit raft when all she had to do was wait on the ship for her boyfriend to turn up. Nothing made any sense.

It didn't take long to arrive at Kuressaare, but it soon became apparent that that was not their destination. Leaving the town on a more major highway, they carried on in what Dawson reckoned to be a northerly direction, passing through a handful of rural communities before the road bore eastwards again and a wide stretch of water appeared in front of them. They rattled over a long bridge.

'Where's this?' ventured Dawson to his incommunicative companions, not really expecting a reply.

'Muhu,' said Prokofiev, shortly.

'There's no need to be rude. Is this Estonia?'

'It is all Estonia. Muhu, then ferry to the mainland. Be quiet or you will travel in the boot.'

'That's going to be difficult,' said Dawson. 'This is a Land Rover and even I know there is no boot.'

'I am sorry, my English is not perfect,' said the Russian in perfect English, turning towards him with the unblinking pale blue eyes which Dawson found quite unnerving. 'There is a box in the back of the car. Like a boot but smaller. Maybe this is a good idea. I do not want to have to kill you just yet and it is not my business to kill anyone else you may cry out to. Not unless it is necessary. It would not be good for international relations.'

Me and my big mouth, thought Dawson as Galina turned into a side road just past the bridge and pulled over. Alexei's gun ushered him round to the back of the vehicle, where Prokofiev opened the big, single door and lifted the lid of a large steel box that took up half the floor space. There was no passing traffic. Birdsong filled the air and the woods alongside the road were alive with new growth. Spring came late to this part of the world but it was an undeniably beautiful setting in which to be incarcerated. He sighed and climbed into the box. 'You will be able to breathe. There are air holes,' said the Russian. 'You are a sensible man so you will not cry out. You would not wish to have innocent deaths on your conscience.'

As the lid clanged shut and Prokofiev turned a key in a lock on the side, Dawson heard Galina, or maybe Sofija, mutter from the front seat, 'He is not sensible, he is idiot.'

Downton had thumped me over the head with the butt of his gun, the second time in only a few hours. Not much original thinking going on there, but at least he hadn't used the business end. I had been in no position to resist, sprawled on the floor hard up against the door and with the remains of the tattooed troll pinning my legs to the ground.

When I woke up, I had a stinking headache and a temper to match. In a bruise versus bruise competition, my ego was giving my poor battered body a run for its money, but I now had so many bits of me physically aching that my ego quickly gave up the fight and started to work out how to improve my situation. Which didn't look great. Number one, my hands were securely tied behind my back by what felt like nylon rope and linked to another rope around my ankles. Basically, I was hog-tied. I'm quite bendy, but it was extremely uncomfortable. I certainly wasn't going to be standing up any time soon unless I could find a way to undo or cut the ropes. And number two, I was gagged with a wad of something which I preferred not to speculate about, held in place by what I hoped was only a dirty old tea towel and not something that Inkman had recently been wearing.

I looked around. There was a little natural light seeping in from somewhere, enough to tell me I was in a large cavern of some kind. Both the ground and the wall at my back were made of rough rock. The most obvious thing about the cavern was that a river ran through it. No, not the name of my favourite film but an actual, genuine river, some three metres wide, flowing past my feet. It seemed to emerge from a tunnel in the rock wall over to my right and disappeared into the darkness ahead of me. The water was rushing along almost in spate. I had no idea how deep it was, and the only way I was going to find out would be by shuffling myself along until I fell in, which didn't seem to be the most sensible plan in the world. I became aware of something else. The rock face against which I was leaning was distinctly damp.

I didn't like the thought of what that implied one little bit. Unless there had been a recent underground downpour, which seemed unlikely, it could only mean that, impossible as it sounded, the river was tidal, or whatever the inland equivalent of tidal might be. I hadn't heard of such a thing but I had to assume that, sooner or later, the river was going to start rising and, if I didn't move, I'd be drowned. I certainly wasn't going to be doing much swimming, tied as I was.

It was only a few minutes after I'd reached this dispiriting conclusion that I was proved correct. It would be sooner rather than later. My feet were getting wet.

The unlate, unlamented Alan Flannery, currently languishing in HMP Bullingdon, and who had recruited me in the first place, had always urged me to be resourceful. I think that's the one piece of advice he gave me that I've taken on board, but it's hard to be resourceful when you have no resources. I managed to shuffle backwards and push myself a little way up the wall behind me, so that my head was slightly higher, but even during the short time that manoeuvre took, the river had risen enough to submerge my calves.

At that point, with my eyes slowly becoming more used to the dimness, I noticed something else on the far bank of the river. Two somethings else in fact. Two shapeless humps, but shapeless in an undeniably human sort of way. One I assumed was the bodily remains of Inkman, *whose name I had never discovered, a fact that wouldn't be keeping me awake at night, assuming I managed to make it to another night. However, identification of the second mound was beyond me although it looked equally as lifeless. Whoever it was, I couldn't work out why I wasn't currently a third body but perhaps I'd annoyed Downton so much that he preferred me to know I was going to drown slowly, rather than put a bullet in my head first. By now, the water had risen to my waist and was lapping against the body of Inkman. That would significantly increase pollution levels in the river, I thought inconsequentially.*

And then I heard voices, muffled and indistinct, but definitely voices, followed by a thump. Momentarily forgetting the wodge of material in my mouth, I started to call out but even I struggled to hear myself. I tried to think. Downton had obviously dragged me or, more likely, given the size of him, carried me into the cavern. Also, the remains of Inkman and unidentified body number two. So clearly there was an entrance of some kind and the thump I had heard could easily have been made by something hitting a door. I stared hard into the dimness beyond Inkman and his chum and thought I could just about discern a darker shadow in the dark rock face that could have been a door. Maybe the voices were just Downton and Marj Bojangles come back to watch me submerge, but I'd far rather take my chances with them than drown helplessly.

So I shouted again. Well, not so much shouted, bearing in mind the gag, but squealed, as high-pitched as I could make it, until I ran out of breath. I stopped and listened. And then I heard someone call, as if from a million miles away. 'Lucy?' the voice was saying, over and over. I knew that voice and a million miles away wasn't far from the truth as the person it belonged to was in Australia. I knew

I'd been unconscious for a while, but surely not long enough for Downton to transport me to the other side of the world. So, what the hell was Elaine Bates doing here? Not that I wasn't delighted that she was, of course.

___ In which Elaine dives in,
   and Sam decides against
   a group hug

When the backup arrived, the big-toothed, smiley face of PC Sam formed part of it. Sam was carrying a circular saw and had a small portable generator slung over one shoulder. He was preceded down the steps by two other officers carrying flashlights and firearms and kitted out in Kevlar vests. They were introduced as Gerald and Ronald although neither looked old enough to own those names.

'Hello again, Aussie sarge,' Sam said, beaming. 'I hear you've got a door needs cutting open. I've been wanting to use this thing for ages.'

'Just get on and do it, constable,' grunted Gulliver. So Sam set to with the saw. It didn't take him long to cut around the lock sufficiently for a solid shove with one hefty shoulder to throw open the door, leaving the small piece containing the lock jutting out of the frame. The door burst open so suddenly that he lurched into the cavern and toppled into the river the other side, together with the saw and generator, which sank beneath the surface with what Sam feared was a terminal gurgle.

He briefly wondered why the equipment hadn't electrocuted him but as it hadn't, he turned his mind to the problem of getting out of the river. This was easier thought than done, however, as swimming was not one of his strengths. He was always careful not to fill his bath too deep, just in case. Arms flailing, he was already heading fast towards the far end of the chamber, where the darkness seemed likely to swallow him up even if the river didn't. Elaine, noticing straightaway that there was rather more drowning than swimming going on, dived right in after him. She hadn't been the Shepparton and District Under 15s Hundred Metre Freestyle Champion twelve years earlier for nothing.

Luckily, Elaine's dive was a shallow one but even so she only just managed to stop herself cracking her head on the rock at the bottom of the river, which turned out to be not much more than a metre and a half deep for all its riotous passage. She stood up, bracing herself against the current, and called to Sam to do the same. A few seconds later, Elaine and the others were rewarded with the sight of a bedraggled, embarrassed but utterly undrowned Sam stomping stolidly up the river towards them, pushing the onrushing water out of his way with a distinct air of crossness.

Gerald reached down and helped Sam drag himself out of the river. Elaine, just as wet, hoisted herself nimbly out and stood on the bank shaking herself like a small dog, her brown hair frizzing.

'Christ, cobber,' she said. 'You're not Dawson's brother, are you?'

She was interrupted by Ronald, addressing Gulliver. 'Sir, woman at eleven o'clock, alive by the looks of her. Two more people, possibly deceased, at three o'clock. No bandits in sight.'

They looked up and across the river to where the dimly discernible figure of Lucy was lying half-propped against the rock wall opposite them, trying desperately to stop herself being washed away. Elaine and Sam slipped back into the river, holding on to each other's hands for mutual support, and waded relatively easily across.

'Hello, girl, fancy seeing you,' said Elaine, reaching Lucy and rapidly untying the gag and ropes.

Sam enthusiastically put his large hands under her shoulders and hoisted her to her feet. 'Yes, fancy you,' he said, possibly getting his words mixed up.

'I thought it was you,' said Lucy to Elaine, after taking a few deep breaths. 'What the hell are you doing here? And what's happened to your hair?'

'Water's always had that effect on it. I blame my genes. Anyway, why wouldn't I be here? You're in trouble, I'm not about to stand idly by, the other side of the world, am I?' She impulsively hugged the blonde girl. Sam, busy trying to untie the wet nylon cords with his cold, damp fingers, thought about making it a group hug but wasn't sure if it was appropriate. By this time, Gerald had joined them on the bank and rather ruined Sam's day by picking the shivering Lucy up, unasked, and wading back through the river with her. She smiled at him and he smiled back. Sam looked on, frowning.

'Thank you,' said Lucy, as they reached the other bank, and after a pause, 'You can put me down now.' He did so and their attention was taken by what Ronald's torch revealed to be two definitely dead people. Up close, Lucy recognised both of them straight away, which was more than anyone else did.

One was Inkman, the remains of his face highlighted horrifically in the torch beam. The second body was that of Marj, the now former proprietress of Mr Bojangles, whose head was twisted in a disconcertingly unnatural position.

'What have we got here, then?' said Gulliver. Resisting the urge to reply in a facetiously Dawson-like way, Lucy told him. 'Are we assuming that this is Inspector Downton's handiwork, Miss Smith?'

'Well, possibly the woman, although I didn't actually witness anything; but I'm afraid I have to own up to the other one.'

Everyone looked at her, small, blonde, bedraggled and bruised, but only Sam put his thoughts into words. 'He hasn't got a face,' he said. 'How did you do that?' He took a step back in case Lucy possessed some sinister face-removal technique that she might wish to re-employ on him.

At that point, they were interrupted by Gerald. 'Ambulance is here,' he said. Either he was trained in telepathy or was wearing a hidden earpiece, probably the latter, thought Elaine.

'OK,' said Gulliver. 'Get them down here. They can take charge of these two people. The rest of us can go back to the station. We're not going to achieve anything more here and we need to dry you three off before you all get pneumonia and we have more bodies on our hands.'

_____ In which Jason Underwood misses
     the opera, and Gulliver's
     travels are rewarded

Jason Underwood loved his job. He loved the underplayed glamour, the subterfuge, the authority, the very word spy itself. Everything about it, apart from the possibility of his phone ringing on a Saturday evening. While he was happy to give his time to official business during the rest of the week, for twelve hours on a Saturday night, only a terrorist atrocity or the outbreak of World War Three should be allowed to disturb him.

So when his phone coughed apologetically early on Saturday evening, he knew that the bomb blast that morning in Surrey had been identified as just such a terrorist atrocity, given that a World War had, on balance, not broken out. It would have made the six o'clock news had it done so. He fished the phone reluctantly out of his pocket and looked, slightly perplexed, at the screen. He was expecting to see one of two names. Either C, his boss, or Borderline, code for the Foreign Secretary herself if things were looking particularly dicey. Instead, it was an unknown number. He thought about ignoring the call, as there was an Uber due any minute to take him to The Coliseum, but the thought of rolling a few heads on Monday morning if some idiot at Vauxhall Cross had called him by mistake persuaded him to answer.

'Mr Underwood?' asked an unfamiliar voice.

'Who is this? And how did you get this number?'

'My name's Chief Superintendent Gulliver, Surrey Police.'

'What can I do for you, Chief Superintendent? Make it quick. It's Saturday night. I have a taxi waiting.'

'You may have heard there was a bomb in Stallford this morning,' said Gulliver heavily.

'That's nothing to do with us.'

'That's not what your agent said. Very interested, she said

you'd be. Gave me your name too. No number though. I had the devil's own job getting hold of it.'

'Colleague, Chief Superintendent, not agent, whoever you are referring to. We call them colleagues these days.' Much more customer focused. 'And I assure you that my organisation has no present interest in this matter.'

'So the name Lucy Smith means nothing to you.'

Underwood did not immediately reply. He moved to the window. His taxi had not yet arrived. 'That's a very common name, Mr Gulliver,' he said at length. 'Can you be more specific?'

Gulliver failed to answer the question. 'What about the name Viktor Nurmsalu?' he asked instead.

Underwood wasn't stupid. He hadn't blundered accidentally into the position of MI6 Control. What the hell was Lucy Smith doing poking about in Stallford without authority? It was way outside the remit of her tiny section, what was it called now? G22, that was it. Meaningless name. There wasn't even a G21 or a G23. He knew she was a troublemaker. Underwood liked troublemakers; he'd been one himself.

And Viktor Nurmsalu. That too was a name he knew very well, although Nurmsalu was now officially Victor Naismith. It didn't take a genius to work out that Gulliver was informing him that Nurmsalu had been the victim of the bombing. Underwood sighed inwardly. His trip to the Coliseum suddenly looked very unlikely.

'OK, Chief Superintendent,' he said quietly. 'You've got my attention.'

'Is this a secure line?'

'I should bloody hope so. This end of it anyway. Not sure about yours. Perhaps we should meet.'

'Good idea. I'm just about to ring your doorbell.' Underwood listened and sure enough there was the bell. 'I'll let myself up, shall I?'

'Not unless you've also acquired two door keys and a seven digit code. I'll be down.'

'I must say you're quite easy to track down for a man who doesn't officially exist.'

I wish, thought Underwood. He opened his front door to find a small, weary-looking man of about his own age who, despite his lack of inches, could only have been a policeman. 'Come through, Mr Gulliver,' and he led the way into a book-lined study.

'Enjoy reading, do you, Mr Underwood?' said Gulliver chattily, but Underwood wasn't in the mood for small talk.

'I'm a single man of impeccable taste. Of course I enjoy reading. What I don't enjoy is having to invite Charlie Copper into my house on a Saturday evening when I'm supposed to be at the opera.'

'Of course,' said Gulliver. 'The victim of the bomb in Stallford this morning appears to have been a gentleman named Viktor Nurmsalu, who I understand could also be called Victor Naismith these days.'

'You say "appears". Are you sure it was Nurmsalu?'

'As sure as we can be.' Then why not bloody say so in the first place, thought Underwood.

'What was he doing in Stallford, Superintendent?'

'What do you mean?'

'He's supposed to be in north Wales, Snowdonia.'

'From everything we know so far, he moved into a flat in a small block in Stallford a short while ago. Isn't that something your chaps are supposed to be aware of? Especially as one of said chaps, a certain Saul Dawson, lives in the flat below. I don't know what the rules are but if you give someone a new identity, it's best to keep tabs on them, I'd have thought.'

Underwood ignored the criticism. Gulliver was right. He should have been told if the newly christened Victor Naismith had moved 250 miles to Surrey, and it could not be a coincidence that it was to the same building occupied by Dawson. 'Drink, Mr Gulliver?' he said.

'Don't mind if I do. Scotch if you've got it.'

'On duty? Surely not.'

'It's been a long day, Mr Underwood and it's not over yet.' And, gratefully sipping the expensive single malt Underwood handed him, he explained about the bomb in the manhole, the rogue Inspector Downton and the dramatic recovery of Lucy Smith and the two bodies in the cavern three hours earlier.

Underwood listened intently and, when Gulliver finally stopped talking, summed up the situation succinctly. 'So, a scientist who is a person of extreme interest to certain people within government has been assassinated, probably by your Inspector Downton. Mr Dawson has disappeared, as has the aforesaid rather troublesome Inspector. Downton's male associate has been killed by Miss Smith and his female accomplice has also passed to a better place, leaving you nobody to question. Three deaths in one day and it's entirely possible Mr Dawson is a fourth since you have no idea where he's gone.'

'That's about the size of it. And we don't know who Inspector Downton is working for.'

Underwood smiled grimly. 'Perhaps we should try to help you find out. We have resources you don't, Chief Superintendent.'

___ In which Elspeth Arundell sits
on a bench, and Lucy spots
Something Wrong

Twice a week, but on different days, Elspeth Arundell collected her lunchtime salad from Pret around the corner from the SIS Building and walked the short distance under the railway line, past Vauxhall Station and into the peculiarly named Pleasure Gardens. Once there, she made a carefully arbitrary circuit of the park, paused briefly under various random trees, and finally came to rest on a worn, green bench beneath a bedraggled alder tree in the south eastern corner. There, she slowly consumed her salad whilst staring fixedly into the middle distance and, finishing it, deposited the plastic container (no eco-warrior, she) into an adjacent bin. Usually the container was empty. Occasionally it wasn't. Then she rose, stretched lightly and left, rather more directly, back under the railway to Vauxhall Cross and up to her pale grey office on the fifth floor.

A short while after her departure, a slightly built young man arrived in the Pleasure Gardens. He invariably wore a long scarf, woollen in the winter months but silk during the spring and summer. It looked, on him, entirely appropriate, even on those occasions when it was matched with a t-shirt, shorts and trainers. The young man always carried a smallish, pale brown bag slung casually over one shoulder, and was accompanied by a small, white, fluffy Bichon Frise, which looked exactly the breed of dog he would own. Observing the bench lately vacated by Elspeth Arundell, the man approached it purposefully but circuitously, sat and, in appearing to deposit some unidentified object into the bin, inconspicuously retrieved the plastic container left there by the woman. This he placed in his bag before rising gracefully to his feet and leaving the Pleasure Gardens, Bichon Frise in obedient tow, by an eastern exit into Tyers Street.

On the second Monday in June, Elspeth Arundell celebrated her fiftieth birthday by inviting thirty of her MI6 colleagues to join her for drinks in the Royal Vauxhall Tavern. Only eleven turned up. One of them, reluctantly, as she had other more pressing matters on her mind and was in any case supposed to be off work, injured, was Lucy Smith, who would have ignored the invitation had it not been for a text message from Jason Underwood suggesting that she should attend.

Lucy was therefore unsurprised to note that Underwood himself was present when she arrived in the pub. Elspeth Arundell, however, was not only surprised to see him, as he had not been invited, but more than a little perturbed. Underwood sought out Lucy in full view of Arundell, but out of her earshot.

'How's it going?' he asked.

'Personally or professionally?'

'Both.'

'How do you think? It's been forty-eight hours. My body feels like it's been through a concrete mixer. My boyfriend has disappeared. An MI6 employee. He may be dead. My boss seems to think her birthday is more important than trying to find him. So, you know, I've been better.'

'I don't doubt it. And we are working on finding Mr Dawson.'

'Does we include she?'

'We're working on that too.'

'Do you ever talk in anything but riddles?'

He smiled. 'Not often, I confess.'

'Why are you here?'

'I wanted to be noticed. In particular, I wanted to be noticed talking to you. We needn't stay long.' He glanced across at a small knot of unhappy looking colleagues standing at the bar trying to hold a conversation with their hostess. There was a great deal of silence in the conversation. Arundell looked up and saw them, and a frown crossed her face. Underwood bent to Lucy and spoke in a near whisper. 'Can you meet me at eight tomorrow morning at this address, please?' He produced a plain white business card, which he didn't bother to hide as he passed it to her.

'Why not at Vauxhall Cross? And have you cleared this with Elspeth?'

'Vauxhall Cross has ears. And I don't have to clear anything with her as you are officially on sick leave. You and she have different priorities. Yours being to locate Mr Dawson.'

'And what's your priority?'

'National security. And I believe that finding Mr Dawson will help in that regard.' He stood suddenly, taking Lucy rather unawares. 'And now I think we have achieved all we can. I will see you in the morning.' He nodded and moved towards the door. Lucy thoughtfully drained her bottle of Becks before following, ignoring Elspeth Arundell and the sparse crowd of miserable-looking staff members further up the bar. She could feel Arundell's eyes boring into her back as she left the pub.

—

'Listen to this,' said Underwood. He fiddled with a few knobs and suddenly the music faded and they could hear words being spoken in what sounded like Russian. Lucy was fluent in the language but still found herself struggling to translate. She looked at Underwood and raised her eyebrows.

'Gibberish,' she said. 'Some sort of code?'

'Exactly.' Underwood wasn't himself a Russian speaker but he had people for that sort of thing, and in amongst the gobbledegooksky there had been one word that had caught their ear. 'Astrid,' said Underwood. 'What's that, do you think?'

'Somebody's name, I imagine, or...' she paused, thinking. 'Could it be a ship?'

'That was my thinking also. I've already checked it out and the *Astrid* left Felixstowe Saturday lunchtime apparently bound for Riga.'

'Latvia.' Lucy's geography wasn't as good as her grasp of modern languages, but she'd liked limericks as a child and had sided with the tiger who had decided that the young lady from Riga would make a tasty snack. Served her right, she had thought. Probably a pointer as to where Lucy herself would end up, career-wise.

'Indeed,' said Underwood. 'And I'm informed that this message may also hail from Riga.'

'So that's where I need to be too.' Lucy stood up so quickly she made her head spin and her chair crashed against the desk behind her.

'Not so fast,' said Underwood calmly. 'And please sit down before you fall down. You are not yet fully recovered from Saturday.'

'Fuck that. I have to get after Saul.'

'Who may or may not be on his way to Riga. The *Astrid* could well have posted a false destination. And the signal may have come from somewhere else close by.'

'Like where?'

'Estonia or Finland.' He paused. 'Or St Petersburg.'

Lucy retrieved her chair and sat down again. 'Russia,' she said heavily. 'So you think Riga might be a blind and Saul's being taken to St Petersburg?' Russia did seem a more obvious destination than Latvia. 'Isn't Valentin Prokofiev back in Russia?'

'As far as we know. Why? Do you think he has revenge on his mind?'

'Saul did shoot him.'

'It's possible, although if Prokofiev is after Mr Dawson's blood, shipping him to Russia seems an unnecessarily complicated way of going about it. And how do you explain the bomb that killed Viktor Nurmsalu?'

'Nurmsalu? What, the scientist guy Dawson found up a tree in Wales? That was him? What the fuck is he doing getting himself blown up in Stallford? How long have you known this?'

Underwood had the good grace to look embarrassed. 'Since Saturday evening.'

'OK, so clearly this is all tied together. Look, I don't want to appear unfeeling, but I don't give a flying fuck about Nurmsalu. My concern is Saul and I'm going to get on a plane and find him. I'm on sick leave. You can't stop me.'

'I have no intention of stopping you. We are tracking the *Astrid*, which is presently well into the Baltic. If it's on its way to Riga or St Petersburg, it will be at least tomorrow before it arrives.'

'All right. Back to the transmission then. There were a couple of other odd things I noticed. Firstly, why would the English words, "something wrong" be in there? Why not the Russian, *chto-to ne tak*?'

'And what's the other thing?'

'*Gidroelektricheskiy*,' she said. 'Hydroelectricity.' Underwood remained silent. 'So, we have the *Astrid* en route to the eastern Baltic almost certainly with Saul on board. We also have something about hydroelectricity, perhaps a new form of hydroelectric power? Something secret, something valuable, particularly in these environmentally sensitive times. Something to do with Nurmsalu, do we think? And we also have the phrase "something wrong" in English. Which could mean that the something wrong is or was in England. The bomb, I'm thinking.'

'I doubt if it would stand up in a court of law,' said Underwood, 'but go on.'

'It doesn't have to. We're MI6. Aren't we above all that courts of law stuff?'

'Don't let the Guardian hear you say that.'

———

It was getting on for lunchtime and Underwood had gone off to find an underling to book a seat on the Air Baltic flight that would get Lucy to Riga at ten o'clock local time that evening. She knew full well though that that was merely the first step in trying to find Dawson, and that there could be several dozen further steps to negotiate, any of which could lead precisely nowhere. When Underwood returned, he had two boarding passes in his hand and was accompanied by someone else: Elaine, rather drier than the last time Lucy had seen her on Saturday evening.

'What are you doing here?' asked Lucy.

'Sergeant Bates is still on secondment to Surrey Police,' Underwood said. 'And now she's on thirdment to us. You didn't think you were going alone, did you?'

'Girls on tour,' said Elaine, grinning. Lucy, who had not had an opportunity to thank the Australian properly for coming to her rescue in the cavern, marched across and gave her a bear-hug. She really hadn't been looking forward to making the trip on her own and Elaine was, after all, a woman in her own image, if not exactly a mirror image.

___ In which Dawson picks a lock,
and Alexei hugs a bonnet

'Ouch,' Dawson more or less said, except he used an F instead
of an O and so on. It wasn't the first time he'd sworn since
being cooped up in the tin box in the back of the Land Rover
two hours ago. In fact, he thought he was probably nearing
his century. This "ouch" was different though. This one wasn't
caused by banging his head, or an elbow or knee against the
unforgiving insides of the box.

This was a different sort of pain, the pain of something
piercing his skin, the skin in question being that of his left
buttock. The box measured maybe a metre and a half by a
metre by a metre and as Dawson was rather longer than the
longest of those dimensions, there really wasn't much room
for manoeuvre. However, he needed to discover what sort of
pointed object had entered his arse, so he somehow squirmed
himself around until he could reach the affected body part.
He found the intruder at once. Gaining an awkward grip, he
tugged and it exited his behind with little effort, leaving
behind a slightly less intense pain. There was virtually no light
in the box but enough to see that he was holding a needle.
Quite a substantial needle, the sort of thing fishermen sew
their nets with. There was blood on it, which explained the
torture it had inflicted on entering his buttock cheek.

Dawson, whilst he had not yet suffered at the hands of
Bulldog in his dojo like Lucy, had been on a couple of less
physical courses during the spring. One of them had included
half a day on lock picking, a skill which he had thus far found
to be of absolutely no use whatsoever. Now, however, he had
a notion that the three hours spent in the company of Kev the
Key, ex-lag and master Houdini of the padlock world, might
come in handy at last. He could see the inside of the lock and,
despite the confined space, was able to reach up and insert

the needle into the hole. He wriggled it about until it made contact with what felt like a relevant cog and twisted, gently but with increasing firmness until, with a loud click which he hoped that Prokofiev and Alexei wouldn't hear over the noise of the engine, the lock sprung open.

He eased the box lid slowly upwards and peered into the compartment. Perhaps another aspect of his intermittent MI6 training was beginning to kick in. Add Careful Reconnaissance to Lock picking. The rear of the Land Rover was walled off from the main cabin and, although the wall contained a window, it had been covered by a sheet of hardboard. Possibly things were wont to go on in the back of the vehicle that needed to be kept from prying eyes in the front but, whatever the case, it was a lucky stroke for Dawson that he was invisible to his captors now.

He opened the lid fully and stood up. Or rather, he tried to stand up, but he had been bent not so much double as triple inside the box for two hours, so his body simply refused. At first, anyway. He relaxed into a sitting position and tried to stretch his screamingly cramped muscles. After two or three minutes some circulation began to return, so he repeated the standing up exercise, this time with rather more success, although the roof of the Land Rover prevented him reaching total perpendicularity.

He had to hang on as the vehicle was still bucketing along at high speed. Clearly Sofija or Galina or whatever she was actually called, was a fairly competent driver of cars as well as lifeboats, if not necessarily home-made rafts. Dawson edged to the rear of the compartment, found a catch and slowly opened the door. The road was rushing by at an alarming speed beneath the Land Rover. It didn't seem the most sensible idea to jump out and risk serious injury, although the alternative injuries that could be inflicted by Prokofiev and Alexei would probably be a few percentage points more serious. Still, he thought, the car was bound to slow down soon, possibly even stop. There was no reason to suppose that Estonia didn't possess the occasional set of traffic lights for example. Dawson pulled the door to, but carried on holding it slightly ajar, ready for a rapid evacuation should the chance present itself. He only hoped that he would be able to achieve a rapid evacuation without a rapid evacuation as it were.

Ten minutes later, the Land Rover did slow down. Quite dramatically in fact, so that Dawson was flung back with a loud crash against the box out of which he had just clambered. Somebody up front must have heard that, he thought, but he wasn't inclined to hang around to find out and, in any case, the car had now stopped completely and seemed to be skewed around in the road.

And then there was a brief burst of gunfire.

Dawson scrambled to the door and slid out on to the road, crouching low in case any of the gunfire was heading in his direction. It didn't seem to be, but he didn't feel like stopping to ask questions. They were in the countryside. For the second time that day, he made for the bushes at the side of the road and this time there was a thickish forest of dark evergreens immediately behind, so he didn't stop until he had gone twenty metres or so into the trees. The gunfire had ended as quickly as it had begun.

Six months earlier, Dawson's curiosity levels had been rather lower than those of the most timid of mice but his life had changed so dramatically since February that now, nothing in the world would have prevented him trying to find out what was happening and who had been firing at whom. He darted from tree to tree, trying to gain a position that would give him a good view of the front of the Land Rover. When he did, he spied an extraordinary sight. It wasn't just the sight, there were sounds as well. The sight told him that Alexei was lying draped across the bonnet of the car. Unless he had a habit of going to sleep in odd places, the likelihood was that he was dead, presumably as a result of the gunfire. Prokofiev and Sofija-Galina were not dead. They were standing in the road, arms aloft in the traditional way, facing two more people whose faces he couldn't see as they had their backs to him. They were both brandishing handguns in a menacing sort of way, although Dawson had yet to see a gun being brandished in an unmenacing way. Both were quite short. Both were in jeans. One had a dark blue fleece on despite the temperature being close to twenty degrees, and was wearing a baseball cap on her head. *Her* head. Dawson stole another couple of steps closer. Yes, it was definitely a woman and next to her, wearing an abruptly familiar green hoody, was another woman. And not just any woman.

'That's all very well, Val, old chum,' said Lucy in English, 'but I think we'll take a peek in the back just to be sure you're not telling porkies. If you would be so kind.'

In which a man with a moustache
falls into an armchair, and
another man growls a lot

Riga's waterfront turned out to be on the River Daugava, a few kilometres inland. That caught both Lucy and Elaine rather by surprise when the taxi dropped them off.

'*Vai tā ir īstā vieta?*' Lucy asked the driver. Elaine wasn't sure what she was saying but the driver's terse reply was clear enough.

'*Jā*,' and he drove off in his elderly Škoda, grinding his gears.

'I don't believe it,' said Elaine. 'A male totally unaffected by your charms. You should have tried your winning smile. That usually works.'

'It's fine, I was just expecting something a bit more, I don't know, seasidy.'

Seaside or not, it was clear enough they were in the right spot. Underwood had suggested the transmission might have been coming from a bar on the quayside, the *Albatrosi*, and sure enough, there it was standing out like a thumb recently attacked by a hammer, squashed between two more prosperous-looking cafés. It looked closed at this early hour, as did the two on either side. A ship's horn sounded loudly behind them and they turned to see a large, seagoing ferry moving into midstream from a terminus to their left. The buildings on the far side of the river were still partly sheathed in morning mist.

It had been too late and too dark when their infuriatingly delayed flight to Riga had finally landed the previous evening for the two women to do more than book into the nearest, least seedy hotel they could find; and getting a taxi out to the docks this morning had also proved more frustrating than it should have been, and not just because of the surly driver.

Lucy spotted a single storey brick building right at the

water's edge a little way along the wharf. The sign over the door read *Ostas Kapteinis.* 'Ah, good,' she said, 'Harbourmaster. He'll be able to tell us if the *Astrid* has arrived.'

She marched off and Elaine followed. Inside, the walls were covered in notices, some so yellowing that they could have been there for decades. They were all incomprehensible to Elaine, but she supposed they would have a generally maritime theme. Lucy was already speaking to an elderly, uniformed man sporting a magnificent walrus moustache but no hair north of that, who was slumped in an unlikely armchair behind the counter and showing no inclination to rise to his feet at the entrance of the two women.

Lucy leant on the counter, arms straight, and glowered at him. She had clearly decided on the officious approach. '*Kur es varu atrast* Astrid?' she said in as stern a voice as she could muster. She flashed her MI6 ID but whisked it away again before he had a chance to read it. The man, presumably the harbourmaster that time forgot, replied, still from a seated position, in a torrent of what was obviously Latvian but, judging by the annoyed expression on Lucy's face, it wasn't a torrent of Latvian that was especially helpful.

'Try the winning smile,' Elaine muttered in Lucy's ear. 'It probably won't let you down twice in a row.' But Lucy, angry now, had other ideas and whipped out the automatic that had been jammed into her jeans under the green hoody. The harbourmaster nearly fell out of his armchair and rose, spluttering, waving his arms about wildly and shedding what looked like toastcrumbs from his belly as he did so.

'*Astrid,* now!' spat out Lucy in English, and the man pointed at a chart further up the counter. They all moved across and he pointed again, this time to the letters AST followed by the figures 0708, written in pencil on the chart, apparently some way out in the Gulf of Riga.

'This is *Astrid?*' asked Lucy in a slightly calmer tone of voice but still holding the gun in a threatening manner, and the man nodded, more toastcrumbs falling from his exuberant moustache as he did so.

'*Jā*,' he said. His eyes moved to a red alarm button a short distance along the counter, the eyes closely followed by a hesitant hand, but Elaine noticed the movement and, deciding that Lucy was having all the fun, gave him a hard smack in the mouth. Most of the effect of the punch was dissipated by the giant moustache but the harbourmaster nevertheless staggered a few steps sideways before toppling into his armchair by way of one of its arms.

'Careful,' said Lucy. 'We don't want to hurt the old boy.'

'Says the woman waving a gun.'

Lucy ripped the chart in half and stuffed the portion showing the location of the *Astrid* into a pocket in her hoody. '*Paldies, jūs esat ļoti izpalīdzīgi*,' she said to the harbourmaster, smiled and turned on her heels.

'What were you saying?' asked Elaine as they left the building.

'Just thanking him for his help. And I added a winning smile at your suggestion.'

'Bit of a waste, I think we'd already won.'

A few metres along the quayside they came across a large, black, inflatable speedboat lying unattended at the top of a short slipway. There was some writing on the side in Cyrillic script which indicated to Lucy, although not to Elaine, that the boat was the property of the Russian Ministry of Defence, followed by the wildly inappropriate slogan, "Service with Solicitude".

'Is that Russian?' Elaine asked. 'What does it say?'

'Nothing much,' Lucy lied. 'Just some company out of St Petersburg. Can't be important or they wouldn't have left it.' She was already trying to heave the boat down the slipway into the water. Succeeding, she jumped adroitly in and Elaine, less certainly, followed. By that time, Lucy was busy surveying the controls. They didn't look too hard to master and a large green button in the centre was a dead giveaway. So she pushed it and the engine roared to life, throatily and rather more loudly than she had anticipated.

A couple of seconds later there was the sound of several pairs of sturdy boots, possibly manufactured in Moscow, pounding over the cobbles outside the *Albatrosi,* but Lucy had already discovered a throttle and given it a good wellying, at the same time spinning the wheel hard to starboard. They set off at some speed, with Elaine sitting down hard in the body of the boat to avoid being flung overboard. She was about to tell Lucy not to be so bloody violent when the first bullet whistled over her head, closely followed by a second, third and fourth. So she had a quick rethink, spun round, flat behind the stern gunwale and whipped out her own gun to return fire. However, the speedboat was already over a hundred metres upriver and although there were a couple more shots from the group of three men back on the wharf, they fell hopelessly short.

'This is fun,' Lucy shouted over the noise of the engine and the flying spray, standing up from the little driver's seat to get a better view over the bouncing nose of the boat, the controls of which had clearly been designed for someone rather taller than five foot four.

'Do you know how to drive this thing?' Elaine yelled.

'Of course. Part of the training. Nothing to it,' and Lucy found the rest of the trip out to the *Astrid* thoroughly exhilarating. Elaine less so.

—

To call the ship unprepossessing would be to endow it with a grandeur it had never known even in its pomp, and whatever pomp that had been was many years in the past. The paint was peeling so much it was hard to discern the actual colour of the hull. Turd brown possibly, unless that was just the rust. In any case, it was the right ship, definitely the *Astrid,* the paint used for the name evidently being of a superior quality to that employed on the hull.

Lucy eased off the throttle of the speedboat and brought its nose around towards a less-than-robust-looking ladder. Cutting the engine, she tied the inflatable to the ladder and started shimmying up it, holding her gun in one hand, a hands-partially-free approach to the ascent which Elaine failed to copy. Even so, she was right behind Lucy when they reached the top.

Having undertaken a quick recce of the *Astrid's* upper deck, they headed for the bridge. It too was deserted but, searching further below decks, they tracked down a grizzled, grey-haired man in the engine room, who turned out to possess a fierce temper and a command of English that was not so much broken as shattered beyond repair. He was singularly unhelpful until Elaine, encouraged by hitting the harbourmaster, kicked him hard in the shins.

'Blimey, love, calm down,' Lucy said. 'I think he was about to tell us something.'

'Just sounded like swearing to me.'

Helping the man into an old chair that had been placed next to the boiler, presumably for warmth, Lucy pulled out a photo of Dawson. 'Has this man been on your ship?' she asked in English.

He nodded sullenly, all the fight kicked out of him. 'Is Misteer Dawsing,' he affirmed in a low growl. Lucy smiled and whether it was a winning smile or not, the man perked up a little. 'He kidnappings my good daughter and takings her in boot to... somewheres.' He waved his hand around vaguely.

'Boot?' said Elaine. 'What boot? What's he talking about?'

'He means boat.'

'Yeah, that would make more sense.' Elaine turned back to the man. 'When was this?'

'Russians,' he said, answering a question that hadn't been asked. He spat at Elaine's feet as he said the word. 'They will be comings and killings me when see Dawsing he gone.' He spat again and Elaine moved a pace or two back.

It took them a few more minutes to decipher what had happened. The man's name was Captain Sesks, he said. Two Russians had approached him ten days ago in Riga and told him to transport "Misteer Name Smeeth", who would be delivered to him in Felixstowe, back to the Gulf of Riga. The same two Russians would then pick the man up from the *Astrid*.

'What's he talking about?' said Elaine. 'Name Smith? What the fuck's that? You're Smith.'

'Don't know.' Lucy turned back to Sesks. 'So this "Mister Name Smith" wasn't Mr Dawson?'

'*Nē*, but when arrives on ship, **is** Misteer Dawsing. I not knowings what goings on, but painted man say I now takings Dawsing to Riga, not Name Smeeth.'

'Painted man?' said Elaine. 'Could that be your tattooed bloke?'

'Possibly.' Lucy shuddered. 'OK, let's move on. We can sort out who "Name Smith" is later. What did they pay you?' she asked Sesks.

He spat again. 'No payings. They havings daughter, showings me picture. Killings her if I sayings *nē*.'

'But you just said that Dawson went off with your daughter.'

'*Nē, nē*,' said Captain Sesks irritably in a hoarse voice. 'Is good daughter, I tellings you, my Sofija. Russians,' and there came the by now habitual spit; 'they is takings other daughter, bad girl, but daughter still, my Guna. They here soon and will killings me and Guna when see Misteer Dawsing he not here.'

'I'm not sure they will, actually,' Lucy said. 'I think we just stole their boat.'

_ In which Chief Inspector Downton
receives a dressing down,
and meets a Bichon Frise
in a cemetery

Perhaps killing Marjorie Tavistock had been a mistake. He'd panicked. It had been the first time, mind you, after years of watching his step, so maybe he was due a small overreaction. And the woman wasn't important anyway. She was just someone who had allowed herself to be duped. An easy convert to the cause, already halfway there, what with all the new age twaddle she peddled. She'd fancied him too of course. And why not? He kept in shape. The natural advantages of being six foot six and possessing the sort of craggy features that looked good staring back at him from the mirror. Oh, yes, women were always flashing their eyelashes at him. And other things. It was a perk.

And he'd needed a local base, an HQ that no one would suspect, one that he could enter at will without attracting suspicion. But Marj had baulked when she'd overheard him telling Terry to kill the MI6 wench. Run scared. She was weak; she'd talk. She'd been fun for a while, in bed anyway, although her conversation levels didn't rise much above Coronation Street and Love Island. She professed to embrace socialist doctrines but had no real understanding of their importance. Now she'd outlived her usefulness. She had proved unexpectedly difficult to strangle, though, what with the fleshy neck and the bangles which kept getting in the way, but he'd managed it eventually. Probably not a completely painless demise, but what the hell. The river would wash away the evidence, along with Terry and the hot blonde.

So, three drown. Good pun that, he liked that one.

That only left the nosey shopkeeper next door, Abbas, the Indian busybody who couldn't keep his trap shut. Maybe not

Indian, whatever, it was all the same. The old boy had definitely seen him lugging the blonde piece into the van. Couldn't do anything about it at the time, Marj would have objected in her brash, overloud voice. And there had been other coppers within earshot of that voice, including bloody Gulliver.

So there he was, on his way back to Stallford to sort out Abbas, when his radio had crackled. His name came up. It was Gulliver talking. There was an Australian voice too, another girl. He didn't know who she was. Anyway, they were on to him. That fucking shopkeeper hadn't wasted any time, fuck him. The river should have done its work but hadn't. And Gulliver had found all three of them, Terry with his blown-off face, Marjorie with her flabby, purple neck that matched her flimsy purple blouse, and the blonde. The Smith girl.

He'd been lying low now for three days.

His phone rang. The name that flashed up didn't fill him with glee, and when he reluctantly answered it, things didn't improve. The man at the other end of the phone was shouting. About the bomb.

'What the hell do you think you were doing? Or did you think at all? You were supposed to be discreet.'

Downton flinched but stood his ground. 'What, stab him, you mean? We don't want a murder enquiry. Apart from anything else, they'd probably put me in charge of it. This way, it's terrorism. We can point the finger at the Russkies.'

'What? Do you really think they're going to fall for that? That Russian Intelligence is going to set off a bomb in a crowded town centre just to kill one old man they're not too fond of? Risking indiscriminate slaughter? It would be Salisbury all over again.'

'But...'

'Don't fucking "but" me. I know that, praise be to some non-existent deity, there was no indiscriminate slaughter. The principle holds. We said quiet. We said untraceable. I believe we suggested a judicious kidnapping followed by a swift knife and a tidy disposal. Not small pieces of human being scattered all over Stallford.'

'No one else got hurt.'

'Really? Let me see. An MI6 agent got hurt. Nearly a lot more than hurt.'

'That was unforeseen. Who knew she'd turn up asking questions? If it hadn't been for that dwarf parody of a copper, Gulliver, she'd have gone away with my flea in her ear.'

'A charming thought. And talking of charming, we seem to have lost the services of your grotesque heavy, what's his name? Terry. Not to mention the Tavistock woman. And now there *is* a murder enquiry. Which, as I believe you just pointed out, we wanted to avoid. And your fingerprints are all over it.'

'Bollocks. I was wearing gloves. The bore was supposed to wash them all away. Anyway, the important thing is, the job's done. Naismith's dead. What now?'

There was a pause. Finally, the man on the other end of the phone said, quietly, 'I'm not sure. Leave it with me. Be at Mickleham Church midnight tonight. I'll have decided by then.'

—

St Michael and All Angels Church, Mickleham was, appropriately, as quiet as the grave when Downton turned up unobtrusively a few minutes before midnight. He waited on a bench, although he was unsure what or who he was waiting for. Even this close to midsummer, it was quite dark, the moon hidden behind clouds scudding across a black sky. He had never met the man on the phone, never known his name. In a rare moment of humour, Downton had saved the number into his mobile under the name P King. Ha-bloody-ha.

He was dog-tired. Saturday had been an exhausting day, mentally, and the subsequent seventy-two hours in hiding hadn't included much sleep. It was the middle of the night. Understandable that his eyes would close. Understandable but unforgiveable. He awoke to the feel of silk round his neck, tightening inexorably. Before he was fully awake, he was already choking. He grabbed at the slippery material gripping him but couldn't find any purchase, so his hands worked their way back towards the operational end of the strangulation. He found some thin wrists. Thin but strong. His grasp was having no effect and he was beginning to black out as the soft but deadly noose continued to constrict.

Was this P King? Unlikely. Downton doubted his phone contact was the sort of man to get down and dirty. Downton wasn't ready to have his employment terminated but he couldn't break the grip and he felt his focus blurring. Then, out of nowhere, there came a furious high-pitched yapping. Some dog. Some small dog by the sound of it. Downton had no idea where the dog had come from but he felt the silk around his neck loosen fractionally as his attacker hissed from behind him, 'Be quiet, Alphonse.' An unknown voice, foreign, effeminate. It was all Downton needed. He pushed up mightily and flung himself backwards over the rear of the bench and into his assailant.

Suddenly he could breathe. The aggressor had been forced to let go of the material that had been strangling him to avoid his surge over the bench. Downton landed on his back and scrambled to get to his feet, but before he was half upright, the man was on to him again, breathing deeply, long fingernails scratching his cheeks and searching for his eyes. Downton staggered into the bench and fell. He landed on something small, soft and, briefly, noisy. A screech more than a yelp, cut short as he came down on top of it. The dog. There was a second screech, this time from his attacker.

'Alphonse!' he screamed, sliding off Downton's back. 'You have killed Alphonse,' conveniently forgetting his own attempt to kill the inspector. He tried to roll the giant policeman off the mortal remains of Alphonse but Downton pushed him roughly away and, grabbing the bench, hauled himself upright. The moon peeked out from behind the cloud cover. There was a small, fluffy, white Bichon Frise lying quite still on the ground and a slim young man in impossibly tight trousers crouching over it wailing softly. He appeared to have completely forgotten Downton.

A broken gravestone stood a little to their right. Downton reached across, picked up a sizeable fragment of marble and brought it down on the back of the man's head. He collapsed across the Bichon Frise.

The moon was still out. Twenty metres away, there was a tarpaulin stretched on the ground, pegged in the corners. Downton stumbled across and lifted one end. It revealed a newly dug, empty grave. It was less empty once he'd tipped the dead Alphonse and his unconscious erstwhile assailant into it. He noticed a pile of earth to one side with a spade sticking conveniently out of it.

Thirty minutes later, Downton, sweaty and dirty, brushed his hands down his trousers and tramped away from the churchyard. If he had felt some slight compunction about killing Marj Tavistock, he felt none for having buried his youthful attacker alive. All in all, though, it hadn't been the most successful of meetings for either of them, and Downton had no idea what to do next.

__ In which Elaine blows on her
    fingers, and she and Lucy
    eat fish

'Do you think Dawson knows how much danger he's in?' Elaine slumped further down on the floor of the speedboat. She had rarely been less comfortable. Even the thick sweater and fleece she was wearing were failing to stop her teeth chattering. She'd been cold ever since leaving Australia but being out on the Baltic in an open boat brought a whole new meaning to the word. How did the locals stand it? How did Lucy? The slight, blonde girl, standing with legs braced and one hand resting lightly on the wheel, pony-tail flapping in the stiff breeze and blue eyes scanning the low cliffs of the northern side of the small island, looked anything but cold, although she at least had the decency to be wearing a hoody over her habitual vest. Flaming June? Elaine could think of several other words beginning with F to describe what was supposed to be a midsummer month, but flaming didn't come close. Also, the sun was getting lower in the sky, its rays bouncing off Lucy's hair. What minimal warmth they were providing was diminishing by the minute.

'I imagine so,' said Lucy. 'He probably picked up on the signs when he was nearly blown up, kidnapped and stuck on a ship.'

'Shouldn't we be getting back? We don't want to be caught out here in the dark. And I'm frozen.'

'Let it go. It's not that cold, and it won't be dark for ages yet. We're nearly in the Arctic. Land of the midnight sun and all that. Where's your sense of adventure? I thought you Aussies were supposed to be rough, tough, outdoorsy types. Anyway, we're not going back to Riga. Dawson's either on this island or that bigger one behind us. Besides,' Lucy continued, 'we can't take this boat back to Riga. We stole it, remember? There'd be too much explaining to do. We'd be arrested and I doubt waving guns around would be an acceptable defence.' She glanced back at Elaine, who was starting to suspect she might have hyperthermia. Or maybe hypothermia. She knew that one meant hot and the other cold but couldn't quite remember which was which.

'We know that Dawson and Captain Sesks' "good" daughter came in this direction,' Lucy said in a conciliatory tone. 'They've got to have made landfall somewhere.' Or sunk, thought Elaine. 'Let's have one more turn around this place, ten minutes tops, then on to the big island.'

Elaine looked at the determined expression on Lucy's face, and realised she was right. 'We should forget this island and go straight to the big one. This is just an empty rock poking out of the sea. Dawson and this Sofija woman aren't here. Why the hell would they be? What could they possibly gain by it? And in any case, there's no sign of the ship's lifeboat. It'd be too big to hide, and we've only seen one beach and it's not there.'

Lucy wiped a hand down her sea-spray dampened face, nodded and looked at the chart she'd found pinned next to the wheel. 'The big island is called Saaremaa, literally Island-land, which shows a lack of inventiveness if you ask me. But you're right. Let's go.'

But Elaine wasn't right. At that moment, Dawson was lying in a cave a few hundred metres away with Sofija's hand clamped on his throat.

—

'How are we doing for fuel?' asked Elaine, after thirty minutes spent gently pootling along Saaremaa's southern coastline.

Lucy glanced down at the instrument panel. 'Not great,' she said. 'You'd think they might have filled it up for us before we nicked it.'

'We'd better head for shore then.'

'True, but I was hoping for a town of some kind. We'll have to start asking questions and we probably won't get any useful answers from sheep.' They were passing a field of fluffy white animals displaying a complete disregard for the two girls in the inflatable.

'Yeah, the answers you get tend to be on the woolly side.' They both laughed, breaking the tension that had been steadily increasing.

They rounded the next headland and suddenly there *was* a small town hugging the bay with a busy little port still going about its business, fishing mainly, by the look of it. Dominating the harbour was a large castle or fortress. Its stone walls shone brightly in the early evening sunshine. It boasted two square towers with pointed roofs covered with red tiles. It could have come straight from Disneyland.

Lucy pointed the speedboat towards a largely unused jetty at one end of the harbour, quietly brought it to a rest alongside and cut the engine. Elaine jumped out and tied up.

'Will we be needing this again?' she asked.

'Don't know, but we can't assume it'll still be here when we get back,' said Lucy. 'Some busybody will report there's a Russian speedboat turned up. We should make tracks. Right, if Dawson's here, where would he be?'

'It's six o'clock. Finding something to eat?' hazarded Elaine. 'Or trying to shake off the captain's good daughter?'

'Yes to the first, probably no to the second. If he believes she's just helped him escape from the Russians, he's not going to leave her stranded.'

They spent a fruitless three hours trolling round the cafés and bars of the small town, which they learned was called Kuressaare, and ended up eating an unappetising meal at an establishment proudly announcing itself to be Saaremaa's foremost seafood restaurant, a description they soon took issue with. Something else they took issue with was a group of four unappealing men who entered the café just as they were deciding they could eat no more of the greasy, indeterminate fish they had been given.

'Hello,' said Lucy, quietly, wiping her mouth on a paper napkin. 'We've got company.'

'Time to leave?' said Elaine.

'Time to leave,' agreed Lucy, and they stood up and walked out into the narrow road outside the café. 'This way,' she added, turning left and ducking into an even narrower alleyway. She pulled her gun from her waistband and Elaine did the same.

Lucy peeped around the corner and saw the four men exit the café. They looked around uncertainly, as if expecting to find the two girls waiting for them. Possibly not the brightest lights on the Christmas tree, she thought. The men muttered amongst themselves, then split into pairs and marched off in opposite directions. Two of them strode past the alley where Lucy and Elaine were concealed. They didn't even glance into the entrance as they passed. Lucy signed to Elaine to follow them whilst she went off on the trail of the other pair, who had headed towards the harbour.

It was Elaine who struck gold. The two men she was trailing from fifty metres back seemed unaware that she was following them and didn't once look behind them. They were both in scruffy, dirty black jeans and greasy looking jackets of the same colour, or lack of, and wearing woollen hats. After a kilometre or so, winding gently uphill through the town, they turned into a nondescript, grey-washed cottage wedged tightly between its neighbouring houses. There was a constricted passage to the side. Elaine waited until they were safely inside the house and, gun in hand, cautiously edged down the passage and round to the back. She heard voices and bent down beneath a window. She couldn't understand what the voices were saying and was unsure whether the language was Russian or Estonian. It could have been Latvian, although it didn't sound much like the guttural utterings of Captain Sesks. She risked a quick glance through the window and wasn't entirely astonished to see that the two men were talking to none other than Valentin Prokofiev, whom she had last seen waving him gratefully off at Heathrow into the custody of two secret service agents some weeks previously. Prokofiev was considerably more animated than he had been on the flight from Melbourne. There was another man with him, with Slavic features, but Elaine didn't risk a longer look.

She crept back into the lane, moved away from the house, pulled out her phone and called Lucy. There was no reply.

The two men I was following had no idea I was behind them. They looked for all the world as if they were going off duty. There was a lot of laughter about something, although I was too far back to hear what they were laughing about. It was still, ridiculously, almost full daylight and there were too few other people about in the small town to provide cover, even for someone of moderate size, like me. I pulled my hood over my head and edged closer. The two men, one of whom looked to be well into his fifties and who walked with a slight limp, the other much younger and friskier, turned onto the wide, almost deserted spaces of the quayside and headed towards the far end. The end where Elaine and I had left the inflatable speedboat over three hours ago.

It was still there. The two men walked up to it and the younger one jumped in, causing it to rock wildly. His colleague shouted at him in Russian to be careful: 'Byt' ostorozhen!' But he was laughing as though it was the funniest thing he'd seen in ages. This was odd to say the least and then things got even odder as the man in the boat, who I could now see was little more than a teenager and one of the few men on Saaremaa not sporting a beard, possibly because he hadn't yet reached puberty, started dancing. In an inflatable speedboat. It was an absurd and, frankly, rather dangerous thing to do. I was enthralled. What the hell was he doing? His older colleague, on the jetty, was still laughing and then I saw him glance my way. Shit, I thought, I've been rumbled. The dancing youth had made me lose concentration. I ducked behind a pile of pallets and tried to work out my next move.

I sensed rather than felt the movement behind me, a wisp of an air current where there had been none previously. I dropped to the ground just in time to avoid the blackjack which thudded into the wooden pallet beside me. Practice makes perfect, I thought, harking back to Abbey Downton in Mr Bojangles. I didn't hang around. My gun was stuck into the rear waistband of my jeans and irretrievable in any usefully rapid sort of way, so I took three quick steps to my right and dived into the water.

Unfortunately, my final step on dry land had been into a coil of thick rope left untidily on the jetty and it wrapped itself tightly around my left ankle as I leapt. Dragging a length of heavy rope didn't do wonders for my buoyancy and I found myself sinking. I wrestled with the rope, which had coiled itself around my leg like an over amorous octopus, for what seemed like minutes, but was probably only a few seconds. Even Bulldog's training hadn't included breath-holding exercises whilst untying knots underwater, but just as I could feel myself beginning to black out, I succeeded in freeing myself and popped suddenly to the surface, gasping uncontrollably.

Inserting air into my lungs was my main priority for quite a few seconds so it took me a while to recall that three Russian agents were likely to be highly interested in my aquatic escapade. Shaking water out of my hair and eyes, I looked up.

I was wrong. It wasn't three Russians interested in my dive into the harbour. It was six. And a dog. I'm not an expert on dogs but I was pretty sure this one was a Dobermann. All I could remember about Dobermanns (or should that be Dobermenn?) was that, if not exercised, they are liable to become irritable and aggressive. This one was displaying all the signs of not having exercised for several years. He also looked like he fancied a swim and it was only because he was being restrained by a chain leash gripped tightly in the gloved hand of another bearded man dressed in black, that he was not joining me in the water.

Apart from the man in black holding the dog, the man in black thumping his cosh in a thuggy sort of way into his palm, and the Dancing Queen in the inflatable, everyone else was holding automatic pistols and pointing them in my direction. It seemed a bit excessive, frankly. It was all I could do to tread water, let alone get at my own gun, still stuck into my waistband but presumably getting a tad waterlogged. I wondered if I should raise my hands in surrender, but nobody was asking me and I really needed both arms to help me stay afloat.

Up to this point, none of my unattractive, black-clothed audience had said anything. The man in his fifties, who had stopped laughing, broke the silence, in English. 'Meess Smeeth,' he said, which was close to being accurate, 'please get out of ze water. You look most uncomfortable.' There was a note of slight concern in his voice which his face didn't share.

The teenager in the boat, grinning wildly, stuck his hand out in my direction. 'Idi syuda, krasavitsa,' he said. I understood the instruction to head his way but objected to being called beautiful by someone who looked just out of nappies and possessed, I couldn't help but notice, one eye with a mind of its own, which was darting uncontrollably about in every direction but mine. In any case, I didn't feel very beautiful, especially as my face was turning blue with cold.

I swam slowly to the inflatable, where Swiveleyed hauled me unceremoniously out of the sea by one arm and one breast. The latter wasn't strictly necessary, but I was too exhausted to do more than store the assault up *for future reference. At the very least, I would have to have a word with his mother.*

Back on the jetty, an elderly, off-white Transit van sporting more than its fair share of rust, had pulled up in a cloud of smoke and another man got out. Unsurprisingly, he was dressed in black and had a thick beard. These were villains with a disappointing absence of imagination. The new arrival brought the number of my captors to seven. I felt quite proud. I'd been an insurance advisor only a year ago, and now the Russian secret service apparently considered me so dangerous that it took a netball team to restrain me.

For the second time in four days I was bundled into the back of a van, and this time I was joined by the dog and five of the men, including the youth with the roving eye and hands, who relieved me of my gun in the process. Somehow, he managed to grab an arse cheek whilst so doing. Inadvertently, presumably. Not. There was no bench in this van, so I was directed to sit on the floor. I did so and everyone else joined me, the youth on one side and the Dobermann on the other, both too close for comfort. It was hard to tell whose breath smelt worse. The van started up.

We didn't go far. After four or five minutes of what seemed to be mostly uphill progress, we stopped and I was marched down a narrow path to the rear of a nondescript grey-washed house, to a storeroom of some kind, linked to the house by an open-sided covered passageway. I was shoved roughly inside and I heard the lock click behind me. It was, at last, getting dark outside but the room was lit by a low-wattage bulb hanging nakedly from the flaking ceiling. There was no furniture but there was a row of coat hooks beside the door with an assortment of smelly old jackets, all black, hanging there. As I was still dripping wet from my dip in the harbour, I was pleased to see there was also a towel left there either by accident or design. Perhaps they didn't want me to freeze to death before they killed me.

Time passed, three or more hours maybe, although my watch and phone had also been taken, so I couldn't be absolutely sure. I could hear virtually nothing from the main house. Perhaps they were waiting for someone or discussing my fate. Maybe they had found Elaine and were dealing with her in some way first. I fervently hoped not.

Eventually there was movement in the passageway outside and the door opened. Two powerful torch beams shone into my face, temporarily blinding me. I was hauled to my feet and pushed out of the door and along the passage to the house. No one said a word and trying to think of something practical to effect an escape attempt seemed to me more important than engaging in pointless chit-chat.

The room we entered was not especially large and there was quite a crowd squashed into it, a dozen or so including the Dobermann, which growled as I entered. I was feeling prouder all the time about the level of importance they placed on me. And in particular that Valentin Prokofiev evidently placed on me. The Russian hitman stepped forward.

'Good evening, Miss Lucy Smith,' he said in hardly accented English, pale blue eyes staring into my own, slightly darker blue eyes from a distance of a metre. 'Or should I say, Lady Joanna Delamere. I am sorry that I was not aware of your elevated position in the English aristocracy when we met in Australia.'

'Don't worry, Val,' I said. 'I'm no lady. You'll find that out in due course. Now, what have you done with Dawson?'

___ In which two gravediggers discuss
filling in and tamping down, and
Gulliver fails to look through
a telescope

Chief Superintendent Gulliver was in his office in Guildford Police Station when his phone rang. The number was unidentified but not unidentifiable.

'Good morning, Mr Underwood,' he said. 'Another lovely day.'

'If you say so.' Gulliver thought that Underwood sounded less than his normally unruffled self, which was interesting.

'Have you found your missing inspector yet?' continued the MI6 man. 'How are the investigations into the tidal surge or whatever it was in the cavern going?'

'Unfortunately, nothing to report on either score, Mr Underwood.' That was the truth. Gulliver did indeed have nothing to report. Not necessarily nothing discovered though, at least as far as the river in the cavern was concerned. However, Gulliver was not quite ready to share any information about that with Underwood. His copper's instincts had not yet decided whether the shadowy intelligence controller was being especially secretive, or whether there was anything more concerning afoot. Whichever it turned out to be, Gulliver had decided he needed to keep something back. As regards Downton though, he genuinely had no information, which was frustrating. The giant, rogue policeman should have been apprehended by now. He hadn't left the country, the coastguard and Border Force were pretty certain about that, and all Gulliver's instincts – those again – told him that Downton had not gone very far. But he had also not been found.

'We don't know if Downton is a traitor yet. And until your people find him, the truth will remain buried. Do you need more resources to dig stuff up?'

'No, thank you, we can cope. I'll let you know if anything

turns up.' Gulliver disconnected and frowned at his phone, which promptly rang again. Another unidentified number, but not Underwood's.

'Chief Superintendent Gulliver.'

'Good morning, Chief Superintendent,' said a clipped, female voice down the line. 'My name is Elspeth Arundell. I work for the government. I believe it would be mutually beneficial for us to meet.'

———

'So how the hell do you manage to bury the wrong body?'

The two Council workmen looked at each other sheepishly. One was tall and lank, no more than nineteen years old. His colleague, in his sixties and presumably in charge, although trying his best not to show it, coughed.

'I'm waiting,' said Gulliver.

'It was Wayne's fault,' said the older worker, scratching his ear and clearly consigning the phrase "the buck stops here" to the bin.

'Eh? What you talkin' 'bout, Reg?' said his younger colleague, mouth falling open to reveal a set of teeth long since due a dental visit.

'You fills 'em in, I tamps 'em down,' said Reg. 'I turns up with the coffee, grave's been filled in, I assumes you've dragged your arse outta bed on time for once and filled the bugger in. So I tamps it down.' He crossed his arms in front of his pot belly. 'Your fault,' he repeated.

'And I *assumed* you'd done me a favour and filled it in yerself,' retorted Wayne. 'You've done it afore.'

The contretemps at the late Mrs Fothergill's burial service had been brought to Gulliver's attention at lunchtime, following his phone conversations with Underwood and the intriguing Elspeth Arundell, whom he had yet to meet. That meeting was scheduled for this evening. In the meantime, he had been informed about the unexpected discovery of a body, or two if you include a Bichon Frise. The vicar of St Michaels and All Angels had expressed quite a reasonable concern about who, if not Mrs Fothergill, was buried in the grave earmarked for her everlasting rest, so he'd ordered it opened up again.

The investigation into the demise of the person who was clearly not Mrs Fothergill was in its infancy but the young man had carried a credit card and driving licence, both in the name of Sacha Tarkovsky and providing an address adjacent to The Oval cricket ground in Kennington, South London. Officers were there already and after leaving the two gravediggers to try to explain their mistake to the vicar and the relatives of Mrs Fothergill, Gulliver joined them.

'Decent place, this,' he said to the inspector in charge of the team in the spacious, immaculate third floor flat, which enjoyed an impressive view over The Oval. 'Do we know what our young friend did for a living? These places don't sell for much less than a million, I'd have thought.'

'As far as we can tell, sir, nothing. Or at least, nothing that involved regular hours. The neighbours say he was polite enough and pretty quiet, although that didn't go for his dog, about which complaints had been made.'

'Ah yes, the squashed Bichon Frise. Noisy little buggers, aren't they?'

Gulliver wandered out on to the balcony. He was a cricket lover and could imagine himself spending long summer days watching Surrey or England from this balcony, once he was able to retire from his current travails pursuing embezzling stockbrokers, crooked car dealers or, to take a case at random, people who blew foreign scientists up for no apparent reason and kidnapped junior employees of MI6. He sighed. It was never going to happen. Not on a police pension, even a Chief Superintendent's.

A telescope was clamped to the balcony railing. Presumably, the late Sacha also liked his cricket. Gulliver wandered over to the telescope. He could see some players practising in the nets strung up at the far end of the ground and, being a Surrey supporter, was keen to see who was taking part. Unfortunately, he was too short to put his eye to the telescope. He collapsed a folding chair and laid it flat to stand on, boosting him several inches. As he strained for the eyepiece, his foot slid on the uneven surface. Naturally low to the ground, he went lower still. And that's when something caught his eye on the shadowy underside of the telescope. The slot for the screwhead of a small compartment had its sides stripped, as if the wrong size screwdriver had been used. He leant over the railing to get a better view.

Gulliver wasn't an expert on the detailed workings of telescopes and the compartment probably just contained some sort of focussing machinery or power pack, but he was a copper and a good one, so he took a closer look, leaning at a precarious angle, one toe on the collapsed chair and his left hand gripping the railing tightly to prevent him toppling into the Harleyford Road three floors down. Never without a Swiss army knife, he slid the screwdriver attachment into the already widened slot and unscrewed it.

Holding his breath and thinking that he should really have pressed a more expendable subordinate into service, he finally managed to insert finger and thumb into the aperture and make contact with what felt like a small plastic wallet. Carefully, he extricated it. He didn't know what the wallet contained but doubted it was the warranty document for the telescope. Clasping it tightly, he clambered down and was just straightening up when the Met inspector leant through the French window. 'Call for you, sir,' he said. 'One of your boys. Says it's important.'

Gulliver stuffed the plastic wallet into his pocket, stepped inside the flat and took the phone from the inspector. 'Gulliver,' he said.

'Hello, sir,' came the enthusiastic voice of PC Sam Bunter.

'We've found something.' He corrected himself. 'Actually two things. Me and forensics that is.' He paused.

'Be nice to know what they are, constable. Forensics first, please.'

Another voice came on the line. 'Chief?' it said. 'Anne here. Our friend, Inspector Downton. His pawprints are all over the spade from the graveyard.'

So at least we know where Downton was last night, thought Gulliver. 'Thanks, Anne,' he said. 'Put young Bunter back on, would you? Sounds like he's got something else for me.'

Sam's voice came on again, sounding as eager as a gundog. If he'd had a tail, he'd be wagging it. 'It's the cavern sir. You know, where we found Miss Smith and the bodies.'

'And?'

'I think I've found out why the water was getting deeper and faster, sir.'

_ In which Valentin Prokofiev commits
a minor grammatical faux pas, and
Elaine checks her gun for bullets

Valentin Prokofiev laughed. 'Mr Dawson?' he asked, his pale blue eyes wide and a mocking smile playing about his thin lips. 'Do you see a Mr Dawson?'

Whilst the living room in the cottage was full, one thing it was not full of was Dawson. Lucy had to acknowledge that fact. 'Well, I didn't think he'd be part of the welcoming committee,' she said tightly. 'But I promise you, Val, if you've done anything to him, you'll pay.'

'So melodramatic, Miss Spy. You should read less James Bond books.'

'Fewer,' said Lucy automatically. She shook her head. Correcting Prokofiev's minor grammatical mistake made in a language not his own wasn't really a priority, she reflected. She should leave that sort of thing to Dawson.

Prokofiev shrugged. 'Your language is ridiculous. And your weather too. They are all you talk about in your cosy clubs and cold pubs while the rest of the world is conducting important business. You British are relics of a bygone age. You do not matter anymore. Your language does not matter anymore. Mr Dawson will be joining us soon enough, and then, as you and him do not matter anymore either...' He trailed off and smiled the thin smile again.

'He.'

As if the room wasn't already crowded enough, what with Prokofiev and ten of his men, plus the dog, which was staring balefully at Lucy through the forest of legs, another person now entered. A woman this time, of indeterminate age, Chinese by the looks of her, who would have been unusually tall even for a western female, let alone a Chinese. She sported cropped, jet-black hair, swimmer's shoulders and dark glasses perched on top of her head. She too was dressed all in black, although minus the black woolly hat favoured by at least six of Prokofiev's mob. A hat would have got in the way of the dark glasses. The crowd parted like the Red Sea as she approached the head man, which indicated that she probably held some influence in Prokofiev's organisation. Exactly what that organisation was, Lucy was unsure about, but it seemed increasingly likely that the Russian, previously a mere SVR hitman, might be more detached from the state apparat now. Had he gone rogue? Was the Chinese ethnicity of the new arrival significant? If so, things were becoming even more interesting. And more confusing. Probably more dangerous as well, if that were possible.

The Chinese woman bent and whispered briefly in Russian in Prokofiev's ear. Her words were heavily accented and Lucy couldn't make out what she was saying but it seemed to please her boss, who again smiled thinly, and looked at Lucy.

'Well, this is a coincidence,' Prokofiev said. 'It appears that our friend, Mr Dawson, has made dry land. Doubtless you will be pleased to hear this news, Miss Smith. I will ensure that you have the opportunity to say goodbye to each other very soon. I am not, you understand, a monster.'

Lucy tried to keep a poker face but inside she was exulting, despite the implied promise that both she and Dawson could expect some form of execution in the near future. For the time being at least, Dawson was alive. She hoped the same could be said of Elaine, who hadn't been mentioned, so was probably still free somewhere close at hand, watching and waiting. Lucy had been relieved of her own weapon, but Elaine would still have hers, although hopefully, she wouldn't go mad and try to rush the building single-handed. That would be a typically Australian thing to do but the odds if she did were distinctly unfavourable.

The tall Chinese swimmer-woman had not left again after talking to Prokofiev but stood next to him, half a head higher in her black trainers, staring down a long, unexpectedly un-Chinese nose over Lucy's head with a supercilious look on her pale face.

'I must leave you now, Miss Smith, but Songsung Rong will take care of you,' Prokofiev said. The woman gave the impression that she might be considerably more efficient in the "taking care of" department than Inkman had been. She probably couldn't be relied upon to blow her own face off, for example. And her name was Songsung Rong. Lucy laughed. So it probably hadn't been Something Wrong that she'd heard on the transmission. It was just poor pronunciation.

A small, black rubber cosh suddenly appeared in Rong's hand and she prodded Lucy less than gently in the upper arm. Blackjacks seemed to be a popular weapon of choice amongst Prokofiev's appropriately black-dressed followers. They must have got a discount for multiple purchases, a sort of BOGOFsky, Lucy supposed.

'Ouch,' she said, glaring up at the woman.

'*Syuda*,' said Rong in bad Russian and gave another prod. And then repeated herself in heavily accented English. 'Thees whay.'

'Don't worry, Princess, I heard you the first time,' said Lucy, moving to the door with Rong beside her and one of the black-woolly-hatted heavies taking up the rear.

———

Elaine had been unsure what her next move should be. She didn't want to leave the grey-washed cottage unwatched in case Prokofiev disappeared, so she remained on a secluded corner some thirty metres down the road from the house. From there she could keep both it and the road leading towards the lower part of town in view. But she couldn't do much alone, other than watch, so she somehow had to drag Lucy back from whatever goose she was wildly chasing. And Lucy was still resolutely not answering her phone, which suggested that something had gone wrong. She had headed off towards the harbour behind the other two black-clothed Russians. Exactly what they were planning to do at the harbour, Elaine had no idea, but they hadn't been going to meet Prokofiev, and Prokofiev was the key to finding Dawson, that much was obvious. Coincidence could only stretch so far and certainly not as far as this.

It was clear that Prokofiev had arranged for Dawson's kidnapping in Stallford and transportation to Saaremaa. But why? Elaine was a policewoman, albeit a traffic officer, but she was a traffic officer with ideas above her erstwhile station and one with recent investigative kudos to her name. She thought quickly. Prokofiev had not expended time, money and energy to drag Dawson over fifteen hundred kilometres to the Baltics just to kill him here. He could have done that back in England. And why would he kill him anyway? OK, Dawson had shot him, that was true, but it had only been a flesh wound, relatively speaking, and he had only remained in prison in Melbourne for a couple of months before the long dull journey Elaine and he had shared back to London, from whence he had presumably returned to Moscow. And now here he was on this Estonian island. No, everything pointed to the fact that for some as yet unknown reason, Prokofiev wanted Dawson alive and kicking.

But Elaine could think of no obvious reason why the Russian SVR should still have any interest whatsoever in Dawson or whether he was alive or dead. He simply wasn't important enough to risk a diplomatic incident. And that suggested that Valentin Prokofiev was no longer taking orders from the SVR. So who was he taking orders from? And why? And, more particularly, what had Dawson got to do with it all?

Twenty minutes passed. Then she heard the growl of a vehicle straining up the slight hill behind her. It was still not quite dark – jeez, how did these people sleep in the summer? – but she managed to squeeze into a patch of shade behind a thick bush. A few seconds later, a heavily laden Transit van, low on its axles, chugged past. It came to a stop outside the cottage.

She watched through the foliage as an inordinate number of people, together with one dog, a Dobermann if she wasn't mistaken, disembarked from the Transit. One of their number was Lucy, who appeared unhurt but very wet, although it was hard to be sure from thirty metres away. The whole troop disappeared into the grey-washed cottage.

A rescue operation seemed like a good idea to Elaine. The only problem was the odds. She knew there were at least four men inside the cottage, and they had been joined by seven others. Eleven to one, twelve including the Dobermann, which looked like it might be a worthy adversary. Twelve to two including Lucy, she reminded herself. It would be too much to expect Lucy still to be armed, but even an unarmed Lucy should be capable of keeping one of the Russian goons occupied. Leaving Elaine to take care of ten. Plus the dog. She checked her gun. There were five bullets left. All in all, a frontal assault might not be her best course of action. She had to think of something else.

But she couldn't. She didn't want to leave in case Lucy was taken away in her absence. And in any case, where would she go? To do what? Could she call someone? Jason Underwood was an obvious choice. It would only be the middle of the evening back in London, so she called the number she had been given, but there was no reply and no voicemail. She thought about trying the local police but decided against. A couple of provincial coppers would be no match for the mass of Russians inside the house, and they would probably just haul Elaine herself down to the police station before investigating.

She slumped on the ground, feeling completely at a loss. Time passed until at last it grew dark. Her legs were cramping so she stood and stretched. This was ridiculous. What would Lucy do? She asked herself the question and grimaced. Elaine had no doubt she would be up at the cottage looking for an opportunity. Certainly, there was no harm in going on a recce under cover of darkness to seek inspiration. Elaine left her hiding place, gripped her gun with its five bullets more tightly, pursed her lips, and walked determinedly up the road. Like shooting fish in a barrel, she thought, and laughed to herself. Whatever lay in store, it was a step up from issuing speeding tickets back in Victoria.

She crept down the side passage, peering through a couple of windows. Each room seemed to contain a selection of men in black, eating, dozing or talking, but she couldn't see Lucy anywhere. However, she did spot a pile of thin logs in a small yard at the rear of the house and, in an adjacent shed with a half-open door, what looked suspiciously like a can of petrol. And suddenly inspiration did strike.

At that moment, Elaine heard movement at the front of the house. She scuttled back along the passage and spotted Prokofiev and the Slavic-looking man she had seen with him earlier emerge and climb into a long-wheelbase Land Rover Defender. With Prokofiev's companion driving, the Land Rover executed a nifty three-point turn and sped off down the road.

Again, she heard movement, this time from the rear of the property, so she turned and made her way as quickly as she could back down the increasingly familiar side passage just in time to see Lucy, accompanied by one of the Russians and an unfeasibly tall woman with cropped, black hair, going into a small outhouse a few metres to the rear. The outhouse was conveniently close to the pile of logs.

I wasn't really expecting the fire. Neither was Songsung Rong nor her shorter, slabbier male companion.

I was expecting something though, as Elaine had winked as she passed quietly across the grimy window in front of me. In front of me, but behind Rong and her colleague. Only a few minutes had elapsed since I'd been pushed into the small outhouse at cosh-point, so Elaine wasn't wasting time. Rong was still busy instructing her companion in bad Russian exactly how closely he was to keep watching me as I was apparently more dangerous than I looked. He seemed to be having some trouble understanding what she was saying. I sympathised; I was having trouble keeping up myself and I reckoned I was a tad brighter than he was. Either Prokofiev hadn't mentioned that I was a Russian speaker or Rong didn't care one way or the other.

I presumed that Val's black-clothed heavies possessed names but it didn't seem important that I should learn them so I thought that numbers would do. The man deputed to watch me was Number Six, I decided, despite the fact that it was me, not him, who was the prisoner. I was idly translating "I am not a number, I am a free man" into Russian when smoke started creeping under the door.

I noticed the smoke before Rong and Number Six did. I smelt it first too. They didn't seem to be very quick on the uptake, despite standing close to the door, which they had been careful to lock behind them. I was sitting cross-legged in the opposite corner. I didn't feel it was my job to shout "Fire!" although I was mildly surprised no one else in the house had. All seemed to be quiet on the other side of the door.

Since the imaginative Elaine was doing her bit to rescue me, I reckoned it was probably a good time for me to do something to help. So I stood up. That caught my two captors by surprise. I no longer had my gun of course, but Number Six had one in a holster under his left armpit, which I considered would do just as well, although approaching his undoubtedly pungent pit to take it could be construed as being way over and above the call of duty. Still, I had no choice. The tall swimmer-woman only had her cosh. Nasty thing to be sure, but then so was the cosh, I thought, laughing inwardly as I strolled over to them.

Rong produced her little blackjack and took a step in my direction. However, at the same time, she finally smelt the smoke, which was now enveloping her ankles. As her ankles were six feet below her lengthy nose, I suppose it was understandable that it had taken her so long to smell it. She briefly looked down, so I relieved her of the cosh with my right hand and hit Number Six with a roundhouse, backhanded swipe hard on the temple. He must have had the reactions of a particularly slow-witted tortoise as he was basically just standing there waiting to be coshed. I would have had to jump quite high to hit Rong on the head, so Number Six seemed the easier option and, in any case, he was the one with the gun, and I wanted the gun.

The blackjack proved extremely effective. Number Six collapsed silently to the floor and I plucked his gun out of its underarm holster with my left hand as he passed me, heading downwards.

I had gone from a state of weaponlessness to having two of them in the space of about five seconds, and the opposition numbers had also halved. However, there was still Rong to be dealt with and, cosh or no cosh, she was a foot taller than me and possessed shoulders twice as wide as mine, which suggested that she may work out. So do I though, but rather than start a discussion about the benefits of various fitness regimes, I decided to shoot her. In the foot. To quote Valentin Prokofiev, I am not, you understand, a monster.

She shrieked in an unexpectedly girly falsetto and collapsed across Number Six.

I imagined that if the smoke hadn't brought the black-apparelled hordes of minions running, then probably a gunshot and a scream would. Rong was obviously under orders not to do away with me before I could be reunited with Saul and, hopefully, as in all the best spy films, we would be updated about what the hell this business was in aid of before the said doing away with. So a gun being fired and a feminine shriek of pain should have caused at least mild consternation amongst Prokofiev's men.

On that basis, a second shot wasn't going to do much extra harm, and I had to get out of the room anyway, not least because it was becoming quite smoke-filled and my eyes were starting to water. I stuck the cosh in a pocket, swapped the gun from left hand to right and shot off the door lock before it belatedly occurred to me that Elaine might be on the other side. It was too late to worry about that though; I'd apologise later if I'd accidentally killed her. I opened the door.

The passage outside was firmly on fire. God knows what Elaine had used to start the conflagration but it was already approaching inferno proportions despite the passage being, effectively, outside. It was a covered way leading from the house to this outbuilding and on to what looked like a garage opening onto a rear access to the property. As I paused, uncertain how to get past the fire without being burnt, the covered bit of the covered way gave up the unequal struggle with the heat and crashed to the ground in front of me, giving me a brief opportunity to hurdle the passage before the flames leapt up again. I landed awkwardly and rolled over twice before springing back to my feet with the gun pointing directly at Elaine's face from a distance of ten centimetres. I hadn't accidentally shot her through the door, and I managed not to shoot her now either. Just well trained, I guess.

'Where's everyone else?' I asked frantically, still expecting anything up to a dozen men in black to come running out of the house.

'Thanks for rescuing me, Elaine,' said Elaine.

She was right, despite the fact that I'd had to overcome two armed opponents myself, so I gave her a quick squeeze. 'Sorry,' I said, 'but all the same, where are the rest of Prokofiev's men?'

She held up an oversized key. 'I found this in the kitchen. There was a whole bunch of uncreatively dressed men eating supper in the dining room, so it seemed a useful idea to lock them in. It'll hold them up for a while although I'm not actually sure if they know what the hell's going on yet. I don't think Prokofiev recruits on the basis of IQ and there's a TV on with the volume up high, lots of gunfire and stuff, so the shots here may not have registered at all. As you seem to be holding a gun, I guess that was you doing the shooting.'

At that moment, I spotted a movement behind Elaine, low down, and brought Number Six's borrowed gun up sharply. It was the Dobermann. He and I were not the best of friends and I'd lapsed my membership of the RSPCA, so I had no scruples about sending him to his final kennel, but before I could pull the trigger, Elaine grabbed my arm.

'Whoa, cowboy,' she said. 'He's a pal. Leave him alone.' I paused. The Dobermann growled at me. There was some saliva in evidence. He didn't look like a pal to me.

'Sit, Riley,' said Elaine. The dog obediently did so and started wagging his stump of a tail He looked up at Elaine with a look of apparent adoration, working hard to maintain the sort of soulful expression that has people posting pet pics all over Instagram.

'Riley?' I said. 'Really?'

'Don't you start,' said Elaine, laughing. 'Although I suppose he is "Really Bigg".'

I chuckled too and edged towards the dog with my hand out to show that I held no ill feelings about his earlier inclination to regard me as potential dinner. He growled again. I stepped back.

'Hmm,' said Elaine thoughtfully. 'Another male impervious to your charms. Riley, be quiet.' The dog collapsed onto its side and whimpered quietly. 'Dogs like me. I was in the God Squad for a while back in Shepparton.'

'God Squad?' I said. It seemed to be an odd conversation to be having alongside a raging fire and a house full of armed foreign agents.

'Yeah, the rest of the force thought the canine division was a bit backward.'

Suddenly, we heard a siren approaching, a siren presumably attached to an emergency service vehicle of some description. More than one, maybe, given the fact that the fire had taken a liking to the main fabric of the cottage. Probably the police would be tagging along too.

'Time to go,' I said. 'There's what looks like a garage just down there. I wonder if it's got a car in it?'

It did, a sporty-looking, dark blue Subaru, which had Elaine grinning as soon as she saw it. 'I'm driving,' she said.

I remembered her background in the Victoria State traffic police and waved her forward. We clambered in, Riley included. He plonked himself in the middle of the *rear seat and put his large head right between me and Elaine, glancing at me with a look that said, "OK, you're safe for now, but one step out of line, missy, and all bets are off, along with ears, nose and any other tasty, sticky-out bits I can find."*

Five seconds later we shot out of the rear gate just as the sirens pulled up at the front.

__ In which Dawson trips over a cat,
and Sofija nearly drowns Prokofiev

Lucy had just said to Prokofiev: 'That's all very well, Val old chum, but I think we'll take a peek in the back just to be sure you're not telling porkies. If you would be so kind.'

'Nothing to see there,' said Dawson, emerging from his hiding place in the trees with what he hoped would be a dramatic flourish. Unfortunately, he hadn't accounted for the large cat-like animal that chose at that moment to shoot across his path and trip him up. As Dawson was on a patch of land a couple of metres higher than the tableau on the road in front of him, the trip precipitated a fall and an uncontrolled roll down the slope to the feet of the four people below who, understandably, were distracted by this unexpected display of amateur athletics.

Both Lucy and Elaine had to leap sharply to the side to avoid Dawson, so it was Prokofiev who reacted first. The late Alexei, sprawled across the bonnet of the Land Rover, still had his gun loosely clasped in one outflung hand. Prokofiev grabbed it and got off a single shot at Elaine, hitting her gun and sending it flying into the undergrowth. Lucy hurled herself to the ground, unfortunately a piece of ground currently occupied by the spreadeagled Dawson. Her slight frame bounced over him and she ended up in an undignified heap, still holding her gun but unable to bring it to bear on the Russian as it was pinned under her. She looked up to see Prokofiev raise Alexei's automatic deliberately in her direction. Things didn't look too promising.

'Goodbye, Miss Smith,' said Prokofiev but, before he could pull the trigger, a solid bundle of fair-haired energy jumped on his back and knocked the gun from his grasp. His slim body wasn't designed to withstand such an onslaught and he fell to the ground with Sofija still attached. They ended up with him flat on his back and Sofija with a powerful right hand clamped around his throat. Dawson, whilst glad of her intervention, could sympathise with the Russian, having recently had Sofija's hand around his own throat.

'For God's sake, Dawson,' said Lucy, scrambling to her feet. 'Get off me.'

Dawson could have responded, accurately, that he hadn't actually been on her, but he was just pleased to see her and equally pleased to see that Prokofiev was no longer in charge of proceedings. Meanwhile, although Sofija still had the man whose status as her boyfriend now seemed open to question, pinned firmly to the ground, Elaine stepped across and kicked him in the head for good measure.

'Bit unnecessary,' said Dawson.

'That fucking hurt, being shot,' said Elaine, holding up a bruised thumb and finger. 'Anyway, he's still conscious.'

'Not for long, if our young friend here keeps up the pressure on his windpipe,' suggested Lucy, standing over Sofija and Prokofiev, gun in hand. 'Do you speak English?' she asked Sofija.

'Of course speak English,' said Sofija. 'The idiot, he know this.'

Strangely, neither Lucy nor Elaine, who had retrieved her own gun from the side of the road, had any doubt that the idiot she was referring to was Dawson.

'What's your name, lady?' asked Lucy.

'Good question,' said Dawson, back on his feet and checking for non-existent injuries. 'What's it to be? Sofija? Or Galina Diminutive?'

'Dimitrovna, idiot,' she replied, slightly easing her fierce grip on Prokofiev's throat. His usually pale face was starting to verge on the puce. Seeing that Lucy and Elaine, the latter using her left hand, both had their guns trained on her and Prokofiev, Sofija stood. Looking down at the still gasping Russian, she spat firmly and effectively in his face. Dawson, whose own throat was as dry as the Atacama Desert, could only admire the amount of phlegm she managed to produce. 'But Galina Dimitrovna is not my name. I am Sofija Ingrid Sesks.'

'Sex?' said Dawson.

'You wish, idiot.'

'So why does Val here think you're Galina?'

'He think I am my sister.' She spat at Prokofiev again with equal accuracy.

'Your twin I'm guessing, if you're telling the truth,' said Lucy. 'According to Captain Sesks, her name is Guna. You've got some credit in the bank for saving my life just then, but I need to know a lot more before I stop pointing this gun at you.'

'My sister is in Russian Intelligence.'

'What, the SVR?' said Dawson.

'Maybe. I not know for sure. Russian secret service has many testicles.'

'Pardon?' said Elaine.

'I think I'm learning to understand Sofija-ese,' said Dawson. 'You mean tentacles, don't you? Like an octopus.'

'Yes, of course, like I say. Anyway, we waste time. This *siga* need killing.'

'Let's try tying him up instead, shall we, little Miss Bloodthirsty?' said Lucy. 'Elaine, how's your hand? If you're fit enough, think you can have a hunt around for something to restrain our friend?'

'Sure I'm fit enough. I'll see what I can find.'

'You needn't bother,' said Dawson. 'There's a convenient box in the back of the Land Rover. I can vouch for its discomfort.'

'Why we not just shoot him?' said Sofija, dredging some more spittle from the rear of her throat and launching it for a third time at Prokofiev's face, which was at last returning to something like its normal pallor.

'Careful, you'll drown him,' said Lucy. 'And I've still got some questions to ask. Get up,' she added to Prokofiev, waving her gun persuasively to emphasise the command. However, before he could comply, Sofija bent down and grabbed him by the shirt collar, yanking him abruptly upright, so forcefully in fact that she momentarily had him dangling in thin air. He wasn't more than twelve stone but it was still an impressive feat. Elaine turned her gun slightly more in Sofija's direction.

Even in his current state of recovery from near strangulation, the Russian wasn't inclined to go into the box in the back of the Land Rover without a struggle. However, the struggle had no sooner started than it was ended by a roundhouse right hook from Sofija that felled him like a dapper, grey-suited ox. Dawson, Lucy and Elaine winced as one.

With the now unconscious Prokofiev safely locked in the box and the body of Alexei piled on the floor next to it, Lucy turned to Dawson and looked him up and down. 'Hello, boyfriend. I take it that wasn't a deliberately ridiculous entrance,' she said, smirking, 'but it was certainly very effective in turning the tables in old Val's favour.'

'I tripped over a cat. I'm sorry, it wasn't on purpose.'

'Lynx,' said Sofija, 'not cat. It run off up road while you were doing your poly-rolies. Estonia has many lynxes in forest. They dangerous.'

'See,' said Dawson, 'I was protecting you from the dangerous lynx. Although I don't think I've ever had the lynx effect on women before.'

'Mr Dawson is your boyfriend?' asked Sofija, looking from the tousled, dirty, uninspiring figure of Dawson to the blonde girl with the ponytail and the fresh, freckled face that looked as if it belonged on the cover of Vogue. 'He rich, yes?'

Lucy ignored her. 'Right, everyone,' she said, decisively. 'We're all off to the British Embassy in Tallinn. Elaine and I have a car around the corner, but I think we'll leave it there as it's not strictly ours, and just take this thing.'

'Is not yours either,' said Sofija.

No, but it does have our friends in the back. There are a lot of questions need asking and there's someone at the embassy who'll want to help me ask them. And that includes you, Sofija.'

'Erm,' said Dawson. 'We've got a tyre with a bullet hole in it. Not going to get far on that.'

'Lucky there's a spare then,' said Elaine from the rear of the vehicle.

'Can you see a jack?' asked Lucy.

'If there isn't one, Sofija could probably do the job,' said Dawson, laughing. 'By the way,' he added to Lucy as Elaine rolled the spare wheel to the front of the car, 'Hello back, girlfriend. What kept you?'

'You do realise I'm holding a gun?' she said.

—— In which Gulliver sits in a big
   chair, and Sam Bunter sits
   on a small one

Wednesday evening saw two people sitting in what had until recently been Chief Inspector Downton's office in Stallford Police Station. Gulliver had commandeered it and was sprawled in Downton's big, black leather chair behind the desk. The chair dwarfed him, having been built for someone a good fifteen inches taller. In front of the desk in a rather less comfortable upright chair, looking grim, sat Elspeth Arundell, whilst in an outer office, looking fidgety and worried, waited PC Sam Bunter.

'So, Ms Arundell,' said Gulliver. 'Tell me about Sacha Tarkovsky.'

Arundell paused before answering. 'I can confirm that Mr Tarkovsky was an associate of mine. In what capacity, however, I am unable to be more forthcoming. You will understand that all this is covered by the Official Secrets Act.'

Gulliver grunted. He had expected nothing else. He had only met Elspeth Arundell half an hour before and had already amended his earlier mental description from intriguing to bloody infuriating.

'So, Tarkovsky was working for MI6?'

'That's not what I said.'

'No, you didn't, but the information we have is that Mr Tarkovsky was indeed working for MI6 and was reporting to a certain Jason Underwood, a colleague of yours who I met last Saturday following the bomb blast.'

Arundell pursed her lips and didn't answer for a few seconds. 'No, that is incorrect,' she said finally.

'Who is Control?' asked Gulliver.

'I don't know what you mean.'

'Come now, Ms Arundell. Really? It's probably written down

in your internal phone directory these days. Underwood is Control. I know it and you know it. Now you know that I know it. What you don't know, possibly, is that our late friend, Sacha, had an ID card linking him with the person known as Control at MI6.' He waited for a response which failed to come. 'Which begs the question,' he continued finally, 'was he working for you or was he working for Underwood?' The plastic wallet given up by the telescope and the ID card inside had proved extremely illuminating.

Arundell sighed. 'Sacha Tarkovsky was working for me. Whilst my titular role within the organisation is European Bureau Head, as I have already told you, my remit is rather more complicated than that. We know that Mr Tarkovsky was killed by your Inspector Downton, who was also culpable for the bomb and for murdering at least one further person, not to mention attempting to kill another of my associates, Miss Smith. Your job, Chief Superintendent, is to find and apprehend Downton as quickly as possible. So far, you do not seem to be making much headway.' That much was undeniable. 'Nothing else is your responsibility.'

'One more thing, Ms Arundell. The man blown up by Downton's bomb was an Estonian scientist called Viktor Nurmsalu.'

'If you say so.'

Now what was that supposed to mean?

———

PC Sam Bunter had been waiting for an hour on a chair so small and so hard that by comparison the one occupied by Elspeth Arundell could have been made of the deepest, softest leather imaginable. He stared at the closed door to the office which still bore the name CI Downton. What the heck was going on in there? Who was the cold-looking woman with the Super? Sam wasn't stupid. She wasn't police. Government then, he decided. Senior civil servant perhaps. Or secret service. What with the bomb and the tidal wave in the cavern, that would make sense.

He ran a forefinger round inside his collar. It hadn't felt so tight an hour ago. He knew that what he'd discovered was important, the Super had said so, but he also knew that he hadn't been supposed to go looking for it. He'd done it because something didn't add up. He was a Surrey lad, born and bred, and knew the local area as well as any man alive. His parents had pretty much allowed him to run wild through his teenage years and he'd thought there wasn't a stretch of the River Mole he didn't know backwards, overground or underground. But he hadn't known about the bit that ran through the cavern where they'd found the gorgeous MI6 woman and the two bodies.

So he'd taken another gander on his day off.

The door opened and Chief Superintendent Gulliver popped his head out. Despite the fact that Sam was sitting down their heads were at the same level. 'Come in, lad,' he said. Was that a smile? Sam hoped it was, and certainly the "lad" was encouraging.

He went in and stood nervously by the desk while Gulliver allowed himself to become enveloped by the huge black armchair behind it. He could hear the thin woman beside him breathing in short, sharp breaths but didn't dare look at her.

She spoke suddenly. 'Sit down, man, for goodness' sake. You're blocking out the light.'

Sam glanced across at the Super, who nodded. There was another chair up against the wall by the door, so he moved it in front of the desk and sat down.

'Sam,' started Gulliver promisingly. 'First of all, what's said between these four walls stays between these four walls unless Ms Arundell here or myself says otherwise. Understand?'

'Yes, sir,' said Sam, sitting up straight. 'And may I ask who Ms Arundell is, sir?'

'I'm sitting right here, constable,' said Arundell. 'You can talk to me. I work for the intelligence service. You do not need to know more and if you tell anybody about me, your police career will be very short-lived.'

Sam turned to her. 'Sorry, ma'am. Can I ask – are you M?'

'Inasmuch as M does not exist outside the pages of a paperback novel and as far as you are concerned, I don't exist either, then quite possibly.'

Gulliver picked up two photos and looked at them briefly before placing them back on the desk facing Sam and Arundell. 'So Sam,' he said. 'Talk us through these for Ms Arundell's benefit.'

Sam leaned forward and prodded at a photo with the same finger that had recently been employed running around his perspiring neck. 'Well, sir, I mean ma'am, I came upon this a short way from the cavern where we found Miss Smith the other day.' Although dark, the photo clearly showed a long table hard up against a rock wall with an array of electronic equipment sitting on it. Arundell picked it up and scrutinised it closely. Then she looked at the second photo, which was of a dark doorway seemingly cut into the rockface at the top of a flight of stone steps. Gulliver had already explained what Sam had told him, but she asked anyway.

'And do we know what this equipment does, constable?'

'Well, ma'am, up to a point. I know I shouldn't've, but I had a bit of a fiddle. And that knob there,' and he pointed out the knob in question, 'started up a rush of water like the one we saw on Saturday evening.'

'What, just like that?'

'Well, no, not immediately. It took a little while. I pushed it but nothing happened, so I was having a look further up the tunnel. I wanted to see where it came out in the open air. Then I heard a whirring noise. The river had been virtually still, but I heard the noise and then I noticed the water was starting to move more quickly and get a bit deeper. As the Super knows, I'm not a great swimmer and I was sort of trapped in the tunnel, so I turned round and hurried back to where I found the equipment.'

'Which is in a room off to the side up these steps, yes?' She pointed at the second photo.

'Yes, that's right, ma'am. I thought, well, if it's upstairs it probably had to be kept above the water level so that's where I needed to go to avoid being swept away like I nearly was on Saturday.'

'And presumably you thought it a good idea to switch the machinery off again.'

'Well, yes, I suppose so, but I'd forgotten which knob I'd pushed, if I'm honest.' Arundell's eyebrows headed towards her coiffed, grey hair. 'So I pushed the one I thought it was and, well, there was bit of a commotion and the river started running back the other way. Rivers aren't supposed to do that.'

'You don't say.'

'Thanks, Sam,' said Gulliver. 'I'll take over now. You can go.' Sam stood up and left, gratefully.

When the door had shut behind him, Gulliver said, 'So, PC Bunter went back to Stallford and told his sergeant, who told him to phone me. I was up at the late Sacha's flat in Kennington but I got a team down to Leatherhead with all speed and, to recap, the equipment in the room twenty metres from the cavern under the bungalow starts, stops and changes the direction and power of the flow through the cavern and beyond.'

'For what purpose, do you think, Superintendent?'

'Ah, well, Ms Arundell, I was hoping you could tell us something about that.'

'Why me? What did Mr Underwood say?'

'I didn't tell him.'

'Why ever not? Don't you trust him?'

'That's a very interesting question. Do you?' He carried on without giving her a chance to reply. 'Look, Ms Arundell, I don't want to know about any internal power struggles within MI6.

What I think is this: I think it's all connected to the scientist who was blown up by Downton. I think that Downton was in the room found by PC Bunter and started the flood in the cavern that nearly finished Miss Smith. I think that Downton scarpered when Sergeant Bates and I happened along, and that this is all part of a much larger whole that I'm not being fully informed about. I can't force you to tell me more if it's tied up with some form of national security, but when I get my hands on Downton, he'll talk, I promise you.' He paused to see if there was any reaction from his visitor but her severe face remained unmoved. 'And I think that, national security or not, you, me and Mr Underwood need to work together on this for everybody's benefit.'

___ In which Dawson meets Riley,
   and Sofija discusses
   talkie-walkies

A little way up the road, Elaine pulled the Land Rover over, climbed out and ran towards a blue Subaru, nearly hidden down a track. She returned with a large dog, mainly black but with a trace of tan around its mouth, bounding alongside her. Opening the rear door next to Dawson, she shoved the four-legged arrival inside. 'Meet Riley,' she said.

'Hi, Riley,' said Dawson, stroking the Dobermann behind the ears and getting a friendly nuzzle in response. 'Hope you're nicer than your namesake was.'

With Elaine driving, Dawson was on the rear bench next to Sofija. Lucy was twisted round in the front passenger seat like Alexei had been earlier, directing her gun for safety's sake at Sofija.

'So, what happened to Alexei, then?' asked Dawson, struggling to make sense of the melee of information. 'Have I got this right? Elaine shoots out the tyre, Land Rover screeches to a halt, sideways on, at which point I scarper out the back door, Alexei comes out shooting from the hip but clearly not very accurately, and you, Lucy my darling, kill him.' Lucy nodded, slightly sheepishly.

'And it's not her first kill either,' said Elaine. 'She wiped out another one a few days ago.'

'That was an accident, I told you. And strictly speaking, he killed himself.'

'Who?' asked Dawson.

'Long story, tell you later, but I can promise you, no one's going to miss him,' and Lucy shuddered at the memory.

'She is murderer,' said Sofija. 'I tell you. And you idiot,' she added, in case Dawson had forgotten.

'OK, guys, that's enough,' said Lucy, consulting an elderly

road atlas she'd found in the glove compartment. 'I reckon it's about ninety minutes to Tallinn.'

'Seventy with me at the wheel,' said Elaine, driving over a pothole at close to 100 kph. Dawson's head hit the poorly cushioned roof of the Land Rover and when he landed again, he found that Riley the Dobermann had been bounced on to his lap. Dawson wasn't particularly entranced by this arrangement, but the dog gave his face a friendly lick before turning round and growling in Lucy's ear.

'Slow down, stupid Austrian woman,' said Sofija, whose face had collided with the window beside her at the jolt.

'This isn't quick,' said Elaine, grinning. 'I'll show you quick.' And she added another ten kph to their speed. Luckily, there were no more potholes. 'Hey,' she added after a few minutes of silence, 'if I'm Austrian now, should I try a bit of yodelling to pass the time?' No one answered, but Riley let out a single bark, although whether of encouragement or discouragement, it was hard to be sure. 'I'll take that as a no, then.'

'So, anyway,' said Dawson. 'Exactly where did you two spring from? Especially you, Elaine. You're a long way from home.'

'Couldn't keep away from all the excitement, mate.'

'Did you think I was just going to let you bugger off on holiday without me?' asked Lucy, and she proceeded to bring Dawson up to speed. 'Anyway,' she concluded, 'Val had said they were going to fetch you as you'd just arrived on Saaremaa and, as Saaremaa's an island, it was a fair bet they'd be turning round and heading back to Kuressaare when they'd collected you. So we parked up and waited. And, lo and behold, back you all came.'

'You could have stopped us then,' complained Dawson, 'before I got shut in the box. It was damned uncomfortable in there. Why did you wait until now?'

'The road outside Kuressaare was too busy. We thought at first they'd be taking you back to the cottage and we'd have a better chance of grabbing you there, hopefully surrounded by police and fire crew. But you didn't stop in the town and by now we were behind you and, because we'd stolen their car, we thought it safer to just keep our distance. Mind you, the ferry crossing was dodgy. Luckily, they weren't looking for us. Anyway, it wasn't until they stopped, presumably to stick you in the box back there, that we could get in front of you and set up the ambush on a quiet stretch of road.'

'Hang on,' said Dawson. 'Back up a bit. You said Prokofiev and Alexei set off when he'd been told I was on Saaremaa. That's right, yes?'

'Yes,' agreed Lucy.

'So, who told him?'

'The tall Chinese woman with the shoulders and the hole in her foot.'

'But who told her?'

Lucy twisted further round in her seat and stared at him disconcertingly, blue eyes wide. Then both she and Dawson turned slowly towards Sofija, slumped in the corner. Elaine would have turned too, but she was engaged in keeping the Land Rover on the straight and narrow or, more accurately, the twisting and narrow. The road they were on wasn't exactly of motorway standard.

Sofija shrugged. 'Yes, of course it was me. I needed Russian bastard to come out of hiding.'

'But how?' said Dawson. 'Not to mention when?'

'You had stalked up bank to road, trying to be man and take charge. I stay on beach and catch you up. I have small talkie-walkie under jacket. It belong to Guna.'

Riley pricked up his ears at the word "walkie", which suggested he was a multilingual dog.

'So, Prokofiev, thinking you're your sister, comes running and you hand over Dawson,' said Lucy with a glint in her eye. 'Did you know he wanted to kill him?'

'Yes, of course, but I think he want information from him

before he do that. So, as I keep saying, we should kill the *pätt* first.'

Lucy was still glaring. Dawson was trying but failing to glare too, and Riley was licking his face sympathetically. 'Look, you peoples,' Sofija continued, 'I like Dawson. He is idiot, yes, but nice idiot. I would do my best not to let Prokofiev kill him. But is not important. What the Americans say, Dawson he is collapsed damage.'

'Just who are you, Sofija?' asked Lucy in a gentler tone.

'I show you. Talkie-walkie is not only thing under my jacket.'

'OK, let's have a look at it, whatever it is, and don't do anything to persuade me to pull this trigger.' Lucy's gun didn't waver from the girl in the rear seat as Elaine brought the car to a halt.

'Of course,' said Sofija. 'But I must take something from jacket. Is not gun, OK?'

She slowly unzipped her parka, reached inside and appeared to feel within the lining before, with a small grunt of satisfaction, she produced a small, black, folding card holder with a blue, black and white striped insignia on the front, which she passed to Lucy, who flipped it open. The card inside contained a photo of a woman with short, tidy, dark-blonde hair and a severe expression. It was either Sofija or Guna-Galina, the mysterious twin. Lucy recognised the writing on the card as Estonian.

'*Leitnant* Sofija Ingrid Sesks,' she read. '*Sisejulgeolekuteenistus.*'

'I am officer in Estonian Internal Security Service,' said Sofija.

'How can you be an Estonian security agent?' asked Dawson. 'You're Latvian.'

'I am both. Father Latvian, mother Estonian. I have what is it? Duet nationality.'

Dawson looked astonished but Lucy was less surprised. It was already obvious that his liberator wasn't just the bored daughter of a tramp cargo ship captain seeking fun and excitement on the run with a somewhat dishevelled and confused British agent. Especially as she had successfully impersonated her twin sister, the apparent girlfriend of Valentin Prokofiev. 'So, this twin of yours, Guna or Galina or whatever. We haven't seen any sign of her. Not in the house in Kuressaare anyway. If she's supposed to Val's girlfriend, where is she?'

'She is on *Astrid* of course. In bilge.'

'I thought I was in the bilge,' said Dawson, unsure if bilges actually had a singular.

'More than one bilge. She will have escaped by now, so we must watch out. She dangerous.'

'More dangerous than you?'

'Of course. I am good daughter. Guna not good, not good at all. I hope my father all right.'

'She wouldn't hurt her own dad, would she?' said Elaine in a shocked voice, but Sofija simply shrugged. There was a small pause, while they digested the information that there was another version of Sofija out there somewhere with probable murderous intent.

I'd told the others we were heading for the British Embassy in Tallinn. I only hoped we were expected. Underwood had instructed me to report there if we succeeded in finding Saul and after seven days if not. Ask for the Third Cultural Attaché, he'd said. The words "Third Cultural Attaché" screamed Spy to me. I'd thought that only the pesky Russkies went in for such obviously fake job titles.

The embassy wasn't difficult to find. Just to the south of the old town and next to a small park, it nestled behind a large sliding steel gate, which was closed and failed to open as we pulled up. The building was more impressive than I was expecting, pristinely white-washed and boasting a ground to roof tinted-glass atrium, or possibly portico, or possibly something else entirely, architecturally speaking. I wasn't an expert.

'I see it has its own greenhouse,' remarked Saul.

'Idiot,' muttered a small voice beside him.

There was an intercom next to the gate but when Elaine leant out of the window and pushed the button, no one answered and the gate remained resolutely shut. However, after a minute, an elderly man came out of what I guessed to be a security office to our left and approached the driver's door, putting on a cap over his thinning grey hair and fishing a pair of spectacles out of an inside pocket. He didn't appear to be armed.

'Poms, still trusting everyone,' said Elaine.

'Tere päevast,' said the man in poor Estonian, smiling benignly. He was obviously English, so I leant across Elaine and replied in our mother tongue.

'Hi. We're expected.'

'Oh, you're English,' he replied with obvious relief.

Elaine interrupted. 'Actually, we're a bit of a mixture, cobber. Got a delivery for you.' She nodded towards the rear of the Land Rover, but that just seemed to confuse the security guard, who removed his cap and scratched his head. He looked as if he could be easily confused.

'I'm afraid the embassy is closed to visitors. Could you come back in the morning?' It was only mid-afternoon but perhaps it was early closing on Thursdays.

'We're here to see the Third Cultural Attaché,' I said. I would have shown him my MI6 ID but that, of course, hadn't survived the encounter with Prokofiev's goons so proving our bona fides was likely to be difficult.

Not so, however. 'Would you be Miss Smith, by any chance?' he said.

'That's exactly who I am,' I agreed.

'Park to the left there, please Miss Smith. Mr Wright is expecting you.'

'If we're all going in to meet this Wright bloke,' said Elaine, parking the Land Rover, 'what are we going to do with Prokofiev and the stiff in the back of the ute?'

'Hold on,' I said, walking back towards the gate, putting two fingers in my mouth and producing a loud whistle. More of a screech, if I'm honest. A flock of birds, just settling down to roost in the surrounding trees, took flight, complaining loudly at the disturbance. The whistle was another product of my time with Bulldog and Snape and was more effective than I'd expected. It was the first time I'd tried it.

'Full of surprises, your girlfriend, isn't she?' said Elaine, from behind me, not bothering to lower her voice.

'Common as muck,' said Saul, laughing.

'Fuck off, idiot,' I said over my shoulder.

The elderly guard stuck his head out of the security

office and looked around for the source of the whistle. 'Hey,' I called through the fence. 'Can someone keep an eye on our car while we go in to meet your Mr Wright? We've got a couple of undesirables with us. Neutralised, temporarily or permanently, but probably best not to leave them unattended.'

'I'm not sure if I can desert my post,' he said, sounding like the captain of a sinking ship and making no move to leave the sanctuary of his doorway. However, at that moment a bored-sounding drawl came from behind me.

'That's perfectly all right, Godfrey. You can stay where you are. I have this covered.' I turned to see a man in his thirties with a Roman nose, oily, slicked-back black hair wearing a beautifully cut pale-blue summer suit, white shirt and navy tie strolling towards me from a small door in the side wall of the embassy. 'We wouldn't want to force old Godfrey out of his comfort zone, now, would we?' It sounded unnecessarily rude and was accompanied by a small smirk.

I took an instant dislike to the man. I could feel his eyes undressing me as he approached, which was not an entirely new experience, but one that never fails to irritate. He held out his hand. Despite myself, I took it. The politeness of the English upper classes, inbred in me from an early age by my parents, the Earl and Countess of Etchingham, was beginning to fray around the edges after a year in the secret service and five months in the company of Saul, but it was just about holding firm for the time being. Not if he doesn't unhand me soon, though, I thought to myself.

'You must be Miss Smith,' he said, finally releasing my hand.

'Must I?' The inbred politeness was beginning to unravel.

'William Wright, Third Cultural Attaché,' said the man, my attempt at sarcasm washing over him.

We walked across to Saul and Elaine, who were still standing by the Land Rover. William Wright peered inside and spotted Sofija, who had yet to emerge from the car. A look of surprise momentarily crossed his face but he immediately recovered himself. 'Who is that?' he asked in an unconcerned voice from which a note of concern escaped.

Something about the look of surprise prevented me from fully answering the question. 'She's with us,' I said.

'If you say so,' said the Third Cultural Attaché, sauntering towards the rear of the Land Rover.

'Why you not say who I am?' whispered Sofija, opening her door and sounding cross. 'You still not trust me? What you think I do?' She immediately brightened. 'I probably not kill more than two of you before guards come and shoot me.' She evidently thought this hilarious and climbed out of the car laughing. Her mood swings were beginning to get rather wearing.

The rest of us traipsed round to the back of the Land Rover and Saul opened the rear door. 'What's this?' said Wright, pointing to Alexei's crumpled body.

'Well, we think he's probably a Russian SVR gunman – ex-gunman – but we didn't really get to talk to him before he reached his expiry date,' I said.

'And why is he dead?'

'Just not very good at his job,' said Elaine.

'Hmm,' said Wright. 'This isn't going to go down too well with our Russian friends. Perhaps a surreptitious disposal should be arranged.' He pressed a finger to his ear and almost instantaneously two virtually indistinguishable giants in tight navy-blue t-shirts appeared behind me, possibly straight from a Chippendales performance.

Wright nodded at Alexei and one of the giants picked him up as if he was weightless and flung him over one shoulder. 'Take him to Room 101 to start with,' he said. 'I'll be along later.'

'Boss,' said Chippendale One with a Scots twang, and he moved off towards the side door of the embassy, seemingly completely unburdened by having an Alexei on his back.

'Room 101?' I said. 'Really?'

'Not sure you can successfully torture a stiff,' said Saul, 'but I admire your optimism.'

'Well, one needs a sense of humour in a job like this,' Wright replied smoothly.

'And what job would that be, exactly?' I ventured.

He didn't answer and Chippendale Two just raised his eyebrows. Clearly a man of few words. Mind you, who needs words when you're ripped like that.

'Stay with us, Simmonite,' said Wright.

'Simmonite?' said Saul. 'Isn't that what they make briefcases out of?'

'Samsonite,' I said. Mind you, there did seem to be a sort of metallic sheen to the man, so maybe Saul had a point. He certainly boasted a body to make the original Samson jealous.

'Is that it?' said the Cultural Attaché with a frown.

It occurred to me that Prokofiev, in the box, was being very quiet. Perhaps he'd expired. Not that I really cared; he wasn't our concern anymore.

'Not quite,' I said. Everything about William Wright told me not to trust him but this was the man Jason Underwood had instructed us to report to, so perhaps my instincts were mistaken. Anyway, we couldn't just turn around and drive off again with Val still in his box. 'There's a Russian assassin of our recent acquaintance, name of Valentin Prokofiev, incapacitated in that box there. He was unconscious but may be awake by now, so you'll need to be careful when you open it up.'

'I am always careful, Miss Smith. I will obtain reinforcements. Follow me.'

Saul, Elaine, Sofija and I trooped inside the embassy behind the Third Cultural Attaché, leaving Riley curled up, apparently fast asleep, on the rear seat of the Land Rover. Simmonite brought up the rear, blocking out the sun.

Despite my misgivings about William Wright, everything was going smoothly and we would soon be on a plane back to England, having successfully recovered Saul and reunited Valentin Prokofiev with the inside of a prison cell. What could possibly go wrong?

__ In which Lucy asks for a cup of
    tea, and Dawson prepares to make
    a confession

'Simmonite will, ah, look after you,' said William Wright, smoothing his already too-smooth hair with one hand as he showed the four of them into a lounge with uncomfortable-looking furniture. 'I will just arrange for the more, ah, permanent rehousing of Mr Prokofiev.' He left and the massive figure of Simmonite took up silent station just inside the door. Saul and Elaine flopped down on a minimalist, turquoise sofa, wriggled a bit to avoid its sharp edges, and shut their eyes in apparent exhaustion. Lucy watched Sofija cross to the window, which looked out on to a row of nondescript trees. She saw the Estonian girl move off along one wall, running her hands over the wallpaper. Lucy wasn't sure what she was up to but was too tired to care much.

In any case, several things were worrying her. She had grown to trust her instincts and her instincts about the oily Third Attaché were not, so far, favourable. She'd noticed him flinch for no obvious reason when he'd set eyes on Sofija, and there was something odd about the "ahs" in his last two sentences. "Ahs" were never a good sign in Lucy's book. And, anyway, why were they being guarded by Simmonite? She wondered what would happen if she went to leave the room.

So she decided to try.

Simmonite moved his massive bulk in front of the door.

'Excuse me,' said Lucy. 'I need the toilet.'

'Mr Wright would like you to wait until he returns,' said Simmonite in a monotone.

'Why's that?' Lucy raised her voice to try to gain the attention of the other three. 'A cup of tea would go down well, too.' She noticed a velvet pull cord a few paces to her left, reached across and tugged it hard. There was a distant buzzing from somewhere deep in the bowels of the embassy and Simmonite clasped a large hand around her right arm. Dawson, roused by the buzzing and the mention of the word tea, and spotting this assault on his girlfriend, got off the minimalist sofa and strode across. Elaine also stood up. Both she and Lucy still had their guns but Simmonite's grip was preventing Lucy from reaching hers.

'Get off her, you gorilla,' said Dawson loudly, but Simmonite made no move to relax his hold on Lucy's bicep.

'Do as the man asks,' said Elaine quietly, her gun pointing unwaveringly at Simmonite's t-shirted midriff. He grunted and let go of Lucy's arm.

At that point, the door opened and William Wright walked back in. If he was surprised to see Elaine pointing a gun at his colleague, he didn't show it.

'Apparently, the lavatory is out of bounds,' Lucy remarked.

'A misunderstanding, I'm sure. You are of course very welcome to use the, ah, facilities before you leave but we can't have you wandering aimlessly around the embassy now, can we?' Lucy noted that "ah" again.

'Are we leaving?' asked Dawson. 'We've only just got here.'

'We'd like to call Jason Underwood,' Lucy said.

'That won't be necessary,' said the Third Attaché. 'The British government would like to thank you for your assistance but feels that you have rather, ah, exceeded your responsibilities and the parameters of your allotted task. The United Kingdom is not currently at war with the Russian Federation and having to own up to the death by shooting of a respectable Russian citizen, together with the kidnap and incarceration of a member of their security service, will do little for our ongoing attempts to improve our presently rather, ah, rocky relationship.'

He stopped speaking and minutely adjusted his already minutely adjusted navy tie. They were all speechless. Simmonite reached over and plucked Elaine's gun from her hand before she realised what was happening, but neither he nor Wright seemed to consider that Lucy too might have one. Number Six's borrowed weapon was secured in the rear waistband of her jeans and hidden by the green hoody.

The so-called Third Cultural Attaché held out his hand but none of them made a move to shake it. After a few seconds and with a small twitch of his eyebrows, he allowed his hand to slide back to his side. 'If you would be so good as to wait here, I will instruct my, ah, secretary to book hotel rooms and arrange for a taxi.' He turned and glided out of the room, closely followed by the muscled figure of Simmonite.

There was a small click. Elaine, who was nearest the door, moved across and tried the handle. With no success.

'The bastard's locked us in,' she said unnecessarily.

'Never mind that,' said Dawson. 'Where's Sofija?'

They looked around. The Estonian girl was definitely no longer of the company but the windows were still closed and the door was not only closed but locked.

'Where did she go?' said Elaine.

'And how did she go?' added Dawson.

'Is that important?' Lucy was pointing her gun at the door. 'Wherever she's gone, who's for following her?'

'Excuse me, lover,' said Dawson, 'but are you suggesting we start shooting up the British Embassy?'

'Only one little lock,' said Elaine. 'They'll hardly notice it. I'll do it, if you like. It's not my embassy.'

Lucy didn't waste time answering. She just shot out the lock with the air of someone who did that sort of thing every day and twice before breakfast. The expensive, solid oak of the door proved no match for the bullet and it swung slowly inwards. 'Me first,' she said, and poked her head carefully through the doorway, looking quickly both ways.

'Shouldn't somebody have come running by now?' asked Dawson, stepping into the empty corridor behind her.

'You'd think so, wouldn't you? Let's assume that the

delightful Mr Wright is not who he says he is. So, what does that tell us about Jason Underwood, who pointed us in his direction? Is old Jase perhaps not quite as lilywhite as we've been led to believe all these months? This, don't forget, is a man who has the ear of the Foreign Secretary, possibly the Prime Minister. I don't want to jump to any conclusions, but maybe we shouldn't be ringing him up for instructions until we know a bit more. And the things I want to know include, where the fuck is everyone? And what the fucking fuck is this all about anyway?'

'Perhaps everyone's gone home,' said Elaine, although she didn't look particularly convinced.

'They keep funny hours here if they've all gone home this early,' said Lucy. 'I don't suppose they have huge numbers of permanent staff but there must surely be more than Wright and his two goons.'

Dawson realised it was probably time to come clean about his visit from Elspeth Arundell in May. The meeting where he had been instructed, under pain of a long sojourn in Wormwood Scrubs, to keep his mouth shut, especially where Lucy was concerned. Still, he reflected, time moves on and priorities alter. He had failed in the first part of his task, to keep watching the newly christened Victor Naismith and ensure no harm came to him. And, as that failure had been immediately followed by his own kidnapping and transportation to the Gulf of Riga to meet, it had turned out, Valentin Prokofiev, his future back in England could hardly be said to look particularly rosy, whether or not he broke his word to Arundell. Having kept her instructions secret from Lucy for the last month, it might well mean the end of a beautiful, if unlikely, love affair, but here goes nothing, he thought.

'Look,' he began, 'there's something I need to tell you.' Lucy and Elaine looked at him enquiringly but before he could continue, a recognisable voice piped up from behind them.

'Here you are,' said Sofija.

Lucy spun round. 'Where the fuck did you come from?' she asked.

'And where did you go?' added Dawson.

'The same place,' explained Sofija. 'I came from the same place I went to. Obviously.'

'And where's that?' asked Lucy, lowering her gun.

'From the room where everybody is asleep. Six people.'

_ In which Sam finds sticks and
   stones quite helpful, and an
   elderly professor is quite
   unhelpful.

Downton knew he had to move soon. He couldn't lie low in the woods for much longer with only a camping stove and a sleeping bag for company. It was only a matter of time before he was discovered. But if he did move, would he be any better off? The only transport he had was the bright purple Mr Bojangles van, currently well hidden, but which would be on the radar of every police force in the country. And where would he go?

He really hadn't planned for this. It was supposed to have been a long game. The infiltration into national security systems by Huawei was just the start. None of this was anything that could be achieved overnight, as his mysterious phone contact had always emphasised. He had never discovered who the caller was. Something told him that "P King" would be issuing no further instructions following the succession of balls-ups starting with the bomb, followed by his failed attempt to remove the MI6 blonde from the game. Not to mention the death of the poof with the ridiculous dog. No, the only future communication he expected was another attempt on his life. Maybe he'd let them succeed this time. The only alternative seemed to be a lifetime detained at Her Majesty's deep pleasure. All in all, his future options looked distinctly unhealthy.

And then he heard the noise.

—

Sam Bunter had not finished his personal exploration. He'd been relieved to escape the meeting with the Super and the scary secret service woman with his job intact, although Gulliver had told him to take a few days off. Sam couldn't go back to the cavern and the underground river itself but that didn't stop him pulling on sturdy walking boots and approaching the problem from another angle.

He still hadn't worked out where the Mole had dived underground or re-emerged the other side of the tunnel, which he took as a personal slight on his knowledge of the area. It had to be a tributary, some sort of unmapped loop that left and rejoined the main flow. Or maybe it wasn't the Mole at all but an entirely different, completely underground river.

He had been tramping around west of Leatherhead for a couple of hours now, trying to avoid trespassing on private land, which was quite difficult in this congested part of Surrey. Having started out as the early morning mists were beginning to be burnt off by the sun, he now found himself on the edge of the woods at Bookham Common. He pushed on into the woods even though the river itself was at least half a mile to his rear. It seemed unlikely that any hidden tunnel entrance was going to be on an industrial estate in Leatherhead.

It wasn't a new stretch of river or hidden tunnel that he found though, but a van. A brief flicker of purple away to his right didn't register at first and he'd taken a few more steps before it did. He wasn't actually looking for the Mr Bojangles van, but then he recalled that it was still missing and that it was purple. He retraced his steps, but it took him a few minutes before he glimpsed the flash of colour again. He pushed through the trees and suddenly there it was, mostly concealed by a screen of cut branches and other assorted greenery.

He pulled out his phone to call in the discovery, but a crack of a twig behind him made him spin round just in time to see a thick branch heading rapidly for his skull. He dived sideways, caught his foot in a tree root and sprawled on the ground. Looking up, he saw Chief Inspector Downton take two steps towards him and raise the branch again. Sam's hands scrabbled under him to try to gain leverage to rise but instead, his right hand found itself on a small rock which he instinctively grasped and hurled, still from a prone position, as hard as he could in Downton's direction. It didn't hit his attacker but did knock the branch from his hand.

This, however, didn't improve the general situation as Downton simply reached into a pocket and pulled out a gun. Sam briefly wondered why the inspector hadn't utilised the gun in the first place instead of buggering about with sticks, but he had the presence of mind to roll sideways just as Downton pulled the trigger.

The crack of the gunshot in the quiet woodland brought a flurrying of wings and a screeching from the trees all around. One of the awakened birds flew right in front of Downton's face as he prepared to fire again. Sam jumped up as his attacker was momentarily distracted and hurled himself at the inspector. His momentum brought Downton, large as he was, to ground and the gun flew off into the undergrowth. Sam picked up the same stick that Downton had tried to use on him and, in a satisfactory turning of the tables, gave him a hefty blow over his left eye. Downton, on the half-rise, slumped back, fully unconscious.

Or possibly worse, thought Sam, suddenly stricken with worry that he had actually killed the rogue inspector; but no, there was definitely a pulse. Still, he didn't look like he'd be particularly active again any time soon. Sam wiped his brow and, breathing heavily, picked up his phone.

———

Chief Inspector Gulliver, who normally possessed the sort of equilibrium that Zen Buddhists would have gone apeshit for, was decidedly unhappy. MI6 were trampling all over his patch in their Oxford brogues and the trampling was coming from two different directions. His copper's nose, although smelling fish, was failing to tell him which direction was the smelliest.

So the phone call from PC Sam Bunter was especially welcome.

Sam himself turned up shortly after accompanied by four armed officers and a secure van containing Abbey Downton, sporting a significant cut over his left eye. The inspector was led inside in handcuffs. He was inclined to struggle, which, due to his mountainous physique, gave the four officers a few difficult moments, but eventually he was safely locked in a cell at the back of the station. It wasn't an especially hygienic cell. Stallford had ceased being a custody station two years ago and the cells had remained unused and uncleaned ever since. Gulliver, though, wasn't concerned about either Downton's comfort or the cut on his head.

'Needs stitches, sir, does that,' Sam remarked as he locked the door.

'I imagine he'll survive,' said Gulliver. 'Come in here, constable.' He showed Sam into Downton's old office and shut the door. 'Take a seat. First off, very well done. This isn't going to do your career any harm. Second off, regarding the machinery in the cavern, I've just received a report that says the frogmen have been down and found all sorts of interesting paraphernalia in an artificially created trench at the bottom of the river. I don't have full details yet, but there's an array of sluice gates, things that could be turbines of some description, propellers or rotors and other whatnots. All very unusual so we've called an expert chappy from the British Hydropower Association up from Dorset to take a look-see. I'll be meeting him there about two o'clock and if you like – and I know you're officially off duty, however loosely you appear to have taken the instruction – you can come too.'

'Yes, sir, of course, as long as I don't have to do any swimming.'

'Probably not necessary. First though, we have a very large rogue inspector waiting for us. A spot of questioning is in order and quickly, before MI6 relieve us of him. Come on young man, let's go chat to the bastard.'

—

The chappy from the British Hydropower Association, a Professor Walkinshaw, turned out to be pushing eighty but, as he explained, he'd pretty much been around when water was first invented, so was sure he could be of assistance. Gulliver took that as his idea of a joke and smiled politely as he led the old boy carefully down the stone steps from the bungalow, now fumigated and installed with some temporary lighting, to the cavern and along the tunnel to the little room that Sam had discovered.

The professor fiddled around with various knobs and switches for a while. This caused the flow of water to increase its velocity and change direction three times. The frogmen had managed to take some surprisingly clear photographs of the submerged paraphernalia, as Gulliver had described it, which Walkinshaw stared at interminably, standing on the bank of the river, brow furrowed. Eventually, he sighed deeply, shook his head and turned to Gulliver.

'Unfortunately, I can't help you, Superintendent.' He appeared to take the admission as a personal afront to his professionalism. 'A lot of this is pretty basic stuff, the sort of thing that a group of intelligent sixth formers could have come up with. However, somewhere between down there,' and he pointed into the river, 'and up there,' and he turned and indicated up the steps to the room carved out of the rockface, 'something's going on that's on a wholly different level.'

'What do you mean?'

'If the parts of this that we can see are League Two, say, then what we cannot see, what I'm afraid I cannot work out at all, is Champions' League. I hate to admit it but it's way over my head.'

Gulliver had not provided any information about the Estonian scientist who had been blown up in Stallford, nor about the involvement of Her Majesty's security services, and he felt no need to do so now. 'Thank you for your time, professor. We'll get you back to Dorset and I'd be grateful if you could let me have a written report on your findings – or lack of – tomorrow morning.'

His mood had already taken a dent following the arrival at Stallford of Elspeth Arundell, who had turned up at lunchtime with one dark-suited, dark-glassed agent in tow and expressed herself to be singularly unimpressed with the delay in informing her of Downton's capture. She had not been inclined to hang about.

'You don't want to question him here then?' Gulliver had asked. He had not achieved much success with his own questions so was actually quite keen to see if MI6 could cut any interrogatory corners that he himself was forced to circuit. Downton had basically blamed everything on Saul Dawson and Lucy Smith. He was an upstanding member of the constabulary, and Smith and Dawson he reckoned, either alone or acting on orders from above, had framed him. It had been Dawson who had set off the bomb. He'd been following the Estonian scientist, hadn't he? He lived right underneath him for Christ's sake. And as for the blonde bitch, she'd killed the entirely innocent Terry and Marjorie, hadn't she? He, Downton, had managed to escape and had been hiding in the woods, fearful for his life.

'So how do you explain the fact that we found Miss Smith bound and gagged in the cavern alongside the bodies of Terry and Marjorie?'

'Must have been Dawson.'

'Who wasn't in the country at the time. And, in any case,

why would he want to kill his own girlfriend?'

'She was putting it about. She had me, you know. She's a slut. He'd had enough of her, I reckon.'

'And what was Marjorie doing there in the first place? Why were you and she in her van in Leatherhead?'

'She was my girlfriend and I needed a lift.'

'We're not short of police cars you could have requisitioned.' At that point, Downton had clammed up. Gulliver had tried a different tack. 'How come your prints were all over the body of Sacha Tarkovsky at Mickleham Church?'

Silence again. Eventually, he'd given up and shortly afterwards Arundell had arrived. It had seemed a tall order for just her and the not particularly imposing agent with her to remove the massive Downton alone but they hadn't seemed to have much trouble getting him into the back of the large BMW with blacked-out windows in which they'd arrived.

'Where are you taking him?' Gulliver had asked.

'Do you want a receipt, Superintendent?' Arundell had said obtusely.

'That would be a start.'

'I'll arrange for one to be drawn up.' And the BMW had driven away.

_____ In which Dawson goes into
a ladies' toilet, and Sofija
wears her birthday suit

'Six people?' said Lucy. 'What, embassy staff? Are they all right? Where are they?'

'I think so.' Sofija shrugged. 'They are breathing. They are unimportant, though.'

'Depends on your point of view.' Lucy's hard-won warmth towards Sofija was starting to cool again. 'Personally, I think the health or otherwise of six British Embassy staff is anything but unimportant. Lead us to them.'

She was still holding the gun and moved it slightly in Sofija's direction to emphasise the order.

'OK,' said Sofija. 'Follow me then, but you are wasting time. The man in the blue suit is getting away. And he has Valentin with him.'

'You were only gone a few minutes,' said Elaine as they set off up the corridor. 'You seem to have found out a hell of a lot in a very short time.'

'I work fast. I am a good spy. You are not so good. You stand around talking. You must be quick if you want to chase Valentin.'

'I think they'll wait awhile,' said Lucy. 'We'll get the word out on them as soon as we know who we can trust.'

'You can trust nobody. Trust me on this.'

'How did you get out of the room, anyway?' asked Elaine.

'There is a hidden door.'

'Which you knew about, how, exactly?'

Again, Sofija shrugged. 'I just found it.'

Dawson, having failed to admit to the secret mission given him by Elspeth Arundell before Sofija's sudden reappearance, was lagging back, deep in thought as the three women reached a nondescript door at the end of the corridor. 'In here,' said Sofija, who opened the door and stood back to let them enter first. Lucy and Elaine immediately saw the six embassy staff lying on their backs on the carpet on the far side of the room. Whether they were asleep, as Sofija had suggested, was hard to tell as they were bound hand and foot and had dark green velvet cushion covers pulled over their heads. However, the two girls hardly had time to take in the sight before hands were clamped over their mouths, hands holding soft cloths giving off sweet-smelling vapour. Simultaneously, they each felt a pinprick in their neck.

If the first drug doesn't get you, the second one will, thought Lucy drowsily before darkness overtook her. Before she passed out, she just had time to hear a gruff voice say, in Russian, '*Gde chert voz'mi* Dawson?'

Good old Saul, she thought sleepily. He's got himself lost again.

———

Dawson saw Lucy, Elaine and Sofija disappear into the room a few metres ahead. He hadn't consciously stopped following the women but something apart from his secret job with Elspeth Arundell was troubling him. Something didn't quite add up. Well, quite a lot didn't add up, but this was something new. Something about Sofija. Her English had improved. Dawson wasn't used to being the one who spotted stuff like that. He usually left that to Lucy, but she had been more concerned with the wellbeing of the embassy staff and, in any case, Lucy hadn't known the Estonian girl as long as he had. There was another thing too. Sofija had referred to Prokofiev as Valentin, which seemed a bit too friendly, bearing in mind how recently she had been so enthusiastically spitting at him.

He had a sinking feeling that the reappeared Sofija must in fact be the "bad daughter", Guna, or Galina; he still hadn't quite worked out which name was correct. But whatever she was called, she had disappeared into a room with his wholly unsuspecting friends.

He stopped, uncertain what to do. No, he thought, I'm going mad. Guna is marooned on a ship in the Gulf of Riga and this girl had to be Sofija. She looked exactly like the Sofija he had spent days arguing with, she was wearing the same grubby parka and old jeans and she had known who they all were. He shook his head. 'Idiot,' he said, self-mockingly. He was just about to start forward to join the others when his arm was grabbed in a powerful, oddly familiar grip and he was yanked sideways through a door he hadn't spotted and into a ladies' toilet. The door swung shut behind him.

'What the...?' he said.

'Be quiet, idiot,' said Sofija.

Dawson reflected that not long ago, finding himself in a ladies' toilet in the British Embassy in Tallinn would have figured very high on a scale of improbabilities. Improbable would have given way to impossible if someone had suggested that not only would he be in a ladies' toilet in the British Embassy in Tallinn but he would be standing next to a naked, female Estonian Internal Security Service Agent.

'You don't appear to have any clothes on,' he remarked conversationally and almost accurately. He noticed Sofija was wearing a tiny pair of panties to cover at least part of her modesty. They weren't doing a particularly effective job. Dawson wasn't sure what kind of panties he would have expected Sofija to be sporting but it definitely wouldn't have been the pair of ivory-coloured, sheer silk ones dotted with pink flowers that he found himself looking at. He tore his eyes away from them, at the same time trying hard not to stare at her breasts. It was difficult not to as they were quite large and they were, when all is said and done, breasts.

'Yes, is not important,' said Sofija. 'Guna has my clothes. Wright's giant friend, Samsonite, hit me when I leave room.' She pointed to a small patch of blood, already starting to clot, just on her hair line. Dawson moved his eyes upwards to where she was indicating. She hadn't seemed particularly concerned that he had been staring at her boobs, but then she genuinely didn't seem at all disturbed about the whole lack of clothing thing. 'I was knocked out,' she continued, 'and Guna was putting clothes on when I wake up. Not pants though. She has enormous white ones. She look ridiculous.'

Dawson couldn't help but feel that a sisterly rivalry in the underwear department was the least of their worries right now. 'So, your "bad daughter" sister has Lucy and Elaine and may have killed them,' he said.

'Maybe,' said Sofija. 'But she and Samsonite have not killed embassy people. They are drugged only, I think. Lucy and Austrian girl will be drugged too, then Guna and Samsonite will follow Russian *pätt*. We must hurry and follow too. Must not let Prokofiev get away.'

'Drugged?' said Dawson. 'Do you mean chloroform?'

'Maybe. Chloroform slow. Lucy would fight it, I think. They may use something else.'

'Is your sister's name Guna or Galina? It's been confusing me.'

'That is because you are idiot.' At least that confirmed that this nearly naked girl was definitely Sofija. 'She is Guna, but call herself Galina to Prokofiev, as I tell you already.'

Dawson thought of something else. 'Samsonite – Simmonite – had a mate, equally large, who went off with Alexei's body. Do we know where he's got to?'

'No, I not see him. He not important. Come,' and she opened the toilet door, peered into the corridor and set off towards the front of the embassy, away from the room where Lucy and Elaine had gone.

'Hold up,' said Dawson. 'I'm not going to leave Lucy and Elaine. I don't give a shit if Prokofiev and Wright get away. They're not my concern.'

Sofija didn't stop. 'Listen, idiot, if you go in room, you will be killed. Prokofiev wants you dead now. He not need you. Also, Prokofiev and Wright *are* your concern. Your Arundell woman send them to electric facility. Samsonite has big mouth as well as big chest.'

'What? How the hell do you know about Elspeth Arundell?'

'Of course I know. Nice lady, no?' And she looked over her bare shoulder and grinned at him.

They came to a door marked reception and Sofija was just about to go through it when it was opened from the inside and there was Simmonite's hefty, blue t-shirted, "not important" mate. He seemed surprised to see Dawson and Sofija, perhaps especially a naked Sofija, and stood in slack-jawed appreciation for a couple of seconds, all the time it took for the confrontation to end badly for him. Sofija punched him hard in the balls with a powerful fist and, as he collapsed forward, hit him equally hard on the jaw with the same fist.

'Good,' she said and proceeded to strip him of his t-shirt and chinos almost before he hit the floor. She was dressed within another thirty seconds and was rolling up the trouser legs to fit her own, considerably shorter, legs and pulling on the man's trainers before Dawson could think of something to say.

'Congratulations,' he managed, finally, in a weak voice. 'What now?'

'Now we find car and follow Prokofiev and Wright.'

'How? We don't know where they've gone.'

'We not know, but Riley knows,' she said mysteriously.

Dawson had forgotten all about Riley the Dobermann, who they had left asleep in the Land Rover which, however, was no longer where they had parked it. Sofija bent down and picked something off the ground where the vehicle had been and put it in her pocket. She started trying the doors of other cars in the car park and soon found one that opened, belonging to a small, white Fiat 500. 'Get in,' she said. She fiddled under the steering column, the engine sprang to life and she drove towards the security gate, which failed to open. As the Fiat would have been no match for the gate, Sofija was forced to stop. Old Godfrey wandered slowly out of his security hut, putting his peaked cap on his balding head.

'Hello, again,' he said. 'Are you going? Mr Wright said you'd be staying overnight. Are your friends leaving too?'

'Change of plan,' said Dawson. 'We've got to leave but Miss Smith and our other friend are still here.' He was about to ask Godfrey if he could go to check they were OK, or perhaps summon the police, when Sofija elbowed him none too subtly in the ribs.

'Be quiet,' she hissed. 'You want old Godfrey killed?' Godfrey, meanwhile, had strolled back to his security hut and the gate started to roll open. As soon as the gap was wide enough, she floored the accelerator and the small Fiat shot out on to the road and swung left.

'So, back to Riley the Wonder Dog,' said Dawson. 'How exactly does he know where they've gone?'

'He has GPS tracker on collar. I put it there. It was also inside jacket with talkie-walkie. We track it with this.'

She produced the thing she'd recovered from the car park, a tiny black box with a tiny map on a tiny screen. A flashing red light on the map pointed to a position some way ahead of them.

'See,' she said. 'They only three kilometres ahead. Relax. We not lose them.'

'It's lucky they took Riley with them,' said Dawson.

'Of course they take him. He is Russian *pätt's* dog.' He love him. He will be happy he has him back. He not know Riley turn traitor.'

It was dark when I woke up. That was strange. Whilst I had obviously been drugged, it had only been mid-afternoon, so I doubted I'd been unconscious long enough for night to have fallen, particularly in this part of the world. Then I realised that I had something over my head, and I remembered the dark green velvet cushion covers that had been slipped over the heads of the embassy staff. Still, I suppose I was hardly likely to be at my cognitive best having just come round from anaesthesia. I couldn't work out the purpose of the cushion cover. It seemed an unnecessary embellishment.

Mind you, it was preventing me seeing what was going on and, as my hands were tied behind my back, I wasn't sure how I was going to remove it to find out. My ankles were also restrained but at least I wasn't hog-tied this time. Were our captors still with us? What about the other captives, the embassy staff? Was I now alone? Had Saul been taken too? He had been lagging behind for some reason known only to himself as we entered the room, so it was possible he'd escaped. Or not. Or been shot. I had no idea and I could think of only one way of finding out.

'Saul?' I called. 'Elaine?'

Neither answered but another voice, male, called back in heavily accented English, muffled presumably by a green velvet cushion cover.

"Ello?" said the voice. 'I em Rasmus. Oo is ziz?'

'I'm Lucy,' I said. 'Is anyone else awake?' There were a few indistinct murmurings and shufflings, and a cough or two. Clearly Rasmus and I were made of sterner stuff than most of the staff. Or Elaine for that matter. I tried not to

worry about Saul. 'Rasmus?' I said, as clearly as possible. 'Who are you? Are you OK?'

'Yes, I em goot. I em caretaker et embassy. I do not enderstend vot iss heppening? Mister Wright end one of ze security men, zey hef guns end tie us up. I do not know vot iss it about. Zere vos bluddy voman too.'

Who was the "bluddy voman"? Sofija? Then it struck me. It wasn't Sofija who had reappeared out of thin air and led us into this room but Guna, the "bad daughter". How dense was I? Anyway, on the plus side, it looked like she, Wright and Simmonite were no longer with us. They were being very quiet if they were. Also on the plus side, if that had been Guna, that meant, of course, that the real Sofija, as well as Saul, was still unaccounted for.

'What the fuckin' bejeesus was that?' Elaine had joined Rasmus and I in the land of the swearing.

'Well, it wasn't laughing gas,' I said, trying to keep my voice level.

'You can say that again. Right, stay where you are and keep talking. I'm coming over.' There was the sound of a bottom being shuffled in my direction. The carpet was quite thick, so the shuffling wasn't too rapid.

'Over here,' I said. 'Keep coming.'

'Vot iss goink on?' said Rasmus. 'Oo is ziz?' Then there was the sound of what could only be two bodies coming together accompanied by a sort of whoomphing noise. That would be Rasmus.

Elaine swore again, then said, 'Well, either this isn't you, Lucy old girl, or you've grown a beard while we've been under.'

'Elaine, meet Rasmus,' I said, slightly pointlessly because they'd already met, after a fashion at least. The shuffling started again and thirty seconds later,

Elaine made contact with me. I refrained from making a whoomphing noise.

'Right,' she said authoritatively. 'Back to back, girly, let's undo these bits of string.' I did as I was told, and felt Elaine working with quick fingers on the rope encircling my wrists. She obviously knew her way around knots and took only a few seconds to untie me. I reached up, whipped the cushion cover off my head and took a few deep breaths. I hadn't realised quite how suffocating it had been. I pulled off Elaine's cover and untied her.

Removing the ropes from our ankles, we looked around the room. The man who was obviously Rasmus was unsuccessfully trying to stand up, so I thought it best to undo his ropes before he did himself serious injury on the marble-topped table next to him. It looked like the other five staff members were all coming to as well, so Elaine and I worked our way around the room doing the necessary. Rasmus tried to help too but kept bumping into things and tripping over other things. I didn't like to ask him if he'd always had balance issues or whether it was a temporary thing brought on by being drugged and enveloped by a cushion cover. But, as a caretaker, he definitely needed to take more care.

By this time, quite a lot of chatter was breaking out amongst the staff as they became more compos mentis. So far there had been no indication that any of the forces of the ungodly were still around but then I heard a noise from outside the room. 'Quiet!' I hissed and, remarkably, I was obeyed. No one else was volunteering to take charge of proceedings so I filled the vacuum. The noise was coming from the corridor. I looked at Elaine and nodded towards the door. We tiptoed across the room. The noise was right outside, a sort of huffing or *grunting accompanied by a scraping sound. I mouthed 'one, two, three' at Elaine and she jerked the door open and I leapt out into the corridor, heart beating and fists raised.*

And fell over something lying outside the door.

___ In which Dawson fails to hear
some Chinese whispers, and
discovers that rain is not
always what it seems

Earlier in the day, Sofija had demanded that Elaine slow down, given the poor state of the roads and the Land Rover's unforgiving suspension. She was, however, clearly a girl for whom the phrase, "practise what you preach", meant nothing. Reckless didn't come close to describing her style of driving. The little Fiat had never been put through such an ordeal.

Neither had Dawson. 'Hey!' he shouted as a brick wall on his right removed the nearside wing mirror in its entirety and left it bouncing along the road behind them. 'We know where they are, we don't need to drive up their arse. Slow down before you kill us.'

'I not kill us. I kill them.'

'Or the other way round. We need to keep our distance. Fucking slow down.'

'Wimp,' said Sofija, but eased off the accelerator, although not before she'd cut up a bus full of pensioners.

It was just as well they did slow down or they would have missed the unexpected left turn on to the unmarked and nearly invisible side road that the Land Rover had taken. Sofija took the corner on two wheels but would have rolled the car had she still been demolishing the speed limit. "Road" was a wholly inaccurate description for the rutted lane on which they found themselves. There were a couple of blind, hairpin bends which forced even Sofija to change down a gear.

Round the third blind bend, they came upon a roadblock by the simple expedient of ploughing into it. They were only going 50 kph but the collision didn't do the front end of the Fiat much good. Both airbags exploded into life and left Dawson and Sofija winded. As the bags gently deflated, the flatbed truck into which the Fiat had crashed was revealed. It was parked at ninety degrees across the lane, its cab pointing up a side road to the right which was no better maintained than the one they were on.

On top of the flatbed were two Chinese-looking men. They must have possessed an enviable sense of balance, given that the truck was still rocking on its springs following the forceful coming together of the two vehicles. Like Prokofiev's Russian colleagues, the Chinese were dressed in black, although there was considerably less oily wool involved. These two bought their clothes in the local version of Harrods, not off a market stall. However, their clothes were the least interesting thing about them. Of much more immediate significance to Dawson's way of thinking was the fact that both of them were holding submachine guns and pointing them through the windscreen of the Fiat.

Not a-fucking-gain, he thought wearily.

One of them was opening and shutting his mouth in a way that suggested he was saying something. If he was, he couldn't be heard over the engine of the Fiat, still gamely trying to drive the little car forward through the immoveable mass of the truck. Chinese whispers, Dawson supposed. It seemed likely he was suggesting that Dawson and Sofija exit the car. Getting out of the Fiat, which was emitting smoke from various orifices in an alarming manner, did seem to be sensible. He smiled ingratiatingly and tried to open the door on his right, but the car had buckled so badly that the door was wedged shut. Meanwhile, Sofija was showing no obvious signs of planning to go anywhere, despite the fact that the door on her side of the car was hanging drunkenly off one hinge.

'I think they want us to get out,' suggested Dawson. 'You first, and I'll shimmy along past the gear stick and follow you.'

'Yes,' said Sofija in a thoughtful tone of voice that Dawson had not heard her use before. She was looking through the broken door as she spoke. 'Look,' she whispered. 'Gap in rocks there, opposite back of car. Go quick. I will distract Chinese pigs.'

Dawson couldn't imagine quite how Sofija was intending to distract two heavily armed men, especially as she was no longer naked. With her hands held over her head, she edged out of the car and stood up, then, without warning, she grabbed the partially connected door, wrenched it bodily off its one remaining hinge, and hurled it forcefully towards the two Chinese, who were late to come to terms with the absurd thing she was attempting. The first man managed to get off an all-too-brief burst of gunfire, which spattered ineffectively into and through the door that was heading in his direction, before it slammed into him, knocking the gun from his grasp and hurling him into his colleague. Like a pair of dominoes, they toppled off the far side of the flatbed. Sofija and Dawson ran to the gap in the rocks and launched themselves through it.

And down a steep, scree-covered slope, ten metres into a river.

As they plunged into the water with two loud, almost simultaneous splashes, the Fiat in the lane above them exploded.

———

It was raining, but that made no sense. It had been a calm, clear, if chilly late afternoon only a few seconds earlier, although the buffeting Dawson had received as he tumbled in an uncontrolled tangle of limbs into the river had rather discombobulated him, so perhaps it had been hours, not seconds. Perhaps he'd been knocked unconscious and the clouds had rolled in and started dropping persistently heavy raindrops into the water over his head. But that still made no sense. He wouldn't have woken up underwater, would he? He'd have drowned.

And he was definitely underwater. His lungs were bursting and all he could make out was a thick green, impenetrable soup. A soup that was swirling around him, grabbing and tugging at him, treating him like a pair of underpants caught up in a high-speed spin cycle. He needed to breathe, rain or no rain, that was definite, so, coming more to his senses, he began to pull himself upwards. He wasn't a bad swimmer and it turned out he wasn't far from the surface.

It also turned out that it wasn't raining. They weren't heavy, plopping raindrops disturbing the water. They were bullets. As his head broke the surface, the bullets that were being sprayed across the river in a random sort of way started heading more purposefully in his direction, like wasps zeroing in on a picnic. Dawson had often been accused of being slow on the uptake, but it took him only a microsecond to realise that keeping his head above water could be construed as a form of suicide and he ducked back under the surface and kicked hard downwards. As he did, he collided with something else that was heading upwards. It was either a fish of unlikely magnitude or, he guessed, Sofija.

Sofija it was. He just had time to make out her pale, round face a few inches away through the green murk before his wrist was grasped in an uncompromising sort of way and he found himself being pulled sideways. He decided that it would be a gentlemanly thing to try and help their combined progress, especially if he didn't want a broken wrist, so he started thrusting with his legs and free arm and twenty seconds later he and Sofija broke surface together, this time concealed from whoever was firing into the river by an overhang of thick semi-aquatic foliage hard up against the bank. He grabbed hold of a convenient branch and turned to Sofija, who was doing something similar and grinning.

'That was fun, yes?' she said.

'If you say so.' Dawson was still in the process of recovering his breath and talking started a minor coughing fit.

'Be quiet, idiot,' said Sofija. 'Chinese pigs will hear us.'

'I don't care,' panted Dawson. 'Anyway, the firing's stopped. Perhaps they've run out of bullets.'

'We not know that. They just not see us.'

'So,' said Dawson, in between the panting and the coughing. 'You hate Russians, now we discover you hate the Chinese too. Any other nationalities you don't get on with?'

'No, although English are idiots, of course. Anyway, we need to get out of river. We cannot hang on branches for long.' She turned and started pulling herself up the steep bank, being careful to keep the overhanging trees between her and any gunmen high up on the other side of the river. It was hard work, even for her. As Dawson tried to follow her example, he found himself making more backwards than forwards progress. Finally, though, Sofija managed to clutch an exposed tree root well above the waterline and, with a truly Herculean effort that Dawson seriously doubted he would be able to replicate, hauled herself out of the water. She turned and grabbed him by the wrist again and, between them, they managed to extricate him too, although he had to admit that it was Sofija doing most of the extricating.

For the second time in what was, remarkably only one day, Dawson lay gasping for breath on dry land after an unwanted swim. He hadn't been able to change his clothes from the ones Sofija had found for him on the *Astrid*, so at least it was good they were getting a regular wash.

There was still no gunfire. Sofija raised herself cautiously to her knees and then into a crouch and Dawson, feeling yet again that it was probably about time he started to pull his weight instead of letting his companion do it for him, followed suit. They peered out through the trees. Not the first time we've done that today, either, he thought, more than half expecting Valentin Prokofiev to emerge from the swirling river in front of them like a Russian Neptune. But neither he nor either of the Chinese gunmen were visible.

'Do they think we've drowned?' he asked, aware before she answered that it was a fairly daft question.

'When will you stop being idiot?' she hissed. 'They Chinese bastards but they not stupid. No, they will come to find us. They not want to poly-roly down bank like us, so will come different way. We must move.'

She turned and started pushing her solid body through the thick bushes and tangled creepers that had made the riverbank their home. Despite the obstacles in her way, she somehow managed to make quite rapid progress, progress which Dawson, suddenly feeling even weaker than normal, found himself unable to copy.

Soon, she was out of sight.

I scrambled to my feet, embarrassed. I could really do with a lot more training, I reflected. Looking down to see what had tripped me up, I saw the other Chippendale lying in the corridor, the one we'd last seen lugging Alexei away to Room 101. He was completely naked apart from a pair of boxers. It was, I have to admit, a nakedness that was worth looking at but, having just fallen over him, I needed to recover some professionalism so tore my eyes away and up to his face. This had seen better days. Indeed, it was possible he had a broken jaw. He attempted to speak but it was unintelligible and not just because of the touch of a Scottish burr I detected. However, it was probably the best he was going to manage by way of sparkling repartee until we could get his jaw working. He also didn't seem capable of standing up and the fact that he had both hands clasped around his, shall we say, midriff, gave a clue as to why not.

'Is this Tweedledee or Tweedledum?' asked Elaine.

'If Simmonite's Tweedledee, then this one's Tweedledum. Do we think he's crawled along the corridor in that state?'

'Well, the noise he was making definitely got louder, so maybe so.'

'And who did this to him?' I guess we were both thinking that it was unlikely to have been Saul. Someone who could swing a fair old punch, for sure. His mate, Simmonite, maybe. In which case, not so much a mate. We definitely needed to get this bloke talking.

It occurred to me that I had no idea how much time had passed. My watch had been the one thing not taken from me back at the cottage in Kuressaare but it too had joined the list of items I no longer possessed. All six embassy staff had now joined us in the corridor. 'Do any of you have the time?' I asked. It turned out that none of them did. Their watches had been taken too. Perhaps the Russians needed a bit of extra cash. Or maybe they'd had the hare-brained idea of trying to make this look like a robbery.

However, Rasmus stuck his head back into the room where there was presumably a clock, and then announced, 'Iss jest pest five of ze clock.' Was that all? In that case, we'd been out for not much more than an hour. An hour isn't much time to fully overcome the effects of a narcoleptic drug and if everyone else felt as out of sorts as I did, then they weren't going to be much use for a while. And I didn't think we had a while, however long a while was. I had to force my brain to think.

'Thanks, Rasmus. Do you think you could find some water?' It might help get Tweedledum's mouth working and in any case I was thirsty. I couldn't remember the last time I'd actually drunk anything. Or eaten anything. If I had any weight to lose in the first place, it would be falling off me in lumps.

'Yes, off course,' rumbled Rasmus, and he lumbered off down the corridor and disappeared through a door a few metres along.

'Right, everyone, listen up,' I continued. They all looked at me expectantly. Not one of them gave off an air of authority. 'Two friends of ours are missing. I need you all to search the embassy while Elaine and I attempt to get some answers from this guy.' Rasmus came back with an armful of bottles of expensive and ecologically unacceptable water. Tweedledum had managed to get himself into a sitting position and Elaine started to dribble some water into his damaged mouth.

A bespectacled man in his mid-to-late twenties –

much the same age as me, I reminded myself – put up his hand. He really did. 'Er, miss?' he started, hesitantly. I smiled at him and he seemed to stand a bit straighter.

'Still winning,' murmured Elaine from somewhere below me.

'What's your name?' I asked, gently. The question seemed to add another inch to his stature.

'And there we go again,' added Elaine.

'Peter,' said the man. 'Wouldn't it be safer if we stayed here? We don't know who's still in the building. I don't think we should be looking for trouble.'

'In any case, I've just summoned the police on an office phone,' said a bloke with grey hair. 'Not only is Peter correct but we don't actually know who you people are. For all we know, you could be connected to the rogues who drugged us and tied us up.'

'Rogues?' said Elaine angrily. 'They're not rogues, they're Russian agents who your mate, William Wright, allowed into the embassy with the express purpose of bumping off or kidnapping one of our colleagues. And as the colleague in question isn't here, they've probably been successful. Either way, they're not here now. And us? We're MI6, you dickhead.'

I couldn't have put it better myself but of course I was now ID-less, so it looked like I might have to rely on the winning smile, at least for the time being. 'Look, sir,' I said trying it, 'we can't prove who we are as all our belongings have been taken. You're going to have to trust us. Our only clue as to what has happened to our friends is this inconveniently incoherent gentleman here. Now, we can't afford to hang around for the local police so we're going to be making tracks. You can tell the coppers whatever you like when they get here.' I turned to Rasmus. 'Rasmus, we need your help, buddy. We want a car and *your assistance in getting this guy into it. And if there's anything around to cover him up, then that would be great too.'*

'Off course, ladies,' said Rasmus. He bent down and, with Elaine's assistance, managed to get the still groaning Tweedledum upright and between them they helped him shuffle slowly down the corridor. At the far end, we turned through a door marked reception. Rasmus bent over the desk and came up with a set of car keys. There was a coat rack to one side of the outer door but it had only a single, thin-looking raincoat hanging from it. Better than nothing, I thought, and plucked it off the rack as we passed. I could do without Tweedledum freezing to death. He was in a bad enough way already.

Once outside, Rasmus led us to an inconspicuous grey Ford at the far end of the car park. I managed to manoeuvre the thin coat over Tweedledum's broad shoulders and eased him into the back seat. Rasmus pointed the key fob at the closed gate, which started to open, then pulled a small wad of euros out of an inside pocket and thrust them into Elaine's hand, together with the keys. There was no sign of old Godfrey. I could hear sirens approaching fast from the direction of the town. 'I stays here end districts ze politsei,' Rasmus said, beaming. I reached up and pecked him on his beardy cheek. The beam increased and Elaine shook her head wearily.

As we got into the Ford, four blue and white police cars hurtled in through the open gate, sirens blaring and lights flashing. Rasmus waved them urgently on towards the front of the embassy and Elaine, back in her favourite place behind a steering wheel, drove out as the last one screeched past. 'Which way, boss?' she asked. I had no idea but tossed a mental coin. 'Go left,' I said. The obvious way would have been right, away from the centre of Tallinn, but nothing about this whole fuck-up had been obvious so far.

___ In which Elaine buys some men's
clothing, and Gary admits to
a spot of eavesdropping

Elaine, having successfully negotiated what passed for Tallinn's rush hour, pulled over just shy of a major intersection and glanced across at Lucy, who was slumped beside her looking grim. She knew why of course. Having found Dawson alive and well, which had been their main objective in the first place, they had now lost him again. And they had no idea whether he was still alive and well and with Sofija in hot pursuit of Prokofiev and Wright, or whether he was, to put it bluntly, no longer alive and well.

Her immediate concern though was that she also had no idea where they were heading. She prodded Lucy in the arm. There was little response. 'So, what do you reckon, old girl, north, south, east or west? Shall we just toss a coin?'

Lucy looked across. 'I think we can rule out north. We'd just end up in the sea. That still leaves three possibilities though. I don't think tossing a coin would work. A coin's only got two sides.' She smiled wanly. 'We're fucked, aren't we?'

'We could try asking Tweedledum. I thought that's why we lugged him along.'

'Charming,' came a rather slurred Scottish voice from behind them. 'And what the fuck's with the Tweedledum? My name's Gary.' They turned and looked at him. He was slumped in the corner of the rear seat, shivering, the thin raincoat Lucy had rescued from reception wrapped tightly around his otherwise naked torso. 'If you turn the heater up or, even better, find me something to wear, I might consider helping you. I was wondering when it would occur to you to ask.'

'Since you couldn't actually speak until now, there didn't seem a lot of point,' said Elaine. 'Anyway, why should we trust you?'

'Who else have you got?'

Elaine glanced at Lucy, who was still looking tired and lacking her usual energy. She decided to take charge, started the engine and executed a neat three-point turn.

'Where are we going?' asked Lucy.

'We passed a charity shop with its lights on half a kilometre back, and there's a McDonalds on the far side of that overpass. Clothes for Gary, then food and coffee for us all. I know we're in a hurry but being in a hurry's no use if you don't know where you're in a hurry to get to, or if you're likely to peg out from cold or hunger before you arrive. Wherever it is.'

She had hardly finished speaking before she drew up outside a row of small shops. Most of them had closed for the night but one, the charity shop she'd spotted, was still open. 'What's your shoe size, Gary?'

'Nine.'

'Is that all? Thought you'd be bigger, somehow.' She ran inside the shop and five minutes later emerged with an armful of clothing, including trainers, socks, black Def Leppard t-shirt, some incongruous, checked trousers and a yellow anorak. 'Good old Rasmus,' she said. 'That was nearly seventy euros he gave us. Still got some left for a bite and a coffee.'

'I'm glad one of us is capable of coherent thought,' said Lucy, trying to dredge up a smile from her slough of despond.

'I've been dying to ask,' said Elaine, once they were ensconced at a table with burgers and coffee. 'What the hell happened to your face, mate? And your balls, come to that.'

'That woman you arrived with, she's what happened.' He winced as he tried to take a bite of burger through a mouth that wouldn't completely open. He continued with a mixture of embarrassment and defensiveness. 'She took me completely by surprise. Thumped me in the bollocks and knocked me cold. She had your mate with her but it was all her work. I've never been hit so hard in my life. Oh, and she was completely starkers, so I guess we know where my clothes are.'

'She's a tough little madam, we know that. Listen, are you sure it was her? What about her twin sister?'

'Och aye, the twin sister. We'll come to her in a second, but no, it wasnae the twin. Look, I think I can help you ladies but I may need protection if I do. You're secret service, right?' He didn't seem to find that strange.

'Why would you help us if you work for William Wright and therefore, by association, Valentin Prokofiev?' Lucy seemed to be perking up at last. She'd already demolished half her burger and drunk most of her coffee.

'I only work for Wright because I'm paid to. He's always been a tosser but until today I didnae know he was anything worse than that. He's certainly never got me to carry a body into the embassy before but I figured it was above my pay grade to ask. Anyway, I dumped the stiff in Room 101, as asked, and went down to the basement. I've been doing a bit of research work down there. I think the tosser forgot about me. Anyway, when I came back upstairs, everything was quiet, naebody about the place, so I snooped around and came upon him and James Simmonite talking to some Russian guy in a grey suit, and a woman who I thought at first was your pal but who clearly wasnae her at all. I stayed out of sight and listened.'

'How could you tell it wasn't the woman who'd arrived with us?' said Lucy.

Gary shrugged. 'Different hairstyle. Not much different, granted, but enough to know there were two people involved.' Elaine and Lucy looked at each other, wondering how they, who were women themselves, could have failed to notice the different haircuts.

Gary continued. 'Anyway, some of the conversation was in Russian, which I'm nae too hot on, but a lot was in English, probably because Simmo doesnae speak Russky either. They'd tied up the staff and were waiting for the four of you, but the one they really wanted was your pal, Dawson. Anyway, Wright and the Russian left and I heard the woman say they were going to Tuhala. I ducked back into reception and called the cops.'

'You too?' said Elaine. 'No wonder they arrived so sharpish.'

'I thought I'd better lie low until they arrived, and I was just on my way back to the basement when your lass jumped me and rearranged my face. And that's it.'

'Tuhala,' said Lucy. 'Where's that? And what's there? Any idea?'

'It's about twenty miles or so south of here. We'll need to take the T2, which is literally just there, right outside the restaurant. It's a region rather than an actual place, I think. I've nae been there but they also mentioned the Pirita River. Again, it's not specific but it might help.'

'Our first job is to find Saul, but I'd also quite like to know what the fuck's going on beyond that.' Lucy paused. 'Look, you're right, we're going to have to trust you, so this is what we have. This whole thing is linked to a bomb last Saturday which killed an Estonian scientist called Viktor Nurmsalu, and it seems to be about some sort of experimental process involving hydroelectric power. Something the UK government is tied up with. There's a river back in Surrey where something very odd is going on and I'm guessing now, but could it be that there's something bigger in this neck of the woods? Somewhere on the Pirita possibly?'

'Wow,' said Gary. 'That's quite something. Is that classified, what you just told me?'

'Absolutely. I'll have to shoot you as soon as I can get my hands on a gun.'

'I'll bear that in mind.'

'So, does your local knowledge extend as far as knowing whether the Pirita could be a source of hydroelectric power?'

'No, it doesnae, but we're nae going to find out sitting here.'

'You're right. Let's go, Elaine. Look, Gary, you've been great but this isn't your fight. We can drop you at a hospital if you point us in the right direction, and they can sort out your face.'

'There may be a crack in my jaw but it's nae going to keep this red-blooded Scotsman down. And in any case, look at you two wee lasses, there's nothing of you and neither of you look as if you've slept for a week. Besides, there's nae much to do in Tallinn on a Thursday night. I could be your bodyguard.' He grinned, as much as his swollen jaw would allow him to.

'Bodyguard?' said Elaine. 'Listen, pal, this one could put you in hospital permanently in about thirty seconds. She's been on courses.'

'I couldn't put an enfeebled mouse in hospital at the moment. All right then, Gary, welcome. You're co-opted to the cause. We'll get ourselves a map at that garage over there. As we no longer possess a phone between us, we'll need something to point us in the right direction.'

Five minutes later, they were heading south towards the Tuhala region, not knowing what – if anything – they would find.

Lucy was soon lost deep in thought. If William Wright was Jason Underwood's man, then Underwood himself was probably not the upright member of the secret service she had taken him for. But where did that leave Elspeth Arundell? Surely they weren't both working for the other side. If they were, MI6 was so compromised that it might as well be shut down entirely. And what other side? The obvious answer was Russia, but perhaps that was *too* obvious. Where did Songsung Rong fit in? She had certainly appeared to be on an equal footing with Prokofiev. So, did that mean that China and Russia were working hand in hand on this? But if Prokofiev was still with the Russian SVR, surely he wouldn't have quite so many black-clothed thugs dancing close attendance. So could it be that China was the main protagonist here and not Russia? On the other hand, Guna was with Prokofiev and Sofija had said that her sister was working for Russian Intelligence.

OK, so what else did they know?

Chief Inspector Downton was taking orders from someone.

It seemed unlikely to be Prokofiev directly but more likely, Underwood, if he was the round peg in MI6's square hole. Underwood had directed them to William Wright, who was now hightailing it, hopefully to Tuhala, in the company of Prokofiev. Or was he? That information had come indirectly from Guna via Gary. All they could be sure of was Prokofiev, Wright, Guna and Simmonite, had hightailed it out of the embassy. The snippet of conversation Gary had overheard was their only clue as to where. And what of Saul and Sofija? Either they too were in hot pursuit or they were held captive. Or lying dead in a ditch somewhere.

Basically, despite Gary's assistance, they were floundering around in the dark and Lucy didn't much like floundering in the dark or the light or anywhere really. People were going to get hurt if there was much more floundering to be done.

After their return from Australia in February, Dawson and Lucy
had been provided with fancy watches in a basement room at
Vauxhall Cross. Rolex, eat your heart out, Dawson had thought.
Despite looking at it every which way and pushing every knob
he could find, his watch had stubbornly failed to shoot lasers
or reveal a garrotting wire. 'What does it do?' he had asked the
bored young man who wasn't Q.

'It tells the time,' the young man had said. 'Sign here.'

And now, four months later and after several scrapes of a
violent nature and lengthy immersion into, first, the Gulf of
Riga and now, the river from which he and Sofija had recently
clambered, it was still telling the time. It was telling him that
it was seven thirty in the evening.

Shortly after losing touch with Sofija, exhaustion had
overtaken him and he had fallen asleep in a small, sheltered
hollow at the foot of a spindly silver birch. He knew it was a
silver birch because it was silver, not because he knew what
a birch looked like. Waking up, he reviewed his situation. He
was hopelessly lost in the middle of what seemed like an
endless forest of largely spindly trees, many of them not silver.
Making progress wasn't an issue but deciding on a direction
of travel was. He had no idea where the nearest town was and,
apart from several large mouthfuls of dirty river inadvertently
imbibed during his submersion earlier, he'd had nothing to
drink since a can of cola bought en route to the embassy in
the early afternoon.

The fact that he was still wearing the MI6 watch was
something of a miracle as, way back on the *Astrid*, he'd been
relieved of all his other belongings and Sofija had never
returned them. Sofija herself had an infinite supply of stuff
hidden in her parka but as she no longer had the parka, just

Tweedledum's tight blue t-shirt, she was probably no better off than he was, wherever she'd got to. Except that she was local and might therefore know where the nearest town was. He couldn't quite understand why she had suddenly left him behind now when she had always been pretty enthusiastic about retaining his company previously.

He started to push his way through the forest but hadn't got very far when he came face to face with half a dozen pigs. These were not pigs of the Russian or Chinese kind so unpopular with Sofija, nor of the farmyard variety with which Dawson was familiar back home. No, these were boars, wild boars if their size, hairiness, snorting, small but potent-looking tusks and malevolent gaze were anything to go by. Dawson could see no obvious way around them but was damned if he was going to end his days boared to death in an Estonian forest so he did what anyone in his position would have done. He yelled 'Shoo!' at the top of his voice. And it worked. The boars stopped snorting, looked at each other quizzically, and turned tail.

Eventually he came to a track. Tracks led somewhere, he thought. Tracks usually meant there was an A and a B involved, although he had no idea which direction led to A and which to B, nor which was more likely to result in food, drink and friendly assistance. He tossed a mental coin and turned towards B. Or maybe it was A. And suddenly, standing twenty metres in front of him, hands on hips, grinning like the Cheshire Cat's happier sibling, stood the extremely large man who wasn't called Samsonite.

'Goin' somewhere, are we, lad?' he asked in broad Yorkshire.

Dawson had learned a lot over the last few months, mostly from Lucy, so kept on walking towards the man-mountain, figuring that was probably the thing he would be expecting least and also that Simmonite did not appear to have possession of a firearm. The t-shirt really was too tight to conceal a weapon and the jeans were also rather snugger than

Dawson would have considered comfortable for a night out on the town or, for that matter, an evening's sinister mayhem in a forest.

Dawson carried on walking towards Simmonite and Simmonite carried on grinning at Dawson. The nearer Dawson got, the bigger Simmonite appeared to be and it wasn't just a matter of perspective. He was hoping to spot some signs of weakness but apart from the lack of a gun, he wasn't seeing any. Simmonite's arms, being thicker around the biceps area than the trunks of most of the trees alongside the track, birch or otherwise, certainly didn't suggest an encouraging level of frailty.

Keeping his eyes on the man meant that Dawson wasn't really looking where he was putting his feet and he unexpectedly half-tripped on something, something which turned out to be a tree branch of moderate thickness. Not as thick as either of Simmonite's arms, naturally, but it seemed to Dawson it might improve his chances from zero to about 2% in the tussle of some description that looked likely to take place imminently. Stopping himself from sprawling entirely onto the track, he reached down and grabbed the branch by its thicker end. As he did so, an angry hornet buzzed viciously past his left ear.

Momentarily thinking how strange that was as he had so far heard nothing in the forest larger than a few thousand mosquitos, he looked up to see Simmonite's expression change from a grin to one of complete astonishment. This could have had something to do with the third eye that had appeared between the two he had sported previously. They were deep brown, Dawson noted inconsequentially, whilst the new addition was bright red. Dawson was still in a half-crouch, rooted to the spot, as Simmonite's giant, muscular form toppled slowly backwards and landed thunderously on the ground.

Dawson stood up slowly, still clinging to the broken

branch. He knew that by rights he should be turning around to see if there was anything behind him, as it seemed very likely that there would be, if not another angry hornet then probably something more humanoid. With a gun.

'Drop your little stick, Mr Dawson,' came a voice. 'It would not have helped you against Simmonite and it will not help you against me.' There was a pause. 'Even if I did not have this gun.'

Dawson turned, dropping the branch as he did so. 'Hello, Guna,' he said, trying to smile. 'Or is it Galina? You'll have to forgive me, your sister wasn't clear on that point.' Guna, still wearing her sister's clothes, spat into the undergrowth by the side of the track. It seemed that Sofija was not the only Sesks with a penchant for expectoration. She returned her gun to its holster beneath the half-open parka and, as if to emphasise how little she regarded Dawson's likely threat quotient, zipped up the parka.

'It is chilly, yes?' she said.

'How are you going to defend yourself if I pick up that stick again?'

'Oh, no, I have made a terrible mistake. Please do not hurt me.' She paused and smiled. 'Trust me, Mr Dawson, I would not need the gun to kill you.' Dawson trusted her. 'But I do not wish to kill you.'

'Why not?' Dawson was genuinely confused. This, after all, was the "bad daughter", the one in Russian Intelligence, Valentin Prokofiev's girlfriend. He gestured behind him, to the body of Simmonite sprawled across the track. 'You killed him.'

Guna considered this long enough for Dawson to think that it might not have been the cleverest suggestion he'd ever made, from a long list of unclever suggestions he had made during his life. 'Several reasons,' she said, finally. 'Firstly, Valentin wants to kill you himself, and he is still unsure about whether you possess information he needs. Secondly, my sister likes you, I think, and I do not wish to provoke an unnecessary family argument. And thirdly, idiot,' and she laughed at what she obviously considered to be an uproarious joke, 'you and me, we are on the same side.'

Elaine, as usual, was driving and, also as usual, wasn't worrying too much with trivialities like speed limits. I was less concerned with coming across any traffic cops than with trying to read the map we had bought by the weak illumination provided by the courtesy light. Gary, bracing himself against the jolting progress of the car, peered over my shoulder.

'There's the Pirita,' he said, pointing a stubby forefinger at the map. I held it up closer to the light and we both squinted at it.

'It's there too,' I said, looking at a completely different part of the map, back near Tallinn, several kilometres behind us.

'That's the trouble with rivers,' said Elaine out of the side of her mouth, her eyes still reassuringly glued to the road. 'They're not like lakes. They tend to go on a bit.'

'Yeah, thanks for that,' I said. However, I was feeling more positive now. Something was telling me that Saul remained alive, maybe the thought that he was still with Sofija, who I doubted would let him come to harm if she could help it. 'Where's Tuhala? I can't see it.'

'It may not be marked,' said Gary. 'As I said, I think it's more of a region than an actual place. This light seems to be getting dimmer. We're nae about to run out of power, are we?'

'I certainly hope not,' I said. 'It's a long way to walk.'

'Have you looked in the glove compartment?' said Elaine. 'Rasmus seemed the practical type. Might be a torch in there.' I opened it and, of course, a torch there was, sturdy, rubber-coated and about a foot long. 'Told you,' she said in an annoyingly smug voice. Somehow, smugness sounds even worse in an Aussie twang. Gary relieved me of the torch and shone it at the map. It was certainly more effective than the feeble overhead light.

'There it is,' he said. 'We were looking on the wrong side of the road. The river goes under the T2 here and there is an actual place called Tuhala. Just a village by the looks of it. Near something called the Witch's Well. I've heard of that. Some natural spring, I think, floods sometimes. Odd place, tourist attraction. We should've turned off a little way back, but if we hang a right just up here at the Vikingite Küla and double back, we can get the road across to Tuhala.'

'What's the Viking-whatever-you-said, a pub?' asked Elaine, hopefully.

'Viking Village,' I said. 'Perhaps we should pick up some horned helmets on our way past. What with those and the torch, we'd be unbeatable. Mind you, wherever Val and William Wright are going, I can't believe it's to a tourist attraction.'

—

'Is that where we're headed then? This Witch's Well place?' asked Elaine, fifteen minutes later. 'As the driver, it would be nice to know.'

'I guess so,' I said. 'Let's be honest, you couldn't power a fart from the energy this river's giving off. Maybe the witches will have the answer.' The Pirita River, alongside which we were driving, was as flat and placid as any river I'd ever seen. If we didn't spot some kind of clue soon, we'd have to give up until the morning. And even if we found somewhere to stay, we only had ten euros left, which wouldn't go very far.

Gary had obviously been thinking along the same lines. 'Look, why don't we get ourselves to the Witch's Well, see if there's anything there and if not, we can go back to Tallinn, freshen up, have something to eat, catch up on some sleep which, looking at the bags under your otherwise beautiful eyes, you could do with, and start again at first light. Perhaps you could phone home, get some instructions. You've done your best, but we have nae resources and nae idea what we're looking for.'

'Just to clarify, Gary old pal,' said Elaine. 'Whose beautiful eyes are you referring to? Mine or blondie's?'

'Both of you have beautiful eyes, obviously. I'm nae falling into that trap.'

Suddenly, without warning, Elaine yanked on the wheel and turned the Ford sharp right down a lane just before a bridge over the Pirita. Almost immediately she slowed to little more than a crawl, peering forward through the windscreen as the car negotiated a series of bends before emerging on the right-hand bank of a different river, smaller and rather faster flowing.

'Hey, lass, where are we off to now?' said Gary.

'Something big's been down here recently. I spotted the tyre tracks. Just a hunch.'

'Hunches are good,' I said. 'Let's give it a whirl. Witches are too much toil and trouble anyway.'

After a few minutes, something up ahead caught my eye. 'Is that a weir of some kind?'

'Looks like it. Could power up a few farts with it if so, I guess.'

As we drove closer, we could see that it was indeed a weir at the mouth of another tributary flowing off to the right, smaller still and considerably wilder than the river to our left, which was itself rather more animated than the main Pirita had been.

'Now we're getting somewhere,' I said, just as a hail of bullets rattled into and through the car, although miraculously failing to hit any of us. Elaine swerved violently to the left off the lane and towards the river, having spotted a small outcrop of rock which might give us some sort of shelter from the gunfire.

'Out!' she yelled and, without bothering to turn off the engine, flung open her door and dived through it. She was followed by Gary, who catapulted his muscular bulk out of the rear door on the same side. I was slightly slower but managed to scramble out of the passenger door just as the Ford plunged into the river. As I rolled over and came up in the lee of the rock, I saw the car come to a standstill, still upright, wedged on top of the weir.

'I hope your government isn't going to expect us to pay for that,' said Elaine. I have to say I was less concerned with the thought of paying for a replacement embassy car than with trying to work out how to stay alive for more than the next few seconds. The gunfire had stopped but presumably only because we couldn't be seen. However, as we were clearly no longer in the car, it wouldn't take a genius to spot our hiding place. Whilst the gunmen probably weren't geniuses, all things considered, and were definitely as bad at shooting straight as the villains in virtually every movie ever made, they didn't need to be good if they simply appeared around the rock to pick us off at point blank range.

Which they did.

Well, the appearing around the rock bit anyway. They didn't start shooting again though. There were two of them and they were Chinese. That caught me by surprise; I'd been expecting reacquaintance with Val's men in black. They both carried rather nasty-looking submachine guns. One of them started shouting in Mandarin. My Mandarin isn't quite on a par with my Russian but I caught the odd word and there was no doubt he was inviting us, in time-honoured fashion, to raise our hands over our heads. So I did, and Gary and Elaine followed my lead. We were pushed roughly around the rock and on to the riverbank, where the same one, who was presumably more than an extra and therefore the only one allowed to speak, started spouting in Mandarin again. I shrugged at him. He spoke in English. 'We wait,' he said.

'Who for?' I asked, but he'd clearly reached his linguistic limit. However, we didn't have to wait long to find out. A chunky Merc appeared along the lane from around the rock outcrop, drew up and two people emerged. Two very familiar people.

One was William Wright, still smirking. I was looking forward to desmirking him and, judging by the expression on Elaine's face, she was harbouring similar thoughts. The second was the ridiculously tall Chinese woman, Rong, last seen in the cottage in Kuressaare with my bullet – well, strictly speaking, Number Six's bullet – in her foot. She was limping slightly and holding a solid-looking walking stick, not that she seemed to have much need of it. That was disappointing. I obviously hadn't done as much damage to her foot as I'd hoped.

Rong limped straight up to me, completely ignoring Elaine and Gary, and swung her stick without preamble straight at my head. Fuck me but it hurt.

___ In which Guna discusses two-humped
camels, and Dawson sees a car on
a weir

'How can we be on the same side?' said Dawson. 'You're
Russian. You're working for Prokofiev.'

'Ah, yes, him,' and she spat into the undergrowth again in
the usual Sesks-like reaction. 'You are right about one thing.
Only one thing. I work for the Russian Federation. I am a
Captain in the SVR.' She outranked her sister, then, thought
Dawson. That could cause friction across the family dinner
table, although they might have bigger fish to argue about. 'But
I do not work for Valentin Prokofiev. It is a cover. Sometimes, it
is necessary to do unpleasant things.'

'Like killing Simmonite?'

'I was thinking more about having to make the two-humped
camel with Valentin. Very unpleasant. Killing Simmonite less
so. He might have harmed you.' She looked Dawson up and
down. 'Would definitely have harmed you. He was first on my
list.'

Dawson was intrigued. 'How long's your list?'

'Not long. Valentin, eventually, and Songsung Rong,
naturally. Possibly your embassy man, Wright, although I think
the British would like to talk to him.' She shrugged. 'Others
may die in the course of events, but they are the important
ones. Above them, I do not know. It would be best if the
person Valentin reports to is kept alive. If that is a diplomatic
possibility.'

'What was the second name? Something Wrong?'

'Yes, that is right, Rong. She is a Chinese government
agent, quite high up I believe, in more ways than one,' and she
laughed for a reason Dawson couldn't work out. 'We should
walk.' She grasped him powerfully by the arm and turned
him back towards B. Or was it A? Quite a lot had gone down

in the last few minutes, so Dawson's already sketchy grasp of direction had deserted him completely. As they passed the body of Simmonite, Guna gave it an experimental kick. Experimental or not, it was still powerful enough to roll the probable sixteen stones of body on to its front. 'Huh, not such a "babe magnet" now, are you, James?'

'Tried it on, had he?' asked Dawson, edging away slightly.

'He never stopped, Valentin or no Valentin. I would have killed him a long time ago but I needed to keep my cover story. Still, everything comes to those who wait.'

Dawson started to look at Guna and, by implication, Sofija, in a whole different light. There was a certain, undeniable attractiveness to the pair of them, albeit in a women's WWE sort of way. Clearly, she had had no trouble ensnaring Prokofiev, and an ability to act wouldn't have been enough. He remembered Sofija's boobs again. They were quite difficult to forget.

'Lucy and Elaine,' he started. 'You took them into that room back at the embassy. Are they all right?' He found he was holding his breath waiting for Guna's answer, no mean feat as she was setting quite a pace along the track.

'Lucy Smith, ah yes, the beautiful English milady, and the Australian policewoman. They will be fine. And the people from the embassy. They were drugged, knocked out, but the effects wear off very quickly. I had to do that, you understand. I think Valentin wanted to do more, to your friends at least, but he was in a hurry, so they were unharmed.' She paused. 'Anyway, they will not be getting in the way now. The police will probably be at the embassy questioning everyone. It is just you, me and Sofija.'

'Where are we going?'

'Back to the river.'

'Why? Is the river significant?'

She stopped and looked at him. 'Of course it is, and now we know which part of it is most significant. You did not know about the river?' Dawson shook his head. 'The Arundell woman did not tell you?'

'No, she didn't.' He'd heard of need-to-know but since it was his life on the line, he felt that the principle could have been stretched a little down that line to include him. They started walking again and after a couple of minutes of thought, he said, 'So, let me get this straight: you work for Russian Intelligence, your sister works for Estonian Intelligence and I, laughably, work for British Intelligence. That's an awful lot of intelligence but very little shared knowledge. If we are all on the same side, as you put it, who the hell's on the other side? And who does bloody Valentin work for, because the last time I met him, he was a member of the SVR, like you?'

'Would that be when you shot him?'

'Oh, you know about that too, do you?'

'Yes, and I also know this shit would not be quite so shitty if you had been sensible and killed him instead of nearly missing. He was dismissed from the SVR for incompetence, my superiors understandably believing that he should not have allowed you to outwit him. So he has a grudge, two grudges, one with you and one with Russia.' She turned to him and smiled. 'Who does he work for? China. Which is why Songsung Rong is here. And I believe you have already met some of her men, yes? Back by the river, with machine guns?' He nodded.

'One more thing. Why is your English so much better than your sister's, two-humped camels apart?'

'Please, will you tell her that to her face? She would squish you like a ripe tomato. She is proud of her English. Two months ago, she had very little. My training is more comprehensive than hers. The SVR makes sure that its agents are fluent in at least three useful languages. One is always English, although not because of England, of course, which is largely irrelevant, but America.'

'Even the Americans aren't fluent in English.'

Rounding a sharp bend, they came to a halt as the track

they were on was crossed by a tarmac road hacked through the forest. Dawson realised that the terrain had changed, the birches and other spindly trees replaced by thicker, taller evergreens, which he amazed himself by remembering were Scots pines. The road, which looked new, was in deep shade from overhanging foliage. The light was beginning to dim anyway as evening drew towards night.

Guna held up her hand and said 'Stop,' which was slightly unnecessary as they already had. 'Be quiet. We are almost there.' Faintly, Dawson could hear the sound of rushing water. Guna led the way off the track, keeping parallel to the road, which soon bent away from them as they started to scramble up a steepish rise in the ground. Guna pulled herself silently and athletically from tree to tree as the terrain got steeper. Dawson, a little less silently and much less athletically, followed. Just before she reached the top of the rise, Guna dropped to her stomach, bouncing slightly, and gestured for Dawson to do the same. They crawled to the brow of the slope and peered cautiously over. The river below them was flowing quickly, much as he remembered it from his plunge that afternoon. Then he saw that it had a choice of two directions in which to flow. The main channel headed off to their left, relatively sedately, whilst a smaller stream disappeared around a jutting cliff face straight ahead. This tributary was anything but sedate, careering over a weir as it broke away from the main river and rushing around the cliff in a maelstrom of churning white water. The whole effect was exacerbated by the small grey car which had somehow got itself wedged fast across the weir.

But all that was of little import to Dawson because, standing on the opposite bank with their hands in the air, were Lucy and Elaine. With them was the man he'd last seen virtually naked in the British Embassy sporting the results of Sofija's handiwork, but who was now dressed in a vivid yellow windcheater and somebody's old golfing trousers. Pointing submachine guns at them were the two Chinese who had stopped the Fiat's progress with the flatbed truck earlier.

'You were wrong,' whispered Dawson. 'Not sure how, but Lucy and Elaine seem to have made it. Didn't think anything as trivial as the police would hold them up.'

'It does not seem to have done them much good,' said Guna, 'but this might be to our advantage. There may be more of Rong's Chinese but deciding what to do with their prisoners will distract these two at least. We must find a way past them.' She looked at Dawson and corrected herself. '*I* must find a way past them. This is not your fight, Mr Dawson.'

'Excuse me?' Dawson replied. 'Not my fight?' he was about to expand on his theme when he heard the sound of another vehicle approaching and a Mercedes 4x4 appeared around the cliff in front of them. William Wright emerged from the driver's door and from the other side, uncoiling herself like a snake, emerged an improbably tall Chinese woman holding a walking stick. This must be Songsung Rong, thought Dawson. Determining Wright from Rong was straightforward; the Chinese woman was six inches taller. The two men with submachine guns took a few steps back, deferring to Rong, who limped briskly up to Lucy, Elaine and the man from the embassy and hit Lucy hard around the head with her stick. Lucy collapsed, blood seeping from her scalp.

___ In which Dawson watches another
explosion, and looks down a
plughole

'Give me your watch,' whispered Guna.

'My watch?' Dawson looked at her and then at the non-Rolex still mysteriously attached to his left wrist after all these days of blood and thunder. 'It's just after nine o'clock. Does that help?'

Guna shook her head in exasperation, grabbed Dawson's hand and forcibly yanked off the watch, breaking its strap in the process. Dawson was outraged but still managed to keep his voice down. 'What the fuck are you doing?' he hissed. He glanced across the river but nobody in the small party on the opposite bank appeared to have heard the minor, chronometrically prompted commotion. Elaine was kneeling down attending to Lucy's head wound, having commandeered their male companion's t-shirt for the purpose. The Chinese submachine guns were pointed fractionally more in his direction, their owners being about the same size as him but only if you were to put both of them together. The two women were not much of a threat, although Lucy was trying to get up, ignoring the menace of the Chinese giantess, who still had her walking stick, ready to strike again. Wright was looking on, smirking, with arms folded.

Meanwhile, Guna was examining the back of the watch minutely. There's a pun there somewhere trying to get out, thought Dawson. He'd have it in a second. Then she grunted in satisfaction and pressed a small part of its backplate, which tilted slightly and began to swivel of its own accord before clicking open to an angle of ninety degrees. A tiny red button was revealed. Guna carefully moved the button until it was directly behind the figure VII on the face of the watch. She turned and grinned.

'Seven seconds. That should be enough. Cover your ears,' she mouthed. She pressed the red button, stood up and hurled the watch across the river, aiming towards the two Chinese submachinists, who were standing a little way apart from Elaine, Lucy and the others, including Rong. 'Duck,' said Guna, and dragged him back below the ridge.

A few seconds silence was followed, abruptly, by an explosion. It wasn't as impressive an explosion as the one Dawson had nearly succumbed to back in Stallford, but it was loud enough. They both jumped up, but for a few seconds their view across the river was obscured by smoke. 'Bloody hell,' he said. 'How did you know it did that? They said it only told the time.'

'Russian intelligence. We know all about your Bond-like gadgets. They are not secrets. We have the information about each new piece of British kit sent round on the intranet every Friday. It is very funny.'

'Why didn't you just shoot them? You have a gun.'

'I would only have time to shoot one before the other starts firing back. Anyway, if you polish off one Chinese, you are always left wanting more.' She grabbed him. 'We must go. Quick, come with me,' and she started running along the ridge to their left.

Not entirely certain whether he was going or coming, Dawson set off in pursuit. 'Wait a minute. What about the women?'

'Don't worry, they will be OK. I missed them and they do not have so many Chinese pigs to worry about now.'

Two hundred metres along, around the bend of the main river, they came upon a bridge, a temporary structure that carried the new road they had seen across the river and through a narrow gorge cut into the low cliffs on the other side. Guna scrambled down to the bridge and, without seeming to worry about being seen or not, sprinted over it. Dawson struggled to keep up, despite the high risk of being shot. The light was fading but there was still plenty of it for a half-efficient Chinese marksman to bring them both down with little fuss.

'Do not worry, there is no one to shoot us,' said Guna, stopping underneath the cliff, turning to him and reading his thoughts in much the same disturbing way her sister had done the previous day. However, as he caught up with her, she unexpectedly grabbed him by the arms, twisting them painfully up between his shoulder blades where she held them together effortlessly with one hand, whilst with the other she produced a long, plastic cable tie from somewhere about her person, which she used to bind his wrists together. She stood back admiring her handiwork, leaving Dawson dumbfounded.

'I give up,' he said. 'All that bullshit about being on the same side, Russians and Brits working hand-in-hand for world peace. Another fucking lie.'

'Yes, it is hard to know who to believe. Also, it is too late to give up. You are already my prisoner. Come, this way,' and she prodded him in the back along the road through the gorge.

As they emerged at the other end, the smaller tributary appeared again in front of them, by this time a swirling herd of white horses, leaping and jumping over each other through a rapidly narrowing channel to reach... 'What's that?' asked Dawson, stopping and peering in astonishment.

'It is called *Kiirevesi*. It means "fast water".'

'You don't say. But I wasn't talking about the river, I was talking about that,' and he nodded to their left where the maelstrom seemed to take a deep breath before plunging, the water corkscrewing wildly, into what could only be described as a giant plughole, half-obscured by an overhang of rock.

'Have you heard of the Witch's Well?' said Guna.

'No. Is that what this is?' Dawson could see why local folklore might have deemed this extraordinary cauldron the work of witches.

'No, the Witch's Well is a few kilometres away. It is a major

Estonian tourist attraction. There are not many. This is a similar phenomenon but has been artificially enhanced.'

Guna pushed him forward again. Rounding a bend, they came to a pair of huge steel doors, obviously designed for large vehicles to pass through, set into the rockface adjacent to the now obscured but still extremely loud giant plughole. There was a smaller, pedestrian access set into the right-hand door. Guna rapped on it hard four times. Dawson was slightly surprised she didn't dent the metal. After a few seconds, he heard the rasping sound of a bolt being drawn back and the gate opened inwards to reveal an unsmiling man with a shaved head, dressed all in black. He stood to one side as Guna and Dawson came through the gate into an echoing, harshly lit vehicle bay. Guna prodded Dawson through a door on their right into an equally brightly lit office, sparsely furnished with a metal desk and two swivel chairs. There was a bank of screens on the wall behind the desk. Dawson peered at them but couldn't be sure exactly what he was looking at.

'*Voz'mi ostal'nykh i idi k reke. Tam byla bomba.*' Guna said sharply to the man who had let them in.

'*Da,*' he replied, turned on his heels and disappeared back out of the office at a run, shouting something in Russian as he did so.

'What did you say to him?' said Dawson. 'He ran off like a scalded cat.'

'I told him to get his arse up to the river because there had been a bomb. There are no cameras up there,' and she waved at the screens, 'and this place is soundproofed, thanks to the rock, so I was banking on him not knowing. He will be collecting some of Valentin's other goons, leaving very few for me to take care of, I hope.' She had been rootling around in a desk drawer as she spoke and came up with a short but fearsome-looking knife. 'Turn around.'

'I'd rather not,' said Dawson. 'If you're going to knife me, I'd rather you did it face to face, if you don't mind.'

'Really? That is strange. I would far rather not face my killer. When it comes, I would prefer to be unaware.' While Dawson was noting that she'd said "when", not "if", Guna spun him forcibly round and sliced cleanly through the cable tie holding his wrists. She moved to an inner door beside the bank of screens and opened it a crack. Dawson heard the sound of running boots heading away from them in the middle-distance.

'Only two,' said Guna. 'There will be more. Come on, we must find weapons. This knife will not go far. Well, it will go about fifty metres if I throw it, but it will not come back,' and she laughed.

'But...' started Dawson.

'Oh, yes, I am sorry, I lied about lying, I am afraid. You had to be my prisoner to get us in here. Now we have things to do. And we must say hello to Valentin of course,' and, spotting a shadowy, grey figure walking across one of the screens, she spat at it, accurately. One way or another, the Sesks twins did seem to possess a great deal of phlegm between them.

I must have blacked out because when I came to, I was on the ground and Elaine was wrapping a strip torn off Gary's Def Leppard t-shirt around my bonce. I was beginning to wish I'd aimed six feet higher when I'd shot Rong back at the cottage. I'm too nice by half.

I started to struggle to my feet. I was getting vertigo looking up at her. I noticed the two submachine gunners had taken a few paces back, which implied that Rong was their boss. I was only half upright when the world disappeared in a ball of white light, followed milliseconds later by a booming sound and clouds of acrid, white smoke.

When the smoke cleared, the two Chinese gunmen were lying on the ground, and I thought it unlikely that they'd be getting up again judging by the amount of blood. The rest of us had fared rather better. Unfortunately, this included Wright and Rong but, even so, there were three of us and only two of them, or maybe two and a half given Rong's size. Her stick was lying a little way away and there had so far been no indication that William Wright was armed, so it seemed as good a time as any to start a fightback. However, as I prepared to launch myself at Rong, a wave of dizziness from my injured head came over me and I inconveniently found myself unable to complete the launch. Elaine and Gary though were both in a much better state than me, notwithstanding Gary's possibly broken jaw. It was just bad luck that they both decided to attack the softer of the two targets, William Wright, leaving Rong free to retrieve her fucking lump of wood and, with a turn of speed that belied a person with a hole in her foot, run up to them and swing it at Elaine's head.

I yelled a warning. Elaine, in response, or maybe just

sixth-sensing the rapid approach of the walking stick, ducked and the full force of the blow struck Wright right in the face. I noted a brief look of surprise replace his usual smirk before it was hidden by a sea of blood and he fell backwards into the river a few feet behind him. I have no idea if he was dead before he hit the water but he was immediately lost to sight under the surface.

That only left Rong.

Except it didn't. Two of Prokofiev's black-clothed thugs appeared from nowhere and in the face of the heavy-duty armoury they were packing, our short-lived resistance faded away. I thought I recognised one of them as Number Six although, if I'm honest, they all looked much the same so I could have been mistaken. He certainly didn't respond when I asked him if he'd managed to escape from the Village, but again it's possible The Prisoner had never been shown on Russian TV.

With Rong leading the way, and not displaying much in the way of remorse about her inadvertent manslaughter of the Third Cultural Attaché, we were escorted at gunpoint along a track and through a steel door cut into the rockface. Inside, a well-lit flight of steps led down. And down. I stopped counting at fifty because I was still feeling a touch dizzy and didn't want to fall down the rest of them. Eventually we emerged on to a long metal-floored gallery. The river re-emerged too although I couldn't see it through the railings to my right. I could hear it though. It sounded pretty angry. There had to have been some kind of waterfall to get the river this far underground. I supposed William Wright was in it somewhere but I had other priorities. Mainly concerning the sight of four more of Val's thugs, even though their attention was taken up by a door at the far end of the gallery.

Then the door opened and the four of them started shooting through it.

— In which Dawson gets kissed,
   and several guns appear

It occurred to Dawson that, although a large number of the principal players in the pantomime had turned up, one was missing. 'A little while ago, you mentioned it was just me, you and Sofija. So, do you have any idea where she is?'

'Here, I hope,' said Guna. 'I expected you to be together, but then I thought, why would she not leave you? You are very good at getting in the way and she has a task to perform which is better achieved alone.'

'What task's that?' They were both whispering as they made their way carefully along a tunnel cut into the rock. It was heading steadily downwards.

'You do not know this either?' She shook her tousled, dark-blonde head. 'She has to find the scientist, Nurmsalu, and keep him alive. He is Estonian so it is her job.'

'You mean he's here?'

'Of course, where else would Valentin and Rong want him to be? They have a facility but, without the inventor of the new process, they have nothing.'

'How did he get here?'

She laughed. 'How do you think?'

'I don't... wait a minute. Are you saying he was on the *Astrid*? With me?'

'We all were. You, Viktor Nurmsalu and the whole family Sesks, leaving your brilliant MI6 to think that he had been exploded in your little town.'

They reached a steel door at the end of the corridor. Dawson was still thinking. 'Elspeth Arundell knew it wasn't Viktor who was blown up. She told me about his brother, Kaspar.'

'Arundell, yes, she is a sneaky one. Maybe I will kill her too before your countrymen can get to her.'

'So that implies that Arundell is a double-agent and, as

she is clearly not working for you Russians, she must be in the pay of the Chinese.'

'*Voila!* Congratulations.' Guna silently slow clapped.

'But why?'

'Who knows? It is not my concern. Perhaps they will let you watch while they put the thumbscrews on her. Come, we must move.' She opened the door and stepped cautiously through it. Immediately she disappeared, whisked out of sight so suddenly that Dawson's mouth literally dropped open. He stood irresolutely for a few seconds, listening intently to near silence. He had no weapon, no expertise in hand-to-hand combat and no knowledge about what lay the other side of the door, nor how many whats. Probably several, he imagined, as he couldn't see that one what would have been enough to overpower the redoubtable Guna quite that easily. But when it came down to it, he only had two options and turning tail and sprinting back up the corridor really wasn't an option at all. So he walked through the door.

The brightness of the corridor was replaced by much dimmer lighting and before his eyes could adjust, he was kissed full on the lips. 'Hello, idiot,' said Sofija. 'Did you miss me?'

Guna appeared from the shadows as Sofija took a step back. The latter looked and smelled nothing like the bedraggled girl in tight t-shirt and muddy, oversized chinos who had disappeared back at the river a few hours ago. She appeared to have had a good wash and brush up and was dressed in camouflage fatigues. 'This was good joke, no?' she said.

'Been to a ladies' outfitter, have you?' asked Dawson.

'I borrow it,' said Sofija. 'Woman Chinese guard not need it anymore. Is good fit, yes?'

'So that is one less for us to deal with,' said Guna, 'and I think the bomb in Dawson's watch has killed two more.'

'Two less,' Sofija replied, confusingly. 'There was second guard also watching Nurmsalu. They had no need of guns anymore so it seem rude not to borrow them.' She held up two handguns and passed one to Guna and one to Dawson, who hesitated slightly before accepting it.

'Wouldn't you be better keeping this yourself?' he said.

'No, you have already shot Russian *siga* once and the practice make perfect. Anyway, I have one already,' and she pulled her camouflage jacket open to reveal a gun in an underarm holster similar to Guna's.

Guna had taken the gun given her, although she too already had one of her own, which she pulled out and checked over. 'Three bullets left in this. I will save the new one until later.' She placed the second weapon in her holster. 'Sister, do you know how many of Valentin's men there are? I sent two off to the river but they will be back very soon, and Rong and the Englishman will be with them.'

'No, they breed like flies.'

'How did you get in?' Dawson asked Sofija.

'They think I am Guna,' she said, shrugging. 'Prokofiev's *värdjad* are bigger idiots than you.'

'Where is the scientist now?' Guna asked.

The short, cross-corridor they were standing in had doors at each end. 'Nurmsalu is in store cupboard that way,' Sofija said, pointing to the left.

'And the river is this way,' added Guna, striding off in the opposite direction and carefully opening the door at the end. Not carefully enough though. '*Kurat!*' she shouted, flinging herself to the floor and firing the last three bullets in her old gun through the open door, where they were met by considerably more than three coming in the opposite direction. One of them hit Dawson high up in the left shoulder, causing him to drop the gun he had just been given, but Sofija, following her sister to the ground, scooped it up as she did so. Dawson had always imagined that being shot would be quite painful and whilst it was satisfying to know that he had been right, the pain itself was less satisfying.

The fusillade of bullets stopped as suddenly as it had started and a voice came from behind them. 'Ah, Mr Dawson, here we are again. You appear to have met my girlfriend, although I must confess I had not known that there were two of her. Galina, moya dorogaya, you have been keeping something from me. That makes me unhappy. Up on your feet, ladies, and through the door, if you please. You too, Mr Dawson.' The vicious little automatic he was holding backed up the request.

__ In which Dawson and Lucy discuss
   blood types, and Riley takes
   matters into his own paws

Sofija and Guna placed their guns on the ground and stood up. Dawson, clutching his shoulder and trying to stay conscious, followed them through the door. They found themselves on a broad metal-floored gallery running down one side of a large cavern. A sturdy set of waist-high railings ran the length of the gallery over to their left and on the right, up against the rock face, there was a long workbench containing banks of electronic equipment whose likely function was a mystery to Dawson. The sound of rushing water coming from the darkness beyond the railings suggested that the turbulent river Dawson had last seen disappearing down the giant plughole above ground had emerged here.

Dawson's head was beginning to swim but he vaguely noted that neither the embassy bloke, Wright, nor the two Chinese gunmen were amongst the group of people standing on the gallery. Presumably the watch bomb had ticked them off the list of opposition. In their place were four black-clothed men with a definite air of eastern European thuggery about them. The guns they held looked effective enough in the right hands, although the fact that the recent spray of bullets through the door had only produced one flesh wound on three people didn't suggest that the right hands were necessarily theirs.

Right in the middle was the tall Chinese woman Dawson had last seen hitting Lucy around the head with a stick. She still held the stick. Behind them stood Elaine and Lucy, the latter with a black bandage emblazoned with the word Def tied roughly around her head. The big bloke from the embassy was still with them, but even he wasn't as tall as the Chinese woman. Two further gunmen had their weapons trained on them. The odds didn't look particularly favourable. Seven guns against the one which Dawson knew that Guna still had hidden under her parka. He smiled wanly and called across to Lucy. 'Wotcher, lover. We must compare blood types once we've got rid of this lot.'

Lucy grinned back. 'Attaboy. That shouldn't take too long.'

It was bravado, they were both aware of it, but Dawson couldn't help but be proud knowing that it was a level of bravado that would have been completely alien to him before he'd met Lucy, not to mention the Sesks twins.

'Now, Mr Dawson,' said Prokofiev, coming into view from behind him. 'I need to have a small conversation with you about the Australian diamonds before I dispose of you. There are some unaccounted for and I believe you can help me locate them.'

'Why would you think that? The diamonds went back to Germany. And even if I could help, promising to dispose of me afterwards isn't much incentive.'

'Killing your friends one by one may be though. You and I both know that while enough of the diamonds ended up with the Germans to satisfy them, some were, what shall we say? Spirited away.'

'Well, they weren't spirited in my direction. Perhaps you should have a word with your pal, Elspeth Arundell.'

'I have but, disappointingly, she is not as privy to information as we had hoped.'

He was interrupted by Songsung Rong, who seemed to be the sort of person who only spoke when necessary. 'Arundell will be dealt with. She has outlived her usefulness.'

'As the person who found them,' Prokofiev continued, 'why would you not have kept some for yourself? Some which you would be happy to pass on to me in exchange for your error in shooting me in Australia? I did not appreciate being shot. The river runs deep, Mr Dawson, and you and your friends will not make a significant difference to the water levels. Her Ladyship will be first,' he said, pointing at Lucy. Two men in black moved to take hold of her but as they did so, two shots rang out simultaneously, the noise echoing around the cavern. The two thugs dropped like ebony stones, hitting the steel floor of the gallery moments after their guns, which skittered through the railings into the unseen waters beyond. The momentary distraction had been all the time Sofija and Guna had required to pull out their second, concealed, weapons and fire.

'Very amateur, Valentin, darling,' said Guna as she shifted the direction of her gun towards Prokofiev. But he was too quick for her. He grabbed the increasingly unsteady Dawson and, using him as a shield, held his automatic to his temple. Guna managed at the last millisecond to avoid putting a second hole in Dawson.

The two thugs guarding Lucy, Elaine and Gary had, understandably, also been distracted by the deaths of their comrades, and Gary and Elaine took advantage by hurling themselves at them. Gary, with the benefit of sixteen stones of muscle, flattened his adversary and grabbed his weapon with little trouble. Elaine encountered slightly more resistance but Gary, having obtained a gun and wondering how best he could utilise it effectively, arrived at an immediate decision and shot the man grappling with her cleanly if not lethally through the thigh. He fell with a screech and dropped his gun in order to employ both hands in a wholly fruitless attempt to staunch the gush of blood from his shattered leg. Elaine scrambled successfully after the discarded weapon and fired at Gary's already-winded Russian in a sort of *quid pro quo*. He was already on his knees so didn't have far to fall.

Meanwhile, Lucy, having effectively utilised a similar manoeuvre on more than one occasion already during the past few days, flung herself to the floor and slid into the back of Rong's giraffe-like legs, bringing the Chinese woman satisfactorily down to earth. 'Timber!' yelled Lucy as she continued her slide before bringing one leg up underneath her and launching herself towards Prokofiev and Dawson.

Whilst the launch was more successful than her earlier attempt up on the riverbank, it may not have been an entirely well-thought-out stratagem, what with Prokofiev's gun barrel being only a centimetre from Dawson's head, but luckily Lucy wasn't the only person launching themselves. Well, not so much a person as a sizeable, four-legged streak of black and tan which had appeared out of thin air. A streak emitting a deep-throated growl.

Quite who Riley thought he was attacking and who he was defending was unclear but later analysis suggested that as he had always shown a deep antipathy towards Lucy, and what with Prokofiev being his owner, it was more likely that his target was the woman. If so, he missed. Badly. Lucy had cannoned into Dawson, leaving Prokofiev exposed, a nanosecond before the Dobermann's arrival at their *ménage à trois*. Riley hit his Russian master with all his muscular six stone and knocked him into the railings which caught him at buttock-height. There was a three second pause whilst he stood there, arms flailing, before slowly toppling back soundlessly into the void. The noise of the splash was unheard over the roar of the water and two further gunshots as Guna and Sofija took out the two remaining armed Russians.

'Blimey O'Riley,' said Dawson weakly, and fainted.

In which a body turns up in a skip, and Sam leaves his mouth open

Another body had turned up, dumped in a skip on an industrial site just outside Ashford in Kent. It was wearing a dark suit and there was a pair of broken dark glasses hanging off one ear. Gulliver heard about it on the intranet and was in his car within minutes, collecting Sam from the station rest room en route.

'This would have ended up in landfill if the refuse boys hadn't spotted it,' the local inspector said when they arrived in Ashford ninety minutes later.

'Well, it's not exactly food waste,' said Gulliver. It was, as he'd suspected, the MI6 agent who had accompanied Elspeth Arundell to collect Downton.

'I don't understand, sir,' said Sam. 'Does this mean that Inspector Downton has overpowered both of them? Should we be looking for Ms Arundell's body too?'

'No, constable.' Gulliver sighed. He now knew that the bi-directional fishy smell that had been assaulting his nostrils was more feminine than masculine. 'I think we can assume that Ms Arundell and Mr Downton have left the island.' Sam raised his eyebrows. 'The channel tunnel is ten miles that away,' and he pointed over his shoulder.

He did the necessary, of course he did, arranging a security blanket at Folkestone, Dover and every local airfield, but he knew he was too late and Jason Underwood's arrival whilst this was happening confirmed his worst fears.

'I didn't trust you, Mr Underwood,' Gulliver said without preamble. 'I'm sorry.'

'Oh, don't be. You were right not to. I wouldn't be doing my job properly if people trusted me. First thing I tell new recruits: trust nobody and you might live to reach thirty. I certainly didn't trust Elspeth Arundell. I've harboured suspicions for many a long day but I didn't know who, if anyone, she was working for. Nor why. Now, however, I do.'

'Russia, surely.'

'Oh, dear me, no, Mr Gulliver. Not the Russians. This whole business is about mutual co-operation leading to everlasting friendship between our two great nations. Not that we want the Sun to get wind of that, of course.'

'Who, then?'

'For a while, I thought it might be good ol' Uncle Sam.'

'The Americans? What about the Special Relationship?'

'Ah, yes, that would be the Special Relationship where one party is holding a leash and the other party is on all fours with a collar round its neck. No, not them. As soon I heard that Elspeth had flown with your inspector in tow, we were straight round to her apartment to see what we could find.'

'And what did you find?'

'Quite a lot. Either she wasn't particularly good at concealment or she figured that by the time we got there it wouldn't matter because she would be beyond our clutches. Which of course she may well now be. In answer to your earlier question, Chief Superintendent, Elspeth Arundell is working for China. We already knew she'd spent some time in the early nineties in Beijing as a junior diplomat. Perfectly clean record, nothing to arouse suspicion. But we have now discovered that she had enjoyed a relationship with a local intelligence recruiter who managed to suborn her and left her as a sleeper. When she returned to England, she obtained a transfer to MI6 and worked her way up. She probably became frustrated with the quality and honesty of senior British politicians, like most of us if truth be told but, unlike most of us, she concluded that the Chinese communist model would be a less dishonest way of running the country. So she got back in touch with her Chinese contact and became a full-time double agent.'

'We can assume Arundell and Downton are on their way to China, then, can we? It's a long way by car.'

'Perhaps not.' Underwood paused and looked down at the chief superintendent. 'Without wishing to cast aspersions on the quality of your force's investigative work, I'm afraid we have now discovered that Viktor Nurmsalu was not the gentleman blown up on Saturday and is almost certainly alive and well, back in Estonia. I suspect that Arundell and Downton are on their way there as well, to collect him for likely forward transportation to China.'

'So who was killed in Stallford?'

'I hope to have that information shortly. We are still going through Ms Arundell's flat.'

Something occurred to Gulliver. 'Our two agents, Smith and Bates. You sent them off to Riga in pursuit of Saul Dawson, didn't you? Latvia. Next door to Estonia.'

'Yes, thank you, Chief Superintendent, I don't need a geography lesson. In any case the dots are very clearly numbered. Look, I shouldn't be telling you this, but we're talking about a tri-nation scientific project, the three nations in question being ourselves, Russia and Estonia.' He paused again. 'Fancy a drink, Mr Gulliver? I could certainly do with one.' He looked across at Sam, who had been standing to one side, listening to the conversation with wide eyes and a wider mouth. 'And perhaps we can put a cake in your mouth, young man. You're in danger of catching flies.'

———

Once seated in a nearly empty, local café, Underwood continued. 'It appears there was some sort of contretemps at the embassy in Tallinn this afternoon. The ambassador returned from a business trip to find the building swarming with local police and most of his staff in a state of shock. I had asked Smith and Bates to report there when they found Dawson and it seems they did that, but by the time the ambassador returned, they'd all gone again. As had my own man at the embassy, a William Wright, to whom I'd told Smith to report. Unfortunately, the inspection of Ms Arundell's flat also revealed that Wright has been working hand-in-glove with her for some time, and I have not been able to contact Smith or Bates, whose phones are out of action.'

'So we don't know if any of them are actually alive and if they are, we can't warn them that Downton and Arundell may be turning up.'

'That's about the size of it. However, they're all very capable – well, Miss Smith is very capable – and the Estonian Security Service is also working on it. They have an operative on the ground there and are drumming up reinforcements.' Underwood's phone purred in his pocket. He answered it and listened for a while. 'Thank you,' he said. 'Ping it through, would you?' Gulliver raised his eyebrows questioningly and Underwood smiled. 'That was our people at Arundell's apartment,' he said. 'They've found an interesting phone number. Let's give it a try, shall we?'

I was still on my hands and knees and when I turned my head, I found I was face to face with a distinctly unhappy chunk of slavering, growling caninity. It was as if he blamed me for his master's demise. He was right, I suppose. I smiled at him. I already had one injury and could do without the addition of teeth marks.

'Not sure even your winning smile's going to work on a dog,' remarked Elaine, strolling over and grabbing Riley by the collar. The slavering and growling were immediately replaced by some vigorous tail-wagging. How easily they forget, I thought; Valentin had only been dead a minute.

Saul was lying next to me. I gave him a friendly prod, which had no effect, so I carefully pulled back his jacket. His shoulder was leaking blood, so I whipped the Def t-shirt off the less serious wound on my head, screwed it into a pad and packed it over the entry hole. I zipped the jacket up again, hoping it would hold the pad in place. I wasn't exactly an expert – First Aid Training at MI6 was not deemed as important as Bulldog's self-defence class – so my ministrations weren't as gentle as they could have been, and Saul woke up complaining.

'Shut up, you,' I said. 'Sleeping on the job's a sackable offence,' but I gave him a quick kiss to cheer him up. Then Sofija marched over, dragged us both to our feet and gave us the sort of hug that bears would baulk at.

'Fucking hell, ouch!' shouted Saul.

'You well matched,' she said. 'Idiot and idiot's idiot girlfriend. That was mad thing to do.'

'We can't all be sensible and have weapons hidden everywhere,' I replied. 'But thanks, Sofija. You can assume I trust you now. And your sister, I guess, although we

didn't meet under the best of circumstances earlier today.'
I turned to Guna, who was keeping a beady eye on Rong,
still flat-out and showing no signs of wishing to move.
She'd probably need a crane to get her upright.

'I am very cross with you, Lucy Smith,' said Guna. 'I
wanted to kill Valentin myself.'

'It wasn't me. You need to have a word with Riley.'

'Riley? The dog? His name is Maxim.'

'Not anymore,' said Elaine. 'I'm bagsying him, and
Riley he stays.'

'Apparently the SVR and MI6 are on the same side in
this,' Saul said to me.

'And Estonian Security,' added Sofija.

'I'd noticed.' I prodded Rong. 'So presumably this little
lady represents the real villains of the piece. Mind you,
she's not a very effective villain. I did her twice in less
time than it takes to say Kung Fu Panda.'

Gary wandered over and put an arm round Elaine
but before I could remark on this, a phone rang. Everyone
jumped except Rong and Riley. The sound was coming
from the workbench. I walked over and picked up the
phone.

'Hello,' I said and put it on speakerphone.

'Ah, Miss Smith, there you are. I was hoping I might
catch you. Not having too much trouble, I hope.' It was
Jason-bloody-Underwood. I started to tell him in no
uncertain terms exactly how little trouble we'd been
having but he interrupted me. 'I need to warn you that
there may be two people, possibly more, heading your
way. You may want to exercise a degree of caution.'

'Says the man who may very possibly be a traitor,'
I said.

'Don't be ridiculous. The real traitor is on her way to
join you. I'm afraid Elspeth Arundell is not one of ours. She

will probably have Inspector Downton with her, unless she's got fed up with him. When you find them, you can do what you like with Downton but I want Elspeth back here in as near to one piece as you can manage.'

'If you're telling the truth, how do you explain sending us straight into the arms of a certain William Wright, your "Third Cultural Attaché"? Seems he was more culturally attached to Beijing than London.'

Before he could answer, however, the line went dead and all the lights went out.

'Stand still everyone,' I said. 'Wait for your eyes to adjust and keep your ears peeled.' I wasn't altogether sure if you could peel your ears but it seemed a sensible thing to say as we were clearly not alone.

'We are in a cavern with fifty metres of rock over our heads,' said Guna. 'Your eyes will not adjust much. I will find the emergency lighting.' I heard her shuffle over to the far end of the workbench; then there was a click and the cavern was bathed in a dim, red light.

Sofija was already at the door. Guna and I joined her. 'Listen,' whispered Guna. 'There are people here, presumably your Arundell and Downton. Maybe more. Sofija and I will take care of them. Keep everybody else here.' While reluctant to let the twins engage with an unknown number of new adversaries by themselves, they had certainly demonstrated an admirable ability to take care of business. I glanced behind me. Gary and Elaine were with the one remaining Russian who was still inconveniently alive. Mind you, he didn't look as though he'd be alive much longer, judging by the blood flowing from his thigh and thwarting Elaine's attempts at applying a rudimentary tourniquet.

I decided I could be spared to join the twins and went to fetch a weapon from one of the dead Russians. Then I noticed Something Wrong, not for the first time. Rong had gone, presumably under cover of darkness.

'Shit,' I said. I really hadn't made much of a job of shooting her in the foot in Kuressaare if she could skedaddle that quickly.

'She will not get far,' said Guna. 'I will go after her. You and Sofija make sure that your Arundell does not capture Nurmsalu.'

'Nurmsalu?' I said. 'What are you talking about? He was blown up last Saturday.'

'Ask Mr Dawson,' said Guna and disappeared out of the far door, the one that led to the set of steps down which we had been manhandled earlier.

'Elaine,' I said over my shoulder as I followed Sofija into the corridor. 'You and Gary keep an eye on Saul and watch out for more opposition. If we're not back soon, shoot the one you've got, assuming he doesn't die of his own accord first, and come looking.' I was really no less bloodthirsty than the Sesks twins, when it came down to it.

We came to a second door at the other end of the corridor. Sofija motioned to me to open it while she stood ready, gun held in a classic straight-armed pose, but there was no one the other side. There was, however, another open door. Sofija glanced inside. 'Kurat!' she said. 'He has gone. Follow me,' and she led the way back to the corridor and through yet another door.

'Don't we need to be more careful?' I whispered.

'No, is not necessary. Nurmsalu is not dead so he is taken. They will be escaping. If we lose him, he will be in China tomorrow.'

At the end of a longer corridor, which sloped upwards quite steeply, we arrived at a large vehicle bay with a set of steel doors that presumably led outside. There was a small wicket gate set into them. This time, Sofija held her hand up and listened for a few seconds before opening the gate.

'Car,' she said, and as I followed her through, I could indeed see a car, or at least the rear lights of one. I'd long since lost track of time and night had at last fallen, but it wasn't completely dark. It was a small car with a definite air of rental about it, and it was heading away from us at a speed the hire company would probably not approve of. Sofija loosed off a brief volley of shots but the car was too far away and immediately disappeared around a bend to be hidden from sight by a small cliff.

Sofija sprinted off in pursuit and, taking a couple of deep breaths, I followed. Then the sound of a submachine gun from up ahead brought us to a halt. The firing was instantly followed by a surge of engine noise, the shrieking of tyres, a loud crash, some indeterminate screeching which could have been an owl in full flight but was more likely metal on tarmac, a second crash and silence.

The good news was that this suggested the escapees were no longer escaping, the bad news that there was someone with a submachine gun around the bend, and I guessed I was right to assume it must be Rong. Sofija grinned. 'We have them,' she said. 'That will be Chinese giraffe and we have her caught in our pinchers, Guna behind her and us in front. Let us go and kill her.'

However, as we edged around the outcrop of rock, the situation we found was not exactly as Sofija had predicted. The first thing I saw was the hire car on its roof hard up against the barrier of a bridge across the river. It wasn't in the sort of condition that the hire company would be likely to consider reasonable wear and tear, and there was a distinct lack of movement coming from inside it. However, its headlights were still miraculously shining through the gloom.

They were shining straight at Guna, unarmed and hands in the air, standing in the middle of the bridge. Rong was in the process of raising her submachine gun with the obvious intention of ignoring the Geneva convention. I guessed that Sofija was about to take the imminent execution of her twin sister personally, but I didn't give her the opportunity.

I took an executive decision and shot Rong.

In the other foot.

I am, when all is said and done, really not a monster.

She squealed in a satisfying falsetto, dropped her gun and toppled sideways. She took a while to topple. I strolled over. She definitely wouldn't be getting around too quickly this time, I decided, stick or no stick.

In the distance I could hear sirens wailing. 'It looks like reinforcements are on their way,' I remarked to the twins, who were hugging each other.

'Oh, yeah, that was us,' said Elaine, appearing with Gary on the bridge, the latter supporting a still groggy Saul. 'I mean, there was a phone so it seemed daft not to use it.

Three Estonian police cars pulled up and ten cops piled out. Sofija walked over to talk to them. Meanwhile Saul disentangled himself from Gary and bent down to look into the overturned car. I joined him.

'Good evening, Ms Arundell,' Saul said into the car, bending double and swaying slightly. 'I think we need to have words about that job you gave me.'

I stared into the vehicle. I'm not sure if Estonian car hire companies save much money by not including airbags or whether they just hadn't worked, but ex-Chief Inspector Downton was in a bad way. He'd been driving and not only had the steering wheel skewered him in the stomach, but his face had suffered a dramatic coming *together with what had once been the windscreen. He'd need hospital treatment, I supposed, but it certainly wasn't going to be me that drove him there.*

Apart from a small cut on her head, Elspeth Arundell appeared unhurt. This was good news. Saul had been right about wanting to have words with her, but my suspicion was that he and I would be a long way down the list of those doing so. Behind her, scrunched up in a ball with his feet waving about in mid-air was a gentleman in late middle-age who would have looked quite distinguished had he not been scrunched up in a ball with his feet waving about in mid-air.

'Dr Nurmsalu?' said Saul. 'I'm afraid I may have some bad news regarding your brother.'

___ In which Jason Underwood goes on
   a bit, and Sofija talks about fish
   drives

The long hot spell had broken. Rain beat against the windows
of Underwood's office. It was a very big office with a very
big desk and very big, deep armchairs, which were currently
occupied by Underwood himself, Elaine, Sofija and Dawson,
the last with his left arm in a sling. Lucy was perched on the
corner of Underwood's desk, legs swinging idly. It was a lovely
desk, she thought, solid oak, but it must have been a hell of a
job lugging it up to the 6th Floor of Vauxhall Cross. She gazed
out of the window towards the Houses of Parliament a mile
away. Even with the rain, it was a much nicer view than the
blank wall she was used to looking at through the window at
Bulstrode Street.

   Underwood spoke. 'I've been working all weekend to try
to sort this out,' he said. A second successive Saturday visit
to the Coliseum had gone up in smoke, so he wasn't very
happy. Neither was the Foreign Secretary, although she was
far too lowbrow to frequent the opera. 'Viktor Nurmsalu,
Estonian hydro-scientist, discovered a way of utilising the
fast flow of water in underground bores, found plentifully
in karst landscapes, into cheap, affordable, readily available
energy. However, he wrote nothing down. Why, we don't know.
Probably, he was scared of something, with good cause as it
turned out. Needing official backing and money to see if it
was practicable and deliverable, he approached the Estonian
Government, which was immediately interested but did not
have the funds to support the experimentation process nor,
specifically, the cost of building even one production facility
if tests proved successful.

   'The Estonians therefore contacted us to see if we would
be interested in a joint venture. The main facilities would need

to be constructed in the Estonian countryside where karst landscapes are common and there are numerous fast-flowing underground rivers which could be channelled to provide bores to give maximum output. Estonia and the UK identified a site for a full working facility near Tuhala on a tributary of the Pirita River and in particular a secret underground channel which they named Kiirevesi. In other words, the bore in the cavern.

'So it could be said that Prokofiev and Wright were both bored to death,' said Dawson.

'You still funny,' said Sofija, but Underwood merely sighed and carried on.

'I was placed in charge of the security of the operation from the UK's perspective and your chief had the same job in Estonia, Lieutenant Sesks. I must say I'm rather surprised that it ended up being your responsibility.'

'I was appointed because of my sister. And because I am continent.'

'She means competent,' said Dawson.

Underwood raised his eyebrows. 'Yes, you certainly have been. Anyway, the Russians, who have ears everywhere, popped up and offered to help fund Nurmsalu's new power generation process as well and, quite honestly, we weren't going to be turning down the offer. Makes as much sense for them as the rest of us. We're all on the hunt for new, cheap green energy and Russia relies so much on oil that they're no different. And we do want to repair relations with them.

'Valentin Prokofiev had been sacked by the Russian SVR for gross incompetence on his return from Australia and vowed to get revenge on you two. You say he thought you still had some of the diamonds, Mr Dawson. Very strange.' Underwood paused. 'You haven't, have you?' Dawson ignored the question. 'Apparently, he'd been involved in this business from the Russian end before he was packed off to Oz, so utilised that knowledge and got into bed with China. The SVR had already appointed Guna Sesks to keep an eye on him and take him out if necessary. Guna infiltrated his organisation by literally getting into bed with him and confirmed his link with China via its agent, Songsung Rong.

'I had brought Viktor over to the UK to work on a small test facility we'd created in Britain. We didn't want to be throwing too much money at Estonia before we knew whether the idea held water.'

'Held water, good one,' said Dawson. 'So this was the cavern under the bungalow in Leatherhead where Lucy nearly drowned.'

'Actually no, we were preparing a place up in Snowdonia. So, having furnished Viktor with a fake identity, Victor Naismith, we placed him close to it in a safe house in North Wales. However, Elspeth Arundell introduced Viktor's twin, Kaspar, into the equation and arranged for you, Mr Dawson, to "find" him and keep an eye on him when Elspeth moved him to Stallford.'

'What?' said Lucy, scowling at Dawson. 'And you were planning to tell me this when exactly?'

'Sorry,' said Dawson. 'I was about to explain back at the embassy but you decided to go and get chloroformed instead. I had no choice. There were threats made.'

'Not as bad as the threats I'll be making when I get you alone.'

Underwood continued. 'I did not know about the switch of Viktor and Kaspar, and I also failed to spot William Wright. Frankly, I messed up. You know the rest. Viktor is taken to Estonia on the same ship as you, Mr Dawson. Kaspar is killed but we thought it was Viktor. No Viktor, no operation, leaving the process in the hands of the Chinese.'

'Chinese hands, Nurmsalu's head,' said Sofija. 'It all inside his head. All calculations, all notes, whole theory. There was nothing. Not even fish drive.'

'Flash,' murmured Elaine.

'Sofija's done enough flashing for one week,' laughed Dawson.

Sofija punched him on the upper arm, luckily the right arm. 'Ouch' said Dawson, but it hardly hurt at all so she must have been holding back.

'So how exactly were the Chinese going to run a major hydroelectric plant in the middle of Estonia while keeping it secret?' asked Lucy.

'Hidden in plain sight,' said Underwood. 'There are so many direct or indirect Chinese Government contracts in place that in effect they can do pretty much what they like. It's not just in Estonia. It's the same here with Huawei's involvement in 5G and the Chinese government's enthusiasm in helping with our new generation of nuclear power plants. So, yes, Estonia benefits, we do too of course, but who benefits most? China.'

'You're speaking in the present tense,' said Lucy, frowning. 'Surely you mean "would have" benefitted?'

'Well, no, I'm afraid not. Contracts are contracts after all. Really our only gain from all this is that Elspeth Arundell has been uncovered. I believe the Foreign Secretary has given the Chinese Ambassador a jolly good dressing down over that.' The expression on Underwood's face whilst he said it was blander than Wiltshire.

'So what happens to dear old Elspeth now?' said Dawson. 'Does she live out her remaining years in Wuhan or somewhere? Or I believe she's very fond of Wormwood Scrubs.'

'The Scrubs is for males only, Mr Dawson.'

'Shame. How about hanging? Can you still be executed for treason?'

'Unfortunately that is a popular misconception. The Crime and Disorder Act 1998 finally got rid of it. And even if it hadn't, I imagine there is a shortage of qualified hangmen these days. Perhaps you could apply for the job, Mr Dawson.'

'No, I don't think so. I quite like the job I've got now. I'm growing into it.'

'Maybe. But G22 has, I think, outlived its usefulness.'

Lucy jumped up. 'What the fuck? In less than six months,

Saul and I have uncovered millions of quids' worth of diamonds, one rogue MI6 officer, Flannery, one Chinese traitor, Arundell, and any number of minions and hangers on. Oh, and we have removed, twice, one Russian assassin from the scene, permanently now. Something that even the SVR are grateful for. Anglo-Russian relations are better than they've been since the days of Gorbachev.'

'You are of course correct up to a point, Miss Smith. Unfortunately, it is all irrelevant. You may not have been listening when I was talking about contracts. Despite this little contretemps, our current government, post Brexit, is still very keen to expand our commercial interests with China, the second largest single trading nation in the world. Your exploits haven't done much to promote that objective.'

'So they'd have preferred Arundell to carry on quietly gassing all our secrets to them.'

'Huawei are probably doing that anyway, so I don't suppose she was as valuable to them as she supposed. No, all in all, I'm afraid we are going to have to let you go. Both of you.'

'Do we get references?' asked Dawson.

'Of course not. We don't do references.'

'Perhaps we can get one from the SVR.'

'You can try but apparently they have never heard of you.'

'You'll be OK, Dawson. Sofija will give you a job. Sex slave or something,' said Elaine.

'Haha,' said Sofija. 'He only last five minutes.'

'That long?' said Lucy. 'Are you keeping something from me, darling?'

'I am sorry to disappoint you but you not my type,' Sofija said.

'Really?' said Dawson, sounding slightly affronted. 'Who is your type?'

'Lucy, of course. You did not know this, idiot?' and Sofija laughed uproariously.

___ In which four people sit in a pub,
and Dawson opens his wallet

A few hours later, Lucy and Dawson were back at Bulstrode Street, tidying up. Sofija was on a flight back to Tallinn, promising to keep in touch. She'd given them a final hug, after which they'd had to check for broken ribs. Elaine had gone off to meet Gary, who had been recalled by the Foreign Office and was undergoing questioning of his own. Officially, he and Elaine were meeting up "to compare notes" but it was obvious to Dawson and Lucy that the notes would be more like *billets-doux*.

'I'll miss this place,' said Dawson.

'I won't. I'd rather have an office with a better view than some badly painted brickwork a few feet across an alley, thanks very much. So, what now, lover?'

'Golden Eagle?'

'I was thinking more in the longer term, but yes, that seems like a fine plan for starters.'

Sitting in the pub, apparently waiting for them, were Chief Superintendent Gulliver and PC Sam Bunter. They were sitting in the same seats Lucy and Dawson had occupied back in February on their return from Australia, following another meeting with Jason Underwood, when he'd given them the jobs from which he'd just sacked them. They fetched drinks and introductions were made, Dawson never having met Gulliver or Bunter.

'Why so gloomy?' said Gulliver. 'Never mind, don't answer that. I've a proposition to put to you both. Now that we're all looking for work, that is.'

'You two as well?' said Lucy. 'Surrey Police lost its lustre, has it?'

'I'm thinking of drawing my pension. Putting it to good use. Care to join us?' and he waved a hand at Sam, who was beaming, possibly because he knew what Gulliver was about to say but more likely because he was sitting next to Lucy.

'What did you have in mind?'

'Oh, you know, bit of this, bit of that. My organisational brain, your action-girl stuff, your, er... nose for trouble Mr Dawson, world's our blister, wouldn't you say? Sam here's already on board. I'd be a sort of Charlie figure, maybe. You three could be my Angels.' He kept a deadpan expression but there was a twinkle behind his eyes.

'That may need a bit more work,' said Dawson, looking at Lucy and Sam. 'Still, one out of three's a start.'

'It's worth thinking about,' said Lucy, 'although a police pension must be bigger than I thought. I reckon we might need a bit more start-up capital and I've gone off the idea of begging from ma and pa.'

'How much more?' Dawson brought out his wallet.

'I don't know,' she said, 'but I've seen that thing before and it's never got more than a tenner in it.'

'You might be wrong there, sweetheart,' said Dawson, poking about in the wallet's lining. 'It's got these in it too. Do you think they might help?'

And he held up two sizeable and beautifully faceted diamonds.

__ The End

About Steve Sheppard

Steve Sheppard was born in Guildford and grew up in a house with a river at the bottom of the garden. This makes him sound quite posh but it wasn't a very big house and it wasn't a very big river. Nine years at boarding school taught him absolutely nothing about how to be an adult and actually becoming an adult also failed in this respect. One thing he did eventually learn, however, was that he should have tried writing a book much earlier than he did although he also now realises that he ought to have tried to become a celebrity first, as this would have made selling it much easier.

In between the day job and writing *A Very Important Teapot* and *Bored to Death in the Baltics*, Steve has also tried his hand at composing the occasional short story, although he finds it quite difficult to write anything that could be considered short. Most of his stories (which can be found on his website below) have met with blank indifference but one, Geronimo, did achieve 2nd place in the 2019 To Hull and Back humorous short story competition. No pressure on his entry into the next competition this year then.

Steve currently lives in an increasingly empty house in a quirky, not-quite-Cotswold village in west Oxfordshire but may move soon to avoid the paparazzi.

www.stevesheppardauthor.com

About Claret Press

Claret Press shares engaging stories about the real issues of our changing world. Since it was founded in 2015, Claret Press has seen its titles translated into German, shortlisted for a Royal Society of Literature award and climbed up the bestseller list. Each book probes the entanglement of the political and the everyday—but always with the goal of creating a page turner.

If you enjoyed this book, then we're sure you'll find more great reads in the Claret Press library.

Subscribe to our mailing list at
www.claretpress.com
to get news of our latest releases, bespoke zoom events and the occasional adorable photo of the Claret Press pets.

9 781910 461310